HONOR AND DESIRE

GOLD SKY SERIES

REBEL CARTER

D1602793

VIOLET GAZE PRESS

Cover Design by Najla Qamber

Edited by Blair Leigh

Published by Violet Gaze Press

20-22 Wenlock Rd

London

www.violetgazepress.com

❀ Created with Vellum

For my ancestors.
I will keep writing the better story you deserved.

PROLOGUE

*S*eylah had never been a particularly elegant girl. She had little interest in frippery or the latest fashions, and had never been one given to minding her manners. That did not mean that she was uncouth, but simply that her edges may have been rougher than most of the other girls of her age.

After all, Seylah had grown up in an unconventional household. With a former debutante for a mother and a pair of Gold Sky's lawmen for fathers, Seylah's upbringing had been one that favored freedom, discipline, and creativity.

Yet for all that, she was polite, pleasant and well-spoken. Seylah's mind was quick, nearly as fast as her tongue, though her fathers swore it would be a miracle if the two ever managed to pull even of each other. Her heart was bigger than she knew what to do with—the product of her warm family where affection and love were never in short supply.

Seylah had inherited her fathers' collective stubbornness, resourcefulness, and bravery. She was in possession of her mother's spirit, that particular strength of will; a character that had carried a debutante to the frontier. Moreover, she had been given the gift of hope by all three of her parents, and so Seylah saw the world as one endless experience of possibility. Adventure awaited her around every corner despite having grown up on the same collection of avenues in Gold Sky. But the influx of new money and people was rapidly changing the face of the town.

Gold Sky had developed from the burgeoning frontier town still finding its legs at her mother's arrival fifteen years earlier, to a cosmopolitan oasis at the fringes of the frontier. The sheriff's department had evolved past her two fathers and now consisted of a force of ten men, and there was even a fire brigade given the town now numbered upwards of thirty retail establishments and countless other homes.

And while Seylah loved adventure, lately she found it left a bitter taste in her mouth. She could have settled for less transformation and, quite frankly, for more of what yesterday had offered.

When that development had occurred she couldn't quite say.

Maybe it was that she had just had her fourteenth birthday and had noticed differences in herself that she'd rather not dwell on. And maybe, just maybe, those physical and emotional changes were putting a strain on the one thing Seylah prized above all else: her relationship with her best friend, August Leclaire.

The pair had been inseparable since childhood, with August only a month older than her. A fact that he never let her live down, despite her still being able to beat him in a foot race. Every day they had walked to school together and back again, spending as much time as they could, after and in between, with each other. Theirs had been a fast friendship, one that made Seylah feel at home, as if everything in the world were in it's designated place so long as August was on her left. But lately... *lately*, something had happened to their closeness.

What it was she was loath to say aloud, but she knew precisely when it had occurred.

The night the main thoroughfare of town had suddenly become grander, more special—which was an easy task with the arrival of electric street lamps. That was the night something had shifted, or at least it had begun to for Seylah.

It was dizzying to watch the street light up like magic. There had even been a party that evening replete with a countdown to welcome the momentous occasion. Electric lights like this were common in the cities Seylah frequented with her family, such as New York and Paris. But not here, not on a frontier that was still a touch removed from civilized.

August had been with her then just as he always was for any event, big or small. They had stood together laughing with the townsfolk as the excitement mounted, until it was practically buzzing. Perhaps their fingers had brushed and Seylah had forgotten to breathe, her lungs suddenly void of air as the crowd around them gleefully counted down each new number until finally they were at one. Seylah was left blinking in confusion, because when the streetlights blazed to life so did another thing.

Her heart.

The light had formed a halo around August's dirty blonde hair, making it gleam like the nearby river when the sun was high. His boyish features now seemed sharper, more of a man than the boy she had grown up teasing. His shoulders, she realized, had filled out since the summer before and when had he grown a head taller than her?

August wasn't a boy anymore. And if this past summer had told Seylah anything, it was that she was no longer a girl, on the verge of blossoming into a woman. How had she not realized the same was true for August? Her eyes had moved over him, taking in all the changes she hadn't noticed until they had *literally* been put beneath a spotlight.

It was enough to make her dizzy.

He had turned towards her and given a familiar smile, that same smile he had given her when they were 5 on their first day of school. But instead of smiling back, she had been too wide-eyed, too focused on him that she hadn't realized he was calling her name.

"What?" she asked, stumbling back a step. She had been staring at him. And she was caught red-handed when August had said her name. "What is it?"

"Why are you staring at me?"

"I'm not. I was stunned by the light."

He scoffed, reaching out and rubbing his knuckles against her head, mussing her hair. "Liar."

"I am nothing of the kind. I'm a lady," she retorted with a toss of her head. August laughed along with her, throwing an arm over her shoulder. She tried desperately not to notice the gesture as anything more than a friendly touch from her friend.

Her best friend.

She breathed in deeply and fixed a bright smile on her face when August blew out a huff of laughter and leaned against her.

"A lady are you?"

She nodded keeping her smile in place. "Truly."

"Then as the only lady I know, would you accompany me to the fall dance this weekend?"

Her heart warmed, lighting up brighter than the street lights around them.

"A dance?" She squeaked.

He hummed, tweaking her nose. "Yes, a dance. Do me the honor of attending the dance with me?"

"What?"

"The dance this month. May I escort you?"

Seylah nodded dumbly and managed a quick breathy: "Yes."

"Then I shall call on you, my lady!" August's voice rang through the night, carrying above the din of voices and the stray sounds of the gathered band that heralded the lighting of the lamps.

He wanted to call on her.

She didn't care if he tweaked her nose or ruffled her hair like he had done when they were children, nor did she give any amount of attention to the old women giving them knowing looks from across the street. It was common knowledge around Gold Sky that you could not find Seylah without August in tow. Of course, that gave rise to more than a fair amount of gossip and well-intentioned wishes from the majority of the townsfolk. And until that moment, Seylah had brushed off the giggles and hopeful looks from the adults around her as meaningless.

She knew that he thought the same as she, the pair of them rolling their eyes and ignoring the pointed looks or playful comments whispered just loud enough for the friends to hear.

"The pair will marry when they grow up. I know it."

"Isn't it darling how they've always been together?"

"Young love is so exciting!"

Seylah would wrinkle her nose and shake her head while August blew out a weary sigh. The both of them intent on carrying on as if the remarks hadn't been overheard. August was her friend and she was his. They had always been and thus would remain so until they perished, of that she was sure.

There would be no separating them. Never. Not even under the duress of incessant gossip from the townsfolk. She was happiest when she was with August. No other place she would rather be, if given the choice.

Except *now* ... now it felt different to Seylah. As if her eyes had suddenly been opened, her heart made aware of something she had always known but hadn't possessed the words to express it. August. She looked up at him, the bright light of the street dazzling her nearly as much as the boy she had grown up alongside. Because suddenly he wasn't simply August.

Then I shall call on you, my lady!

He was the first boy to call on her. *Her.*

The first to set her heart pounding. The first to make her shiver with a feeling she couldn't quite place. Her cheeks heated with a blush that left her hot and shaky beneath the arm August had thrown over her shoulders.

Heart fluttering in her chest, Seylah felt dizzy with the still new exhilaration that accompanied August's touch. For the first time in Seylah's life, she was happy to be at August's side for all to see.

That night had been startling. A realization in feelings that left Seylah bewildered about her relationship with August. Her fledgling confusion may have registered as nothing at all if August hadn't mimicked her behavior in perfect synchronicity.

In the two weeks that led up to the dance, their easy and steadfast friendship had become strained. The conversation was stilted. No longer did they touch with easy affection, nor was it possible for the two of them to ignore the comments that dogged their every step.

It felt as if the street lights had illuminated every dark and shadowy corner of Seylah's mind, and there was nowhere for her to turn without being confronted by thoughts of August. She swallowed hard and closed her eyes, blowing out a sigh.

It was normal for friends to think of one another, especially best friends. Things were just...confusing right now, but it would go back to normal. She was simply nervous about the dance, nervous about dressing as she was now for the first time. She opened her eyes, taking in the image of her standing in a pale green gown that showed off her girlish figure to perfection. She smoothed her hands over the sumptuous material that was a far cry from the durable dresses she much preferred in her day-to-day life.

As was her hair, a swept up style replete with a pompadour. Such a look wasn't conducive to horseback or field surveying. She patted at her hair nervously and forced herself to not fidget.

A lady does not fidget.

Or at least that's what Mrs. Rosemary had advised her when she'd approached the woman for tips on how to conduct herself tonight. Her mother had also given her thoughts on fidgeting. But the former debutante had strongly advised her daughter to behave as she always did. She was under no pressure to conform to expectations, and anyone that wanted her to do so was not worthy of Seylah's energies.

Seylah knew her mother only sought to help, but she much preferred Mrs. Rosemary's advice on how to approach her night with August.

Forcing her hands still at her sides, Seylah gave herself a determined nod and remained still. She would not fidget. She would not do it. She would not touch her hair. She would not shove August into a doorway if presented with the opportunity.

She. Would. Not.

She was a lady.

She was still giving herself a talking to when August arrived to call on her. Her heart fluttered like a bird against her breast at the thought of him coming to call on *her*. Her fathers answered the door while her mother fussed over the lace of her dress with a watery smile.

"You look so grown up," her mother whispered with misty eyes that had Seylah biting back an *"Oh mama."*

She was the oldest of her siblings, all girls to their

mother's delight and fathers' horror and chagrin. The four Wickes-Barnes' girls, ages fourteen, twelve, ten and nine had inherited their mother's beauty. Tan skin and abundant curls were the markers of Seylah and her sisters, as was their eyes.

All four girls were in possession of differently hued eyes. Seylah had inherited her mother's dark brown, but the next, Delilah, had sky blue. Florence took after Will with her cool slate gaze, and then there was the youngest, Rose, whose eyes were the mirror of their grandfather's clover green. Seylah quite liked the reminder of their family when she looked at her sisters. In each of their faces, a reminder could be found of where they came from, how beautiful their family was, and for that she was happy—they all were.

Though Seylah suspected her fathers would have been a tad happier with the presence of an older brother, August had always filled the space where a son might find himself. This proved a gift for everyone involved, considering August's father had taken work out west when the boy was five, and had never been heard from again. It wasn't easy to be a boy without a father, but Forrest and Will filled the roles nicely, and so quietly, that none thought to show August or his mother pity at the loss of a man that had been flaky at best.

Forrest had taught August how to skin a deer and chop wood. Will had taken care that August understood the importance of accounting as well as how to shoot a target dead on. The men had welcomed him as the son they never had, and with four girls in the family, August's presence had been appreciated as a brother of sorts. Now that he was here for Seylah on the night of a dance, it was plain to see that both Forrest and Will were reconsidering their estimation of August.

"Are you bullying August?" Her mother's voice rang through the foyer, and Seylah squeezed her eyes shut at the grumbling sound her fathers made at the question.

Of course they were bullying August. Once a friend, now a foe given that he was here to escort their daughter to a dance. Gathering her skirts, Seylah set her chin and cleared her throat.

"Leave him alone!" She called, rushing towards the foyer. She skidded to a stop when she saw her fathers looming over August with crossed arms and stern faces.

"You have her home by seven," Will said.

"You'll keep room for the holy ghost between the two of you while you dance, you hear?" Forrest ordered.

August nodded, his face and ears turning red. "Y-yes, sirs. I promise."

"Seven? That's when dinner is served! She won't have any time for fancy dancing!" Delilah cried from the staircase.

"She must fancy dance, Papa!" Florence chimed in from beside her sister where she clutched the banister.

"FANCY DANCE!" Rose cried from the second floor, and Seylah bit back a groan. This hadn't quite been the scene of romance and sophistication she had imagined when daydreaming about this moment. She had anticipated August looking gallant, herself like a maiden with effortless beauty, and they would smile and go together. It would all be perfect, but instead...

She blushed furiously at seeing her fathers crowding

August further against the door. This was not romantic or what a lady imagined when being escorted to an event. At least, Mrs. Rosemary hadn't told her about this. She cleared her throat and took a tentative step forward. How she would restore order she wasn't rightly sure, but she had to do something, and it must be done now. Thankfully, her mother appeared, effectively rescuing both August and Seylah from the scene of familial mayhem. Julie bustled forward towards her husbands with a frown.

"Stop that this instant," she ordered, hands on her hips.

Her husbands automatically dropped back, ducking their heads. "Aw, Julie, we were just givin' him a talkin' to about tonight," Forrest supplied.

"I know precisely what the pair of you were doing. You were scaring August to death and embarrassing Seylah within an inch of her young life. You've scarred the poor girl."

Her fathers glanced back to see her standing red-faced, hands fisting in her green skirts. In unison, they cringed and stepped back from August, who looked as if he might faint at any moment.

"Shoo, the pair of you," Julie flapped her hands at them and then gestured for Seylah to come forward. "Come on, darling. Let's get you and August out the door before I have to put your fathers in line." She smiled at August, smoothing a hand over his suit jacket. "Don't you look dapper, August!"

August offered a weak thanks as Seylah came forward to her mother's side. "Now you two have a lovely time tonight. Come back by nine, not seven." Her mother kissed their cheeks and bustled them towards the door with a warning look at the men who were still standing in the hallway, albeit with a recalcitrant look on their faces.

"Sorry about that sweetheart," Forrest offered, giving her a quick peck on the cheek.

"Home by seven," Will repeated, pointing at August as her father bent to hug Seylah.

"Yes, sirs." August managed to get out. Seylah had had quite enough of her overbearing fathers and looped her arm through August's.

"Come on. If we don't go now, we will never make it," she said, stepping out of the house and into the early evening. August stumbled after her and was silent as she continued to march up the path towards the lane that led to town. Quite a few homesteads had sprung up on the lane, leading from the school to their home, but it was still blessedly quiet, a respite after her family's chaotic scene.

They walked in silence, August stiffly beside her as gravel crunched underfoot. Seylah glanced at him and winced when she saw that he was still pale and shaken looking.

"They won't do anything to you, you know that."

He blinked as if coming out of a trance and looked at her as if realizing for the first time that she was there with him. "I, ah, I know," he sputtered.

She raised an eyebrow. "Do you?"

"They are the law men...sheriffs can't kill people right?" he asked after a moment and Seylah laughed.

"August..."

He cracked a smile then and relaxed slightly against her. "I know they aren't going to kill me."

She nodded, patting his arm. "Good, then it—"

"Maim me? Possibly. Rough me up? More than likely, as they both informed me they would without your mother or you knowing."

Her mouth dropped open. "They did not."

"They did, but," he held up a finger when she went to protest, "I know it's because they love you. I understand."

She drew back, looking at him in confusion. "You do?"

He nodded. "Of course, I do. You're family. They'd do anything for family."

"But you're family too," she protested.

August smiled thinly. "Not like you, Seylah." There was a note of such moroseness in his voice that she nearly stopped walking.

"August," she put a hand on his arm and moved to stop him. "August, what do you mean?"

"Don't worry about it, Seylah."

"But—"

"We will be late for the first dance. We can't have that. Not with how pretty you look tonight."

Her eyes widened at August's words. He had never said that to her, not ever. She hadn't even thought that he had noticed what she looked like with how little he commented on her appearance. And now, now she was pretty.

"You think I'm pretty?" She asked, a hand going up to her pat her hair.

He nodded and cleared his throat. "Prettiest in town."

Seylah felt simultaneously as if the air had been punched out of her lungs and that she was floating. It was on unsteady feet that she made it to the dance that was being held in their school, a favorite site for festivities.

Tonight, the building she saw every day was magical. Lit up and sparkling like a jewel box, ribbons and garlands hung from the trees nearby, making it a picture of romantic perfection. This is where all of her wishful daydreaming would be made reality, she could feel it in her bones.

Tonight things would change between she and August. For the better, she knew it. The strained nature of their relationship would be understood, feelings would be communicated, there would be no lingering awkward nature to their friendship. Not tonight. There couldn't be. Not when he'd called her the *prettiest girl in town*.

She preened and simpered at August's side. The lingering looks they received were no longer covert, but out right. No one was surprised to find them together. After all, they were always together, were they not?

The only difference was that tonight, it wasn't just the grown ups commenting and noticing. No, tonight the girls in their grade had taken equal interest. Seylah tried not notice as they danced their first dance, or again when August excused himself to get them refreshments. But, it was plain to see that the girls had finally taken notice of August, and had also, like Seylah, realized that he was no longer a boy.

Their eyes followed his every move, but Seylah could not begrudge them, as she found that her eyes followed a similar path. It was hard not to stare at August when he was the tallest and broadest of their year, when he was the only boy that could properly keep step in a waltz, or had the forethought to offer a drink after a spirited dance. August was attentive and kind, listening to her and laughing along with her jokes, rather than sticking to the walls in sullen silence as the other boys did.

Given this, Seylah understood why the other girls in attendance had noticed August and wasn't surprised to hear him the topic of conversation when she excused herself to freshen up. But, what she didn't anticipate was August's voice joining in the din of girlish chatter. She was standing at the back side of the schoolhouse, about to round the corner to return to where she had left August waiting. It seemed he hadn't been alone long in her absence.

"She's just a friend," August was saying. The tone was unlike the soft, warm voice he had complimented her with, when he had said that she was the prettiest girl in town. This was nearly a scoff, so unlike her best friend in any nature that she stopped short as if she had been slapped.

Something was going on. Something big.

"Doesn't look like just a friend," a girl laughed. "Looks like you're her beau."

"M'not," August returned.

"Then why are you always together?" Another voice asked, and Seylah leaned against the building feeling as if she was no longer walking on air, only punched in the stomach. There was no air to breathe and this time it wasn't from excitement.

There was a long beat of pause before August spoke again. "Because her pas look after me, so I look after her."

"So you don't *like* her then?"

"No. I couldn't ever see her like that."

"You look after her for her fathers? They make you do

that?"

"I do it to return the favor," August bit out, suddenly sounding uncomfortable. Seylah felt unshed tears pricking her eyes. "Nothings for free out here, and I owe them a debt."

A murmuring of understanding arose from the girls gathered, and Seylah reached out a hand to steady herself as her knees buckled.

"Since you don't *like* her and you're not her beau, will you dance with me?" The girl asked, but Seylah couldn't bring herself to hear August's response. Not with the sudden sick feeling that rose up and threatened to choke her.

The magic of the night, the imagined closeness and changing of their friendship to something more was lost to her. While she had been dreaming of a declaration of affection between herself and August, he had been merely performing a duty, a debt to her fathers for their care. A rushing sound filled her ears, choking off the jovial music that still played inside the school house, the sound of feet on wood turned into a single humming sound as did the chattering and laughter of the gathered merrymakers.

Seylah heard none of it. Not as she pushed away from the school house fighting back tears, not as she rushed towards her home, ignoring the instruction from Mrs. Rosemary that ladies did not run.

Seylah was no lady. Not with her best friend merely keeping her company in repayment to her family.

She was mortified, alone, and most certainly not the prettiest girl in town.

She would take care never to forget the lesson.

CHAPTER 1

1910. A DECADE LATER.

"*S*eylah, did you hear me?"

Seylah lifted her head from the book she was reading. "Hmm?"

Her mother blew out a sigh and crossed her arms. "I said, before you ignored me for the countless time, do you have time to take your sister to get her dress fitted?"

Seylah wrinkled her nose at the question. "Dress?" she asked setting down the book in her hands.

"Yes, the dress fitting for Rose."

"What dress fitting?"

Her mother groaned and tipped her head back, closing her eyes. "Lord give me strength to survive my children."

"Are you giving Seylah grief about reading?"

They turned to see her father enter the room with a laugh. "Never thought I'd see the day you were fussing over too much reading, little bird."

"Oh Forrest," her mother opened her eyes and gave her father a pout. "It's not the books, it's the lack of listening." She pinned Seylah with a pointed look.

Seylah sat up and did her best to present the image of an attentive daughter who wasn't in the least distracted by a book. "I'm listening, Ma!"

"See, look at that," her father pointed at her, "she's listening real nice." He took a step closer and nodded at her book. "What are you reading anyhow, sweetheart?"

Seylah truly brightened at that. "The manual Daddy got me on my new shotgun."

"The one I bought you for your birthday?" Forrest asked taking a seat beside her and looking at the book in her lap with interest.

Seylah nodded. "Yes, Papa. I'm so excited about it. Thank you for it. I love it so much!" She threw her arms around her father's waist and hugged him tightly. "It's my favorite birthday gift."

"You deserve the best. I'm glad you like it. Now show me what you're learning with this book."

"I was learning about what to do in case the pump action locks up. It's a problem with this model," Seylah said, holding the book up for her father to see the diagram on the pages. "But it's an easy fix so long as I have the right tools."

"We have all of that. You'll be fine. What else is in there?" Forrest asked, pulling out the chair next to her and scooting closer to get a better view.

"Oh, lots and lots, Papa. I am very interested in the loading mechanism, but I don't understand why it might catch with repeated use. I'll have to take mine apart to get a better look, I think."

Forrest nodded and tapped his chin thoughtfully.

"That's a fine idea, sweetheart. We can do that after lunch if you like."

"Oh really? That would be—"

"You have to take Rose to her dress fitting," her mother broke in with an aggrieved look on her face. "Not to mention that you have a fitting to attend as well."

Seylah's eyes widened. "What fitting? How am I now a part of the dress expedition?"

Julie's hands went to her hips. "Expedition? It's simply a trip to Rosemary's."

"That is an expedition of sorts," Forrest supplied.

Seylah nodded solemnly. "Nearly a journey to another continent, it is."

Julie rolled her eyes and waved a hand at the pair of them. "Stop being so dramatic."

Seylah pursed her lips, shoulders slumping down, and gave her mother a pleading look. "Must we?"

"Yes, now put the book away and get ready for your fitting."

Seylah sighed and stood, handing the book off to Forrest. "Oh, all right," she said giving her mother a mock salute, "I'll collect Rose and off we go."

She turned, setting off in search of her younger sister, who most likely could be found pouring over the latest news in fashion and beauty. The youngest Wickes-Barnes girl had inherited a healthy interest in the latest and greatest in style that could only be satisfied by a constant supply of periodicals via her grandmother in New York. The pair were holy terrors when the family visited the big city for the holidays, and Seylah was always content to tagalong when Rose and her grandmother had their fun, so long as she was able to stay on the sidelines.

She didn't much think that a dress fitting at Mrs. Rosemary's would allow much time for sideline sitting. What happened when one wasn't enjoying their place on the sideline in terms of the fashion world was a mystery to Seylah. She desperately hoped it wouldn't run long as she had it in her mind to spend her afternoon inspecting the inner workings of her new shotgun with her Papa.

If she were lucky, she might be able to duck out after her fitting and leave Rose to the finer points of frippery and fitting. Maybe her sister could even be persuaded to handle the logistics of Seylah's outfit. So wrapped in her thoughts of how to best avoid an afternoon spent drowning in fabric choices and patterns, she scarcely noticed the journey into town, and it was only when she was standing with Rose in front of the dress shop that Seylah asked the question she hadn't thought of when her mother first told of her of the appointment.

"What dress fitting are we here for?" She asked, turning to look at her sister.

Rose raised an eyebrow. "You've come for a fitting and have no idea what it's for?"

Seylah lifted a shoulder in a shrug. "It didn't seem that important when Mama stopped my reading to tell me of it."

"Mama stopped you from reading?" Rose gasped, a hand flying to her chest.

Seylah gave a solemn nod. "She did."

"But why?" Her sister asked still aghast.

"For this, of course," Seylah said, pointing at Gold

Sky's premiere dress shop, The Modern Dress, and then frowned at the shop window where an assortment of fine dresses in pastel shades were displayed.

"You mean the appointment you have no idea about?"

Seylah nodded in agreement. "I haven't the faintest clue." She turned to look at her sister. "Do you know?"

Rose bit back a laugh at the confused look on her sister's face. "Know what we are doing here?"

"Well, yes."

Rose nodded. "I do."

"What is it for then?" Seylah wanted to know, but Rose only looped her arm through her sister's and pulled her along.

"You'll find out soon enough, darling," Rose said shooting her a mischievous grin that had Seylah digging her heels in.

"I don't know about this. Mama didn't say anything about this."

"About what?" Rose asked feigning innocence.

"About whatever has that expression on your face," Seylah replied giving her sister a shrewd look. "Whatever it is that has you grinning like the cat that got the cream is not an affair that I want to be found getting fitted for."

"Oh you're always so dramatic," Rose sighed sticking her tongue out at her sister. "We are here for a very simple affair."

"Which is what?" Seylah asked, begrudgingly following her sister into the dress shop.

"Mama's in charge of the spring dance this year."

"But she's in charge of that every year," Seylah pointed out.

"Well, yes, but this is the last year she'll be doing it, and that means we have to all be in attendance. It's going to be the finest dance yet, you know!"

"I suppose it--wait," Seylah stopped short and gave her sister a confused look. "Why is this Mama's last year doing the dance?"

Rose shrugged, looking at a swath of periwinkle fabric. "She says it's time she steps aside and lets the next generation take the reins."

Seylah's eyebrows shot up. "The next generation? What does that mean?"

"It means," Rose turned to her sister and shot her a bright smile, "that the way is open for us to plan the next dance! Won't that be fun? Oh, I just can't wait for it, and this dance is when she'll announce that we are taking over."

"I mean, well..." Seylah shrugged unsure of what to say when her sister looked so happy at the idea. The thought of planning the spring dance was enough to make Seylah want to run for the veritable mountains. "What do you mean *we*?" She finally asked when she could think of nothing else to say.

Rose blinked at her sister. "What?"

Seylah pinched the bridge of her nose and let out a long suffering sigh at her baby sister. "I mean, what do you mean when you say we? What do *we* have to do with the spring dance planning?"

This time it was Rose who gave the long suffering sigh. She rubbed her temples and shook her head at her sister. "It means that we Baptiste women are taking over the planning. Carrying on with Mama's good work and all that!" Rose punctuated her statement with a punch of her fist in the air.

"Oh no," Seylah murmured eyeing the door. If she moved fast enough, she might be able to make it outside before anyone was the wiser. Perhaps she would be able to make it home in record time, where the only thing awaiting her hand at planning was when she might take apart her newest firearm, or deciding whether she would head out to help mend the fences before or after dinner.

"Oh yes!" Rosemary sang as she sailed into the front room. "And what brings the oldest and the youngest Baptiste ladies to my lovely shop?"

Seylah darted towards the door but Rose was far quicker than she appeared and caught her before she'd made it more than a foot. "Don't you dare," Rose hissed at Seylah who gave a pitiful moan at being detained.

"But Rose…" Seylah pouted.

"But nothing," the younger woman growled at her sister before she rounded to face Rosemary. "Mrs. Rosemary, how are you? We are here for our fittings for the spring dance."

Rosemary tilted her head to the side and gave the pair a considering look. "Then why is it that your sister looks like she might faint?"

"She skipped breakfast. She's peckish," Rose replied without sparing her sister a look. "Isn't that right, Seylah?" She asked giving Seylah's hand a hard yank.

"Ah, yes," Seylah nodded with a weak smile, "that's the measure of things."

"If that's all it is I'll have something sent over from the cafe, hmm? Can't have you fainting now that I've finally

23

managed to get you to a fitting appointment. I cannot tell you how thrilled I am at the chance to dress you, Seylah."

Seylah cleared her throat. "You're thrilled?"

"Over the moon!" Rosemary trilled waving her arms before motioning them to follow her. "If you both come right this way, I'll start by taking your measurements, Seylah. Rose, I believe we have yours on file from your last visit to us. You looked lovely by the way, in that summer outfit. I have half a mind to start commissioning you to wear our newest looks about town. If enough of the new arrivals see you looking so beautiful they'll be beating down our doors for sure."

Rose flushed, but gave Rosemary a pleased look. "I, ah, do you mean that truly?"

"Of course! How about we talk it over after your fitting? We have the entire summer line in the works and I'm quite sure more than one piece would suit you."

"Like a fashion model?"

Rosemary wiggled her fingers at her. "The one and the same. Why you'll be just like a Parisian girl!"

"I wouldn't let daddy hear you say that," Seylah said, hiding a grin at the dark look that crossed her sister's face.

"Oh pish," Rose said waving a hand. "He never lets me have any fun."

Seylah nodded along, thinking of her overprotective father. He was, for all intents and purposes, aloof and quiet with anyone not of their family or trusted circle of family friends. Will Barnes was downright intimidating to those he didn't love, but even so, the man kept them all close and under strict rules. The effect was only compensated for by Forrest Wickes' tendency to over indulge them to the point of spoiling. Seylah much suspected Will's behavior to be in reaction to Forrest's soft touch with them all. "Then keep this your little secret, hmm?" She advised her little sister.

Rose winked conspiratorially at Seylah. "I think you mean our little secret, big sister."

Seylah held up a hand. "Oh no, I'll not be included in that plan."

"But you just advised me to keep it secret."

"Precisely. I am only involved in an advisory capacity, not a participant."

Rose pouted and turned to Rosemary. "I'll do it, but Seylah is right. We musn't let daddy know or he'll get in one of his moods."

Rosemary tutted while pulling out her glasses and turned towards her work table. "That man is a storm cloud. However, I suspect he'll let you do as you please. We all know it. You're the baby, after all."

Rose preened. "True, true, but I aim to spend the holidays with Grandmama in New York City, so I have to keep up appearances of obedience. You understand?"

Rosemary laughed, unfurling a measuring tape. "I do." She winked at the girls and then gestured for Seylah to come forward. "It's time for your fitting, Seylah. Come stand up on this platform and I'll get to measuring."

"Can't you just use Rose's measurements?" Seylah asked as she slowly walked towards the small raised platform next to Rosemary. Her mind was already wandering, there had been a ruckus at the Yellow Rose saloon just the night before and she longed to inquire if all was well within. Though her job title was secretary to the sheriff's

25

office, it was not outside of her range of duties to check in on townsfolk and do her own fair share of policing. She'd been doing it for as long as she'd had the job and the locals looked to her for their safety as much as they did her fathers, or any of the other deputies.

Rose snorted and pointed at the top of her head. "You're nearly half a foot taller than me, Seylah. That would never work."

"A lady's measurements must be exact to achieve the most flattering silhouette," Rosemary said coming forward to catch Seylah's hand when she made as if to step towards the door.

"I'm not a lady," Seylah said, the words bursting from her before she could stop them, and she winced. The suddenness of her outburst silenced the other two women, and Rosemary froze where she stood, holding Seylah's wrist.

"Why," Rosemary pursed her lips and leaned closer, giving Seylah a scrutinizing look, "would you think that?"

Seylah cleared her throat and looked away. "No reason. I mean to say that I do not aim to present myself in a very ladylike fashion. All of this," she nodded at the dress shop around her, "as lovely as it is, isn't for me. It's more for women like Rose or Delilah."

Rose crossed her arms and pinned her with a stare. "You always get like this when anyone tries to fancy you up a bit."

"Get like what?"

"Twitchy. Odd. Close mouthed and shifty-eyed," Rose said too quickly for Seylah's liking. "And don't think I don't know you're already thinking on how you'd much rather be patrolling, looking for vagrants than here getting fitted for something pretty."

"I do nothing of the sort," Seylah replied with a jut of her chin. "I just am not interested in the same things as you, and that is—"

"Perfectly fine," Rosemary said, breaking in between the two sisters. "You can like what you feel drawn to, but this is a special occasion with the dance announcement, after all, and being your ma's special project...." her voice trailed off, the unspoken implication that it would mean the world to her mother hung in the air between them like a heavy smoke. If Seylah breathed too deeply she would surely choke on it.

As such, she cleared her throat and opted to give Rosemary a delicate shrug. "It is an important event."

Rosemary smiled encouragingly at Seylah, and as if sensing Seylah wavering, she pressed forward. "It is! We need your measurements to make a dress as uniquely lovely as you are. I can make you a dress that will make you shine like the special young woman we all know you to be. Will you trust me to do that?"

Seylah paused and glanced at her sister, Rose, who was staring at her with clasped hands, looking as if she were willing the very words Seylah was about to speak into her sister's mouth. Seylah's lips turned up in a rueful smile at the look of focus on Rose's face. She would not let her down with the wrong answer, she would look presentable for the spring dance announcement, and she would give Rosemary free reign over her attire for the night.

"I will," Seylah told Mrs. Rosemary, and stood up taller where she stood. "Shall we?" She asked giving Rosemary a bright smile. What harm could come of it? It was only one dress fitting, and Mrs. Rosemary was a trusted family friend. If anyone would be able to do this competently and painlessly, it would be Mrs. Rosemary, of that she was sure.

CHAPTER 2

*T*he fitting was, in fact, not painless.

If Seylah were to describe it, she would use the words *laudanum inducing* and *purgatory* to describe her time under Rosemary's pins and tape. She would never utter either of these in front of Mrs. Rosemary. No, never that. But, it didn't negate the fact that Seylah's fitting went on for a grueling five hours, and left her with battle scars in the form of three needle pricks, all of which were inflicted when Seylah tried her hand at escape.

"You're being positively dramatic, nearly as much as your daddy," Rosemary muttered around a mouthful of pins. "If there was ever any doubt you were William Barnes' daughter, let it be laid to rest now."

"It's just so much, Mrs. Rosemary," Seylah protested and glanced at her sister, praying for help, but Rose was much too absorbed in her perusing of the fine silks just arriving from Paris.

"I thought this was only for the one dance?" She tried, hoping Mrs. Rosemary would relent in what Seylah swore must be the fifth outfit, a day dress of purple muslin and ivory lace. Seylah fidgeted and pointed at the ledger that held her measurements. "Mama only wanted the one dress and—"

"One dress is not enough! I haven't been able to fit you for a single outfit in years. I'm quite tired of seeing you in drab riding dresses. They do not flatter you as they should, Seylah."

"Oh Mrs. Rosemary, that's not important."

"It is if you hope to catch a young man's eye. You're of the marrying age."

Seylah winced at the woman's words. "There's no one I wish to marry," she said a little too quickly for Rosemary's liking.

"Oh pish," she said waving a hand, "there are plenty of attractive and eligible men of a suitable age in the vicinity as of late, and I have hopes that one of them will be just the thing to catch your pretty eye."

Seylah colored at Rosemary's words. *Pretty* wasn't a word that she used to think of herself, nor was it one that she particularly thought others used to describe her. Not since ... that night. Her brow furrowed as that fateful night a decade ago flitted through her memory.

Prettiest girl in town.

She shook her head. No, that was not her. Had never been, and never would be. "Then I'll be a tad clearer, Mrs. Rosemary. There are no men of marrying age that would be particularly interested in me."

Rosemary's blue eyes widened and even Rose was roused from her fabrics at Seylah's words.

"No, no." Rosemary shook her head. "Now that is just not true, my dear."

"It is, Mrs. Rosemary. I am not the kind of woman that men notice upon first blush. It is … a delicate thing, but I am at peace with my role as it is."

"Seylah..." Rose sighed, standing from where she had been sitting.

"As it is? What do you mean?" Rosemary put down her measuring tape and spit out her pins. "Dear, you are as lovely as your mother, even more so because you are *you*. There is only one you, and that is the gift of beauty. Everyone has their own unique kind."

Seylah nodded, giving the other woman a tight smile. "Yes, you are quite right. There is only one me."

"Even if there were a hundred, you would still be beautiful," Rose broke in with a wave of her arms, "because you're beautiful." When Rosemary opened her mouth to speak, Rose shook her head. "She needs to hear that she is a beauty for the superficial sake of beauty, no niceties about uniqueness or spirit, Mrs. Rosemary."

Seylah rubbed the bridge of her nose. "Rose..."

"Well, it's true. You act as if you don't have eyes, or that half the men in town don't stop to look when you pass. You are fetching."

"I am nothing of the sort, and those men are looking because they are worried I'll box their ears."

Rose sighed. "You would think that. I blame Papa and Daddy letting you spend so much time with them at the jail."

"Well, that is what one does when their job is in the

jail," Seylah returned, making Rose's lips purse in annoyance.

"And that's the other half of the problem. You spend entirely too much time with that sort of crowd."

"And what exactly do you mean by that?" Seylah asked, stepping down from the platform to stand in front of her sister.

"Law breakers," Rose said simply.

"Not all of them are law breakers. August is there a lot, too, and the other deputies!"

"And not a one of them is allowed to so much as ask you for anything other than a ration of bullets or a new holster."

Seylah laughed. "A ration of bullets, Rose? What do you think it is? A soup hall?"

Rose threw her hands up. "You know what I mean. Those are not the sort of men that will give you the attention you deserve. They're degenerates!"

"That's absurd. There are good men employed there, not to mention Papa and Daddy," Seylah retorted while Rosemary made a sound that didn't sound as convinced of her fathers' not being categorized as degenerates.

"That may be, but you are all far too focused on shooting and riding," Rose replied, undeterred by her sister or Mrs. Rosemary's reactions. "It's getting rougher in town, and I worry about you being out there just like Daddy and Papa."

"If by focused on shooting and riding, you mean keeping Gold Sky safe," Seylah said, though her sister's estimation of the company she kept, working at the Sheriff's office, a necessity given the rapid expansion of the town and the increase in population, were ringing in her ears like gunshots. The people of Gold Sky were good people, but it was easy to get carried away, and life on the frontier demanded a certain wildness in a person. To not expect that wildness to make itself known from time-to-time was unrealistic.

And that demanded a strong presence from the sheriffs in town. If that also meant their secretary of sorts pitched in, then Seylah was more than happy to do so. The work was familiar and satisfying, the men were people she had known since childhood, and a little bit of excitement never hurt anyone. Besides, she was a crack shot who could hit a target from a moving horse sure as anything.

Yet ... for all the job's excitement, Rose was right. Seylah was afforded little opportunity of being admired or of coming into contact with anyone she cared to be admired by. There was something left to be desired when the men in the vicinity were either behind bars or her fathers.

Though not all the men were related to her, but even so, *those men* were not an option.

Rose sniffed. "Yes, that."

Seylah rolled her eyes and slipped off the jacket Rosemary had just been fitting for her. "Thank you for the new wardrobe, Mrs. Rosemary. I trust you have enough to finish any other pieces you have in mind for me? I'll come in for a final fitting of course."

Rosemary gave her a quick nod and a reassuring smile. "Of course. You'll love what I have in mind. I'll send word when I've finished the lot of them."

"Thank you, Mrs. Rosemary." She turned to Rose and wiggled her fingers in goodbye. "I'll see you at dinner, hmm? I have to get back to my job surrounded by degenerates after all," she said shooting her sister a meaningful look as she strode towards the door. She had been away from the office for far too long as it was, if she was lucky, the men there would have kept their noses clean for the most part.

"They don't deserve you," Rose called after her sister.

"Oh, never fear, dear sister, of that I am well aware!" Seylah shot back over her shoulder as she stepped out into the sunlight. The women erupted in a chorus of other well meaning chatter, but Seylah firmly shut the door to the dress shop behind her and kept moving. It was a miracle she had managed to make it out of the shop as quickly as she had. Mrs. Rosemary was notorious for her all day fittings, though Seylah had mistakenly thought those were only carried out at the behest of the person being outfitted.

A rookie mistake to be sure, where Mrs. Rosemary was concerned. Seylah shook her head, all thoughts of the seamstress's pins and tape, or how good a silhouette the draping of this or that silk would afford her, clearing from her mind. It was all a mysterious world of color and pattern that Seylah had walked away from many years ago, not that she had ever truly been a citizen of the world of femininity.

She pursed her lips. No, she had been afforded a one night pass that she had promptly revoked herself. That kind of vulnerability was ... unsettling. She much preferred sturdy wool for her day-to-day, Montana's climate was unpredictable at best, depending on the season, and if given the choice between chiffon or a hobble skirt, Seylah would defer to her tailored serge day dresses each and every time. She didn't understand modern fashions, nor their functionality in a world as rough as theirs. Yes, there were civilized places and soft moments in Gold Sky, but the town, for all its growth and prosperity, was still very much a frontier town.

How was a woman supposed to remain gentle and exposed in such a place? To be stripped of all ones armor and defenses in the name of fashion was far too much for her to endure, even though her sister Rose did so and happily.

Was there something different between them? There had to be even if they came from the same parentage, the same family, the same home. Yet for all their similarities, they were so entirely different. Seylah smiled at the thought. She quite liked how they were different. She knew her sister did as well, even if the ambushing at Mrs. Rosemary's hadn't quite felt as much, and that was what had her in such a poor mood.

That, and remembering her one fateful foray into the world of beauty and style. It had been done at such a tender age and had hurt her deeply. But her sister and Mrs. Rosemary had no idea of it. She hadn't breathed a word of her night at the dance to a single soul, not even her mother, much preferring for the entire evening to to be of the past, to be naught but a memory as she willed the past five hours spent with Mrs. Rosemary.

The women were only trying to help. They hadn't meant for her to recall unpleasant moments that were still sore to the touch. She would thank them for their time and care as soon as she was able. With a determined sigh, Seylah stepped off the boardwalk and made a beeline for the Sheriff's office a few streets over. She only needed to cross the street and round the corner before Mrs. Rosemary's dress shop was left in the dust.

Out of sight and out of mind.

So focused was she on her destination that Seylah forgot to do one very rudimentary and necessary thing. One that she had done without fail since she was allowed to cross the street as a child: *look both ways*.

And that failing caused her to miss the stagecoach barreling down the avenue courtesy of a spooked horse that set both coach and Seylah on a collision track. The resulting crash would have been considerable to both woman and beast, of that there was no doubt. Except that on this particular day when Seylah forgot the most basic of pedestrian rules, there was a newcomer to town in possession of a keen eye and even keener reflexes.

"Look out!" A gruff voice shouted as a pair of powerful arms wrapped themselves around Seylah's midsection and yanked her back against what felt like a wall.

"Oof!" Seylah spluttered, the air soundly knocked out of her from the sudden crash into the wall at her back. She gasped, eyes squeezing shut as she tried to remain calm. Her hands automatically came to cradle her stomach when her lungs failed to pull in air. The stagecoach roared past in a cloud of dust, a cacophony of shouts from townsfolk narrowly avoiding being rundown following behind it.

"Are you all right?" The wall holding her asked. It was

a nice voice, rich and full of dulcet tones that conjured ideas of laying in the sun. Who knew walls could have such lovely timbres?

"Ma'am?" Seylah opened her eyes just as the arms around her moved, turned her so that she was now facing the magically speaking wall.

"Oh," she whispered when she was face-to-face, or rather face-to-chest with the not-so-very-much-a-wall, but very much a man. A handsome one at that. He was built like a house, or what Seylah supposed a very well-built, sturdy, but also handsomely attractive home would look like if it were presented in human form.

This man could provide shelter and warmth no matter what the Montana climate sought to throw at the inhabitant.

"Oh," Seylah said again and tried not to notice how large he was, or how warm his hands felt on her waist, and she very much refused to breathe in the amber and sage smell of him that was both clean and masculine.

The man had disheveled dark brown hair, no doubt a by-product of their crash, and hazel eyes. Hazel eyes that were looking at her in such concern that Seylah was forced back into the present and away from admiring the man's jawline or the fact that his suit fit him perfectly. Though she knew nothing of clothing or material, it was easy to see, and feel, given that her hands had immediately reached for him, the sumptuous fabric beneath her hands was expensive and of a fine cut. She suddenly understood the importance of tailoring and measurements, and what Mrs. Rosemary meant in terms of achieving a flattering silhouette.

It was indeed a goal to be strived for where clothing was considered, especially when a strapping young man was the one to be outfitted.

"Are you all right?" He asked again, and this time the question jolted Seylah back to reality. She jerked her hands up and off him as if she had suddenly been burned.

"I, ah, yes," she managed, taking a hasty step back that would have sent her sprawling if not for the man reaching out again to steady her.

"Are you quite certain?" He asked.

Seylah nodded and looked down at where he was touching her, his hand, a big hand that splayed across her waist. "I'm certain," she whispered, a blush spreading across her cheeks.

"That coach came out of nowhere. The driver should be fined for reckless driving." The man shook his head, shooting a glare in the direction the stagecoach had disappeared. "If I hadn't come along, you would have been seriously injured."

"I should have looked where I was going," Seylah sighed, feeling a wave of embarrassment wash over her for the mistake. She blushed but this time it was for another reason entirely. She should have known better than to simply step out into the avenue without observing basic safety and traffic rules.

The man snorted, still glaring off in the direction of the coach. "A runaway coach like that has no place around a lady such as yourself."

There it was again. That pesky damnable word: *lady*.

She started, stood up straight at the word that served like a bucket of cold water to whatever interest Seylah had felt for the man who was still, inexplicably, holding onto her.

"I'm not—" Seylah began, the words tumbling from her mouth, as if on que, when another shout interrupted her.

"Seylah!"

She turned in time to see August rushing up the avenue, his eyes panicked as he called out to her again. "Seylah, are you all right?"

"Seylah? What a beautiful name," the man in front of her said, pulling her attention back to him. She was not immune to the rich tones of an attractive house-turned-man.

"Thank you?" Seylah tried, blinking in surprise up at him.

"I'm Elliot. Elliot Myers."

"Seylah Wickes-Barnes," she offered politely, as anyone did when presented with another's full name.

"Get your hands off her," August huffed, finally arriving at their side.

"August!" Seylah gasped at the edge she heard in her old friend's tone. "He helped me. I was nearly run over a moment before."

"I saw it," he growled and then pointed at where Elliot's hand was still on her waist. "Take your hands off her."

Mr. Myers held up his hand and took a slight step away from her with an apologetic smile. "Forgive my manners, Seylah," he said, and she did not miss how he pointedly ignored August where he stood fuming beside her. The men were of the same height and Seylah quite found being between the pair of them to be a stifling affair. When she had thought of Elliot as a sturdy house, she had quite forgotten that August was built of the same stuff, if not wrapped in a slightly different material.

Where Mr. Meyers was attired in spotless and expensive clothing, August wore the durable denim and leather required by his occupation as a deputy. The man spent entirely too many hours in the saddle, and was always the first to respond to any altercations whether in town or in the more rural lands that surrounded Gold Sky. At his waist was a six-shooter, the handle of it gleamed in the afternoon light when he moved his duster to the side exposing it to view. Seylah felt a flare of anger at the sight.

August meant to intimidate Mr. Myers with such a display. *But why?*

"You stop that this instant," Seylah blurted out jabbing a finger into August's chest. He flinched and looked away from Mr. Myers.

"Stop what?" He asked with feigned innocence.

"Stop flashing your piece at Mr. Myers. This gentleman helped me and you mean to treat him like a criminal? I'll not have it, August Leclaire! If you keep this up, I'll see to it that you are scheduled for third shift rounds, and only third shift rounds, for the remainder of the month!"

August's eyes narrowed and he stepped closer into Seylah's finger. "Do it, I dare you, but I'll not have some man pawing at you in broad daylight."

"Elliot did nothing of the kind! And besides, you know I am capable of taking care of myself. Why are you in such a state over this?"

"Oh, so he's Elliot now, is he? How long have you been acquainted with him? Is that where you've spent your morning?"

Seylah blushed, furiously, and drew herself up. "I do not have to explain my whereabouts to you. You are not my keeper," she told him with a toss of her head.

"Ah, the lady was in trouble and I merely stepped in to ensure her safety. I did not mean to cause trouble between a couple," Mr. Myers said, holding up his hands.

The pair of them whirled on the man. "We are not a couple!" They roared in unison.

"Are you..." He tilted his head to the side, eyes moving between the pair of them where they stood far too close for propriety's sake, "quite sure on that account?"

Seylah stamped her foot. "Yes!" She blinked at her outburst and cleared her throat. "I mean, Mr. Myers, I—"

"Elliot, please," he said, giving her a warm smile.

She nodded and continued on with a nervous laugh. "Elliot, then."

"And I may call you Seylah?" Elliot asked.

"Of course!" She enthused with far more energy than she meant and colored at the misstep. "I mean to say, yes, please feel free to address me so."

Elliot bent low into a bow that left her struck quite dumb. "My lady, it would give me no greater pleasure." He took her hand and pressed a kiss to the back of her glove, the heat of his lips shot through Seylah like a bolt of lightning. It was like nothing she had ever felt before, perhaps for the reason that Seylah had never been courted by a man, never been given such intimacies as a kiss to the back of her hand, or any of the other things a woman of her age went weak in the knees for.

"Get your hands off—" August began, but Seylah silenced her friend with a well-placed elbow to the sternum.

"Ooof!" August sagged over, hands going to his chest as he struggled to breath.

"I thank you for such a thoughtful introduction, sir," Seylah said, and she was not one bit remorseful over the simper she heard in her own voice. She smiled, broadly, despite the hacking sound of August trying to regain his breath at her elbow. "Are you new to Gold Sky?" She asked, stepping away from August's bent over form.

"I am, just arrived today," Elliot told her, giving her friend a curious look. "Is he all right?"

She waved a hand. "Oh, he's fine. Very hardy."

"I see…" Elliot nodded, though the man didn't look the least bit convinced of her explanation, but Seylah noted he also didn't look concerned at August's welfare. "I am lucky to have met such a lady as you, though I would have much preferred out first meeting to be from less dramatic circumstances than—"

"Than a runaway coach?" She asked.

He held up a finger. "Yes, that, but at least I have made an impression on you, I hope?"

"You certainly have, Elliot."

"Then I can think of no finer way to make my entrance to frontier life."

"Where are you from, then? Where are you staying? Who are your people?" August asked, standing up and finally appearing to breath normally.

"August, really, is that necessary?" Seylah moaned, giving him a cross look.

"Yes. When a man kisses my best friend's hand, it is entirely necessary that I know what he's about."

Seylah glared, and was quite ready to give August a piece of her mind, when Elliot held up a hand and gave them an apologetic smile. "It doesn't offend me," he told her and then addressed August, "a man is right to keep a close eye on who consorts with their loved ones. The world is a harsh place. To answer your questions, I'm new to town, I have no people in the area so to speak, as I am here on my own, and I am one of the new bankers that's been brought in to help with Gold Bank's expansion."

It was common knowledge that the current premier, and at one time, only banking institution, could not keep up with the new influx of clients. Seylah had heard Mister Koch lamenting to her fathers about the matter, and he had told them he had sent for a few new bankers fresh from the east coast.

"How marvelous. We are happy to have you," she told Elliot. "So very, very, happy to have you. Isn't that right, August?" She asked, giving her friend a sidelong look. For a moment, he said nothing, but rocked back on his heels, eyes moving over Elliot's form for a long moment before he jerked his head in a nod.

"Mighty happy," he finally conceded.

"Not as happy as I am, but that may have a thing or two to do with my present company. Far lovelier than I could have hoped for." Elliot bowed slightly, his eyes on Seylah, and she swore that she had never felt more seen.

"Thank you," she demurred.

"Of course, Seylah. I am glad I was able to pay my admirations before I am woefully pulled back to the bank. I hope that we are not strangers after this."

"No, no, not that."

"May I call on you?"

Seylah's smile froze, her voice silenced in her throat. "What?" She croaked. Beside her, August went rigid.

"May I call on you?" The beautiful man, built like a house, asked her once more. In her wildest dreams, men like Elliot asked her if they might call on her, but she often woke from those dreams, confused and fuzzy on the details. But, never in all of her dreaming, had one of her imagined beaus asked her if they might call on her *twice.*

Which meant only one thing—this was no dream. She blanched at the realization. A man was calling on her in earnest. In broad daylight, and she was awake for it.

"I, ah," Seylah cleared her throat and willed herself to keep standing. "Yes?"

Elliot beamed at her answer. "You have no idea how much your answer pleases me. I will call on you two days from now if that is convenient. There is a picnic I was told of, would you accompany me to it?"

"She has work," August butted in, and Seylah grit her teeth in frustration.

"I do not. Two days from now is the Sunday picnic. I am blessedly free on the day the Lord has intended for rest. And rest is exactly what I intend to do," she said, glaring at her friend. August snorted and crossed his arms with a shake of his head.

"Splendid. I will find my way to your home. I believe I met your father this morning while at work. He

44

mentioned where your lovely home is. Shall I call on you at three?"

"That's perfect. I look forward to our outing."

"Until then, Seylah," Elliot gave her another winning smile before he nodded goodbye to August, and just like that, the man was back into motion and on his way to work. There was silence between she and August as they stood watching Elliot's departure. A dreamy sigh escaped Seylah's mouth and the spell of silence was broken.

"What do you think you're doing, Seylah?"

She arched an eyebrow, the soft look on her face vanishing as she turned to face her best friend. "What do you mean?"

August gestured after Elliot. "With that man. That's what I mean." The disdain in his voice was evident, and Seylah found she did not care for it in the least.

"I'm going on a picnic with that man, *that man*, I might add, has a name," she told him, hands going to her hips.

"Do you really think it was wise to accept an offer from him so quickly?" August asked, moving his hands to mirror her posture.

"What's that supposed to mean?" Seylah wanted to know.

August took in a deep breath and looked away from her. "It means...it means that perhaps you should be more choosy when it comes to accepting possible suitors, and not leap at the first bit of attention that comes your way."

Seylah jerked back as if she had been slapped. "You cad!"

"I am no such thing. I am worried about you, Seylah."

"Oh, please, you are a selfish man, August Leclaire."

She shook a finger at him and ignored the looks they were garnering now from passerbyers, all of whom were newcomers to town. The old locals were quite accustomed to the sight of Seylah and August bickering.

"Me? Selfish? If I'm selfish, then you're a violent woman."

Seylah scoffed and set off marching towards the Sheriff's department. "Oh, August, you are so dramatic. I am nothing of the sort."

"You took the breath out of me with that elbow," August told her as he followed her.

"You quite deserved it with your behavior, and I was not going to allow you to spoil such a special moment," she said, speeding up her pace as the Sheriff's department came into view. The quicker she was indoors and at her desk, the quicker today would settle back down, and the quicker August would stop badgering her.

"That's a tall tale you're tellin', Seylah."

"I'm ignoring you now, August."

"Very mature," he huffed when she bolted up the stairs and tried to shut the door in his face, the latter was only deterred by him sticking his foot in to catch the door before it closed.

She whirled then and stuck her tongue out at him. "I never claimed to be mature," she informed him and was pleased at the look of annoyance on her friend's face. August's handsome face twisted in a frown, but he said nothing else while she went about inspecting the office. She was not accustomed to coming in so late, but the day's events could not have been helped or foreseen with Mrs. Rosemary's fitting taking up a goodly portion of her time. She was relieved to see that the deputies hadn't managed to cause too much trouble. The coffee they had prepared was unbearable, but that was to be expected, and of course, the common area was in disarray but still clean, even if there were scattered papers to set to rights given that none of the three other deputies were in the building.

Her fathers' desks were empty and she figured they were making their rounds, which meant she had entirely too much time alone with August. She glanced over at him where he was going through paperwork, he was still frowning, his brow furrowed, and she bit her lip at the sight.

August was agitated. Though, where she was concerned, he seemed to agitate easily, or at least he did as of late. The thought made her stop, her own brow coming to a knot. They had been so close growing up, and after a brief awkward stage as young teens, had come back together as close as ever from the night of Seylah's eighteenth birthday.

That night had been ... *healing*.

All it had taken was a bouquet of flowers and a simple: "I've missed you," from August for all of the distance and walls between them to come crashing down. Seylah hadn't been able to keep herself from hugging him, from telling him how much she had missed their friendship as well. It was as if the years had melted away, and the two had picked up right where they had left off the night of the ill-fated dance. The reconciliation had been so very needed in their long relationship, because as far as anyone was concerned, August Leclaire was family, part of their clan, and there was no possible world in which August was not a part of her, or her family's life.

A heavy sigh escaped August, and she swallowed hard, the fear that distance and coldness might settle between them again, might drive them apart until they were strangers, making her hands shake.

She couldn't bear it again. Not ever.

Seylah didn't expect that August could either, but then why were they so at odds these days? It seemed they misunderstood one another more and more each day. Perhaps he felt it too, and that was the reason for his reaction to Elliot's acquaintance.

It was enough to make her gnash her teeth.

"August?" She tried breaking the quiet of the room.

His hands froze. "Yes?" August said, not looking up from the papers in his hands.

"I'm sorry for striking you," she told him. "And for making you not be able to breath, and for ignoring you when you were unable to breath so that I could talk to Elliot."

He shook his head, hands moving again. "No, you're not."

"But I am, I swear it."

"Even if I wasn't mooning over your new beau?"

"He isn't my beau! He's just-just—"

He looked up at her then. "Just what, honey?" The word rolled effortlessly off of August's tongue, as if it had always been there between them, even if they both looked shocked to hear it. The room around them seemed to grow smaller, the common surroundings of the everyday, of the shelves of booking ledgers and bond releases, all took on a slightly different light, they were all rosier, softer, even the hard lines of the mahogany desks took on a far more elegant element.

All from one word. Honey. It made everything...*tender and soft.*

Seylah was left feeling out of her element, no more in command of herself than a fish with legs.

"It's only a Sunday picnic," she whispered.

He hummed and dropped his gaze back to the desk in front of him. "So it is, but don't forget one important thing."

"What's that?"

"It's a picnic that I'll be in attendance of, *so that man* had better treat you like a lady or he'll have me to answer to."

And just like that, the spell that the word *honey* cast over them was broken and Seylah felt the familiar sense of familial frustration rise up in her. The office came back into sharp focus. and she wondered if she had not been suffering from some sort of shock from her near collision with the runaway coach.

"I'm off to check the mail," she informed him, though the endeavor resulted in her sticking her hand into the mailbox at the side of the building. But, even so, August hummed in acknowledgement, and just like that everything was back to normal, and at least that, Seylah found comforting.

CHAPTER 3

*I*t was Monday afternoon, and Seylah hadn't yet managed to recover from the early chaos the start of a new week had seen fit to bless the good people of Gold Sky with, which directly involved the sheriff's office, and by proxy, Seylah. She ran a hand over her face and blinked against the weariness that was finally settling into her bones. From sunrise that morning, things had been in disarray, and it had all begun with the homesteaders.

Seylah understood the allure of land, the security and stability offered to beleaguered people set upon by low wages and pitiful living situations. She knew why the homesteaders had come west, why they were drawn to the open spaces of Montana. Life on the frontier promised more, it asked for hard work, but most importantly patience.

Rome wasn't built in a day, and neither was a well-ordered and profitable homestead. Most newcomers understood that, planned for the rough months and even years of starting over, but not everyone understood the slow and steady approach. There were those desperate homesteaders who expected instant success. These impatient few had set their sights on claims much larger than the 320 acres afforded to them by the government.

That much land was the start of a manageable farm or working ranch. It was enough that a family and a hand or two could easily tend it, but not the stuff of an empire. Too bad it seemed the homesteaders wanted empires, and they wanted them *now.*

Unauthorized fence lines had begun popping up with the latest migration to the area. Angry cowboys at the head of a cattle drive south had been tangled up in haphazard fences that spanned miles and miles of territory. The result had created an early morning shootout between angry homesteaders and cattle drivers fed up with being detained at every hillcrest and valley.

Normally a small scuffle, even one with guns, was resolved by the deputies in town, of which there were three capable men, including August, but this one had called even her fathers in via a before-sunrise visit from August.

It had been years since her fathers had dashed out before dawn, the last one Seylah could remember had happened when she was thirteen, and a group of outlaws had taken to hijacking incoming trains. Then she'd had to stay at home with her anxious mother and sisters, but this time she'd run out the door right after them. It had been dark as night when they'd ridden hard to the conflict, a spot six miles north of town where the valley emptied out to the plains. It was an advantageous spot for anyone commanding the high ground. The homesteaders knew this and had cordoned off the valley, slowing down anyone trying to make use of the route.

How there hadn't been a full on gunfight before they arrived at the site was beyond Seylah. She estimated it was on account of the homesteaders not having the mettle to follow through on it, and the cowboys having enough foresight to recognize the untried nature of the homesteaders.

After a tense few minutes of assessing the situation, her fathers had gone forward with a plan of brutal honesty: either the homesteaders stood down and went home, taking the fences with them and no more fence lines were erected, or they not only took on a very angry wagon train, but also the full force of Gold Sky law enforcement.

"Son, how sure is your shot?" Will had asked the fresh-faced man Seylah wasn't sure was much older than she. "Because my girl won't miss." Seylah turned then, showing the rifle that laid across her lap. The young man standing in front of her father had swallowed hard when she raised the rifle to rest across her arm.

"You don't want to do this," Forrest said, dropping down from his horse so that he was eye level with the gathered group of homesteaders. He turned, surveying the gathered group of men standing around them and sighed.

"You came here for a new life and this is not the way to do it. You'll be outlaws by the time the sun comes up," he paused, a hand dropping to the revolver at his hip, "and that's if you survive it. Are you ready for that?"

Seylah's heart was hammering in her chest. Another deputy, Tom, was beside her, and she could feel the energy radiating from the man. He was as ready as she to shoot, and she knew he wouldn't miss. August and Wallace were in the shadows, unseen by the homesteaders. They'd fire the moment it looked as if things were going south. The cowboys from the drive were also at the ready, but they, unlike her fathers or the deputies, were not as cool, their fingers far more prone to firing than any of the seasoned law men of Gold Sky.

Her lips had pursed at the thought—well, the men of Gold Sky, and her. On the books, Seylah was a secretary, but here when the situation called for it, she was a crack shot with a steady hand and a cool head.

Thankfully, the homesteaders had relented and packed it in, including the contentious barbed wire fence. They had also agreed to ride ahead of the cowboys and remove the remaining fences between Gold Sky and where the stockyard was located in Butte City. After that, it had mostly just been a matter of waiting it out while the homesteaders and cowboys sorted themselves for the ride ahead. Her fathers and Tom had gone ahead with the cattle drive to oversee the entire affair and ensure that no one did anything they'd regret in the true light of day.

"Keep an eye on the town," Will had said, giving her a kiss on her cheek before riding off.

"Send August in first time anyone gives you trouble," Forrest called over his shoulder. Seylah had nodded at both of them, though they couldn't see her in the dark.

"Be careful." Her voice had been lost in the early hours of the morning and she hadn't uttered a word until she'd dismounted and walked into the office. The rest of her morning had been tense, her mind following every thread of reality that might end with one of her fathers hurt, or worse...she winced at the thought and refused to even think it.

Anything *but that.*

The sound of a telegram arriving set her to her feet and she raced to the machine at the far side of the room. The paper unfurled slowly and Seylah had to clasp her hands in front of her to stop herself from snatching it free and ripping it in half before it was finished. When, at last, it was complete, she took a deep breath and with a trembling hand, read the message.

Arrived safe. Be back by dinner.

All our love.

-W.&F

A sigh of relief escaped her at the brief but reassuring message. All the tension in her body eased out until she sagged against the table at her back. She could breathe again, at least for the moment. She knew the situation with the homesteaders was not over, not by a long shot, but for now, she would put it out of her mind. Her mother and sisters would be so relieved...*her mother!*

She bolted for the door. She had to tell her mother that all was well and her fathers would be home for dinner. If Seylah had been this worried, she loathed to think of how difficult the past hours had been for her mother. The door banged shut behind her, and Seylah was off like a shot, with home and her mother as her only thought.

She was nearly to the edge of town when she heard her sister, Rose, call to her.

"Seylah!" She turned and looked behind her to see her sister hurrying towards her.

"Have you heard anything?" Rose asked, breathless from her near sprint.

"Everything is okay. They've arrived in Butte and will be home by dinner."

"Oh, thank God." The sisters embraced, and Seylah patted Rose's trembling shoulders.

"I was on my way to tell Mama."

Rose pulled back and linked their arms together. "She'll be a wreck until she knows. Let's be on our way, then."

Seylah leaned against her and nodded, content to let the other woman take the lead. It had been a stressful and exhausting day thus far, and she wanted nothing more than to rest, maybe eat a bit of something now that the knot in her stomach was finally loosening enough for her to do anything, but think of terrible outcomes. Her stomach rumbled, and Rose looked at her with a disapproving frown.

"Have you eaten?"

Seylah shook her head. "No. I couldn't manage it. Not with everything."

"You have to take care of yourself, Seylah," Rose chastised, giving her arm a light yank. "You're eating as soon as we get home and tell Mama."

"That sounds wonderful," Seylah sighed in relief. They had only taken a few steps together when August rounded a corner and stopped on the boardwalk in front of them.

The man had a determined set to his shoulders, and he waved a hand at them before he started forward.

"He looks determined," Rose observed giving her sister a nudge, who nodded in silence. It was true. August looked like a man on a mission, with his sure steps and the focused look he was sending them. There was no mistaking that he meant to speak to them.

"Are you all right?" He asked, and Seylah raised an eyebrow, noticing he was out of breath.

"Yes, but are you all right?" She asked, giving him a curious look. "Did something happen?"

"Were you running?" Rose added in, and he sucked in a deep breath.

"Yes," he said and gave them a shaky smile, "but everything is all right. I saw the telegram that your pa's are coming home. Took off to tell your ma. Was hoping I'd run into you on the way."

"Seylah already saw it. We were on our way home now," Rose told him and a look of relief crossed August's features. He closed his eyes briefly and he nodded, a smile on his face.

"Good to hear. I know it's been rough since the morning."

Seylah nodded and reached out, touching his hand, lightly. "Thank you for thinking of Mama."

He opened his blue eyes and gave her a crooked smile. "'Course. Didn't know where you'd gone, but I didn't want to let the message sit in case you missed it." He stopped and stepped closer, his gaze sweeping over the length of her. "Are you well? Have you eaten?"

"No, she hasn't," Rose grumbled and elbowed her sister

in the side. "You know how she gets when she's stressed."

Seylah rolled her eyes at her sister. "I'm standing right here, Rose."

"I do know how she gets. Takes to forgettin' about herself," August answered, as if Seylah hadn't spoken, and this time, she aimed a sharp look his way.

"I do not forget about myself."

"Can you please take her to lunch?" Rose asked.

August gave a quick nod and reached for Seylah's arm. "I can."

"Oh, perfect! I'll head on the way to tell Mama, and you get Seylah fed and keep an eye on her for the rest of the day, won't you?"

Again, August nodded, and again, Seylah glared. "I am an adult perfectly capable of minding myself."

"Then maybe you should take to doing it then, hmm?" Rose asked with feigned sweetness. She looked at August and made a shooing motion. "Go on, take her, ignore her fussing."

"I do not fuss," Seylah protested, but August ignored her as directed, and put her hand on his arm as he started forward.

"I'll bring her home after work," he told Rose as he maneuvered them in the direction of Mrs. Lily's Cafe.

"Have fun on your outing! I couldn't have planned this better than if you had called on her. What lucky timing." Rose waved a hand at them, merrily, and turned off on her heel before she bounded away in the direction of home. Seylah was left disgruntled and dragged along by August.

"This is not an outing," Seylah muttered giving her

arm a shake, but August kept it right where it was and gave her a sidelong look.

"And, why not?" He wanted to know.

"Well it isn't. You did not call on me, for one, and secondly, we are best friends, and lastly, we are only together on account of my pas."

The last of her reasons was related to the early morning goings on that nearly resulted in a gun fight, but Seylah wasn't so sure August understood her meaning when he winced and said, "I would be right here with you, Pas or not, Seylah Wickes-Barnes, and it's about time you got that into your way of thinking."

"What are you talking about?"

He didn't answer, but kept walking, the quick pace forcing her to hurry her steps and take hold of her skirt in order to keep up. They were attracting looks from the other citizens on the street, but August didn't seem to mind or care. Seylah ducked her head at the attention when she saw Elliot Myers stepping out of the bank and catching sight of them. The man looked as confused as Seylah felt, and she offered him a half-hearted wave on their way past, of which he nodded in recognition, but she saw how his eyes lighted on where August was still holding on to her. August's hand resting over hers where it was in the crook of his arm.

"August, let go," she whispered, but he shook his head.

"No."

"People are *staring.*"

He slowed, then. The change was slight, but he did so when he was nearly even with Elliot and gave the other man a nod of greeting, his fingers tightening on her hand.

"Afternoon," August offered Elliot as they continued past.

"Afternoon." Elliot touched the rim of his hat, but said nothing more, and Seylah shot him a worried look over her shoulder. He was still watching from where he stood, and Seylah wasn't quite sure what to make of the look he was shooting her and August. It wasn't angry, or confused, but interested. Why on earth was he looking at them like that?

"Are you out of your mind?" She asked when they came to a stop in front of Mrs. Lily's.

August opened the door and ushered her inside the bustling establishment. He held up a hand in greeting to Mrs. Lily, who beamed at them and gestured them over to a table in the corner.

"Seat yourselves and I'll be right over, you two!"

"Come on, then," August's hand was on her again and the pair of them were in motion once more before Seylah could get another word out. She frowned at him when he pulled out her chair for her and inclined his head.

"Are you going to answer me?" She asked, crossing her arms now that her hands were free.

"Are you going to sit?" He asked, arching an eyebrow in challenge, and gesturing to the chair once more.

Seylah's lips pressed into a thin line, and for a moment, she contemplated not budging an inch, but then August gave her a pleading look and said: "Please, will you sit?"

His voice was soft, blue eyes softer, and she swallowed hard against the warmth in her belly the scene elicited from her. August was a fine looking man, always had been, and Seylah suspected always would be. He was muscular in a way that only time in the saddle and hours of intense farm labor could create. Broad shoulders, thick arms and thighs Seylah desperately tried not to notice that never quite fit in the suits he wore.

Seylah knew the man much preferred the far more casual clothing suited to a frontier law man, than a gentleman. Seylah had thought she preferred the casual look, but then she'd had her little run in with Elliot.

As if on cue, the man walked past the window of Mrs. Lily's and she felt her heart leap into her throat. As before, he looked put together and refined, the hat he'd tipped to them earlier was sitting perfectly on his coiffed head. She watched him, helpless to look away, as the man strode past, looking every bit the gentleman from her dreams.

Well, *hers,* and she supposed, a good number of ladies from Gold Sky.

A gaggle of well-dressed and beautifully made up women bustled after Elliot with bright smiles on their faces. They were trying to catch his eye and Seylah could not fault them for their efforts. He'd swept her off her feet, literally, yes, but it didn't change the fact that Elliot had stirred up a part of her she'd long supposed lost to her.

No man, but August had made her feel a spark of anything, and then Elliot had appeared out of nowhere. The charming man, that set her to blushing and simpering like a schoolgirl, was taking her to a picnic the following week.

Her cheeks warmed at the idea of spending time with

Elliot, and she smiled to herself, looking down at her hands. It would be a lovely day, she was sure of it.

It would be perfect.

A sigh escaped her lips, and she would have continued to smile if not for the scoff that came from across the table.

She narrowed her eyes at him. "What?"

August sucked his teeth and leaned back in his seat. "Nothing."

"Are you sure? From where I'm sitting, it sure as hell sounds like a whole lot of something."

He flashed her a smile at that and held up his hands in surrender. "Oh, it's nothing. Just not used to seeing that look on your face is all." He flicked a finger at her face and Seylah frowned.

"What look?"

August shrugged. "Nothing, Seylah May." When he used her middle name, Seylah knew there was more to it. There always was when he called her by her full name, and knowing he had more to say, but was keeping it close had her itching to get under his skin.

So she did.

"Fine, August Henry."

He smirked at her ploy but to the man's credit he didn't take the bait, and instead turned towards Mrs. Lily who was bustling up with a pitcher of water and a smile. The woman's arrival derailed Seylah's plans to poke at August, but she made a mental note to only table the endeavor, not give it up completely.

"What will you two dears have?" The older woman asked, filling up their glasses with water.

"Special of the day works for me," August replied, and looked expectantly at Seylah. "Sound good for you too?"

Seylah nodded and smiled at Mrs. Lily, "I'll take the same please, ma'am."

Mrs. Lily nodded scribbling on her notepad. "Coming right up. How's your mama? I heard there was trouble out by the pass. Your Pas okay?"

Seylah nodded. "Yes, it's all settled now. Thank you for asking."

"Of course. Glad we have men like your Pas around to keep the peace. These newcomers are a tad energetic about the land around here lately." Mrs. Lily shook her head and then smiled at August. "Glad we've got young blood with deep roots like you, too. Gold Sky will need it if we aim to keep life good."

August nodded at the words of compliment. "Thank you, Mrs. Lily. Happy to call Gold Sky home."

Mrs. Lily stayed for a few moments more, asking after their days and general catching up before she departed with their order, but not before August added on a dessert order which surprised Seylah. August never ate dessert, and she raised an eyebrow in question.

"What is it?" He asked, sipping from his glass, and returning her look with a quizzical one of his own.

"You never eat sweets," she informed him.

He grinned at her. "No, I don't, but you," he pointed at her, "always eat sweets."

"I do not always eat sweets," she replied, her determination to annoy him renewed by his matter-of-fact tone. He was acting smug and that irked her. It was common knowledge that she had an insatiable sweet tooth, she had no idea why he was acting as if it were special knowledge, so she forced her features into a severe look and said, "In fact, I've quite given up sweets. Outgrown them, I think."

"Oh, you have, have you?" He leaned forward on his elbows and gave her a challenging look. "Are you saying that you do not take certain liberties to line your pockets with as many as you can during the holidays?"

"It's a time of festivities, everyone does."

"Or birthdays?"

"What's a celebration if not for cake to be enjoyed later?"

"Then what of your cake-for-breakfast habit?"

She stopped at that and then grinned at him, her motivation to get under skin suddenly leaving her at the mention of her favorite breakfast food. "Every morning deserves to be celebrated with cake."

August grinned at her and nodded, sipping from his glass again. "You're right. It does deserve to be celebrated. That's why I got you dessert." There was a tone in his voice that she recognized, the one that was protective and a touch lower, the kind of voice she'd heard when the boys at school had picked on her for her growth spurt and August had to put them all in line about giving her grief.

There had also been the time she was so sick they feared she'd gotten scarlet fever when she was eighteen. He hadn't left her side then, staying close to her and refusing to care for himself when she was ailing. And who could forget when she'd started riding in earnest two years ago, and she'd taken a fall so hard that she broke her arm and suffered a concussion. For weeks, the man had fussed over her more than her own mother, and every word that came from his mouth had been this low and slow voice.

He'd only ever spoken to her in this voice, one with hushed words and a touch deeper that she felt it in her bones when he was worried for her.

It was a nice voice.

Seylah liked this voice, even if she didn't know why he was worried for her now.

Her fathers were fine. He'd read the telegram himself, hadn't he? What was the cause for his protective streak to show?

And how damnable was it that she liked knowing he was thinking of her enough to be concerned?

That shouldn't be.

"What's wrong?" She tried.

"Nothing," August said, leaning back in his chair once more, eyes moving slowly over her as if he were trying to memorize how she looked.

"I'm all right, I swear it."

He nodded. "I know you are."

"Then why are you fussing over me like a mother hen?"

August lifted a shoulder in a shrug. "What's wrong with me looking after you every now and then?"

Seylah's mouth opened, there was a retort on the tip of her tongue, just begging to be let loose, but with him looking at her the way he was, with those blue eyes warm and open, his handsome face softened by compassion, she couldn't find it in her to let the words fly.

She closed her mouth and swallowed hard. "Nothing...I suppose," she added as an afterthought, pulling a chuckle from August. Seylah felt his hand brush against hers, rough fingertips trailing over her knuckles so light she could nearly convince herself that she had imagined the sensation. She nearly sighed at the sound of it. There was something to hearing him laugh, as slight as it was.

She lived for the moments when it was like this between them. Soft, tender, so akin to that feeling of romance that she was willing to endure the misunderstandings to simply bask in these simple and precious few moments.

"You suppose?"

She raised her eyes to meet his and gave a slight nod. "I find it agreeable."

The corner of his mouth lifted in a smile. "I'll make sure to note today as a lucky day."

"The luckiest," she said, returning his smile. Her heart skipped a beat when she again felt him touch her, this time a thumb against her wrist, and all of time seemed to stop around them so long as he was touching her. Seylah knew she should not feel this way, that it wasn't fair in the least to August, nor herself, to misconstrue this friendly touch as anything but the familial comfort it was meant to convey.

August did not want her as she did him. Of that she was sure.

Of that, he had been afforded ample time and opportunity to act upon, and yet the man remained close but only so much. They were as close as any two people who were not of blood could ever hope to be, and save that one fateful night in their youth, nothing had ever blossomed between them.

Seylah may be untried in the ways of love and romance, but she understood enough to comprehend that given the time and years shared between the two of them, that if their friendship had not grown into love by now, then there was no hope for it.

It made no sense why she continued to lose herself to daydreams and hopeful wishings as if she were still a naive child. It only worked to bruise her heart, to put more distance where she only wanted closeness, and most of all, it wasn't fair to August.

She snatched her hand back from across the table and tucked it close in her lap avoiding the curious look August was now giving her.

"Seylah?" He tried, that low voice she loved, once more assaulting her without mercy.

"Mm?" She asked, pretending as if she were not fighting back tears. Her fingernails dug half-moons into her palms as she clutched the hand August had touched. If she could sever it from her body she would, anything to get rid of the warmth that still ghosted her skin where his fingers had been.

August leaned across the table, a hand reaching for her once more. "Seylah what—"

"And here's your lunch, dears!" Mrs. Lily's voice sang to them and all at once the bubble of peace that had separated them burst, leaving them bare to the sounds and commotion of the busy eatery. "I'll have that cake along shortly, I hope that's all right?"

Seylah nodded, grateful for the interruption, though her senses felt off kilter by the sudden shift, and she blinked, owlishly, as if seeing their surroundings for the first time. "Yes, that's perfect. Thank you, Mrs. Lily."

Mrs. Lily shot her a smile and touched her shoulder. "Of course, Seylah. Enjoy your meal, you two." The woman swept off and the silence that descended on the table was palpable. If she had a mind to, Seylah estimated she could cut it with her knife and fork in place of her chicken and potatoes.

"This looks wonderful. Don't you think?" Seylah asked, spreading her napkin across her lap as if she hadn't just nearly given into her heart and spoiled things between them.

"Seylah," August cleared his throat and ran a hand through his hair, the strands catching the light and creating a halo around him in such a distracting way that Seylah bit the tines of her fork. She winced and cursed at herself silently.

What was wrong with her as of late?

She should not be comparing her best friend to an angel lest that creature be the Archangel Michael. She smiled at the thought, which in turn, made August cross his arms and give her a narrowed eye look.

"Are you all right?" He asked when her face was caught between a wince and a smile. She was certain she looked half-mad, but there was no fix for it.

"Ah, yes, I'm fine," she nodded and swallowed her chicken. "The flavor was just interesting," she lied, banishing all thoughts of sun-kissed blond hair and angels from her mind.

August picked up his knife and fork at her words, but his face clearly told her he remained unconvinced despite her reassurances. "Eat your lunch. You're acting strange. I think it's gone to your head."

She bobbed her head in agreement. "Yes, you're right. I'll be right as rain after lunch. I don't know where my mind has gone."

Seylah then dropped her eyes to her plate and made a show of tucking into her meal with as much enthusiasm as she could muster which turned out to take no acting on her part at all as Mrs. Lily's cooking was delicious and savory, as usual. By the time dessert arrived, Seylah did not have to work in the slightest to convey a sense of normalcy, and she was nearly done polishing off the sweet when August caught her attention.

"I don't think it's good for you to be with us on call."

Her fork tines clattered against the china of her plate. "Pardon me?"

"It was dangerous this mornin'," he said finally, looking uncomfortable as he shifted in his seat and crossed his arms. "You could have been hurt."

"Same goes for you."

"It's not the same."

"Why not?" She set her fork down, thinking she had no more room for dessert with the current topic at hand, which had her thinking August looked less like an Archangel and more an unholy pain in her side if he was about to say what she thought he was.

"I am a deputy," he said simply.

"And?"

"And?" August threw up his hands and leaned across the table in exasperation. "And you are not a deputy, Seylah May. You are a *secretary*." He said the last word as if it were a curse, as if the title of secretary was something foul he wanted to spit from his mouth. It fell between them on the table like a dirty thing.

She jerked back as if slapped. "And what's wrong with being a secretary?" Her hands were now flat against the table pressing hard on the wood, her dessert long forgotten with the time of fire she now felt for August which was far from amorous.

"Nothing," he ran his hands through his hair and closed his eyes, taking in a deep breath. "There's nothing wrong with being a secretary but *secretaries*," he said once more, emphasizing the word with a tone Seylah cared nothing for, "do not pick up guns and follow me to god knows where while a damn gun fight nearly breaks out."

Seylah grit her teeth. "But—"

"Secretaries stay safe at home in their beds, secretaries do not leave the damned office to arrest a drunk when the rest of us are out," he continued, referencing the time *or three* Seylah had done just that.

"Something had to be done," she explained.

"I know that, but it needn't be done by you," he told her.

"Why not?"

"You're too important for that horseshit, Seylah May."

Her fingers curled into fists. "Stop calling me that."

August gave one defiant shake of his head. "It's your name isn't it?"

"I don't like it when you say it like that. You say it like I'm still a child and you have some sort of say in what I do, which," she held up a finger when he opened his mouth to speak, "you clearly do not. I do as I please and as

69

a *secretary* of Gold Sky, I will continue to do my civic duty as needed, which includes providing back up and responding to disputes when deputies are not able to."

A growl was pulled from August, but Seylah was far too worked up to pay it any mind. "Do you understand me, August Henry Leclair?"

"You're being unreasonable. I'm concerned for you."

"I am nothing of the sort."

"You are," he said, his blue eyes flaming to something far more intense than the normal ire Seylah was familiar with when they quarreled, "you're being reckless. About this morning, about that man."

Her eyebrows shot up. "About that man?" She asked and then she gasped. "Elliot? Are you truly bringing him up? Is that what all of this is about?"

He scoffed. "This is not about him, but he is a symptom of your recklessness."

"You're just jealous," she blurted out, unable to stop the words before they came out. She clapped a hand over her mouth, shocked at the words that she'd uttered before scarcely having a moment to think them over.

They were silent for a moment before August spoke. "Might be you're right."

"What?" Her eyes widened. She had never thought he would say such a thing. "I don't understand."

"What's to understand, Seylah?" August asked, his words coming faster now, the words tumbling over each other as if they had a life of their own. "He's new in town and you're mooning over him. That is something you only —" he stopped, abruptly, as if he had been punched and shook his head.

"I have to go," he said standing from the table so quickly his chair nearly toppled over. He looked as shocked as she felt by her accusation, as rattled as she was by his sudden declaration. *What was happening? What was this constantly shifting ground between them she couldn't quite gain her footing on?*

"Where are you going?" She asked, confused by his sudden change of tack.

"I'll pay for this. You get on home."

"But August, what were you saying? Why—"

"I'll, uh, be 'round later to check in with your pas. Goodbye, Seylah." And then, the big man Seylah had thought of as her mountain, as the man with deep roots in the place she loved the most, the man that made her think of avenging angels, and what it might be like if only things were different, turned on his heel and strode out of the restaurant.

Once again, Seylah was left with the agonizing possibility of what might have been if only they'd had a moment more.

CHAPTER 4

"I hear you are to attend the picnic with a charming newcomer."

Seylah looked up at her sister Delilah's voice. The other woman was grinning at her like the cat that got the cream, and Seylah huffed in annoyance.

"How do you know about that?"

"Everyone has taken to talking of it," Delilah informed her upon entering the room. They were in the home library their fathers had built for their mother.

The room was stuffed with books of every genre, but there was no mistaking the larger than normal romance section. Her mother had a soft spot for the genre, and she had imparted it zealously to her daughters, all of whom made no secret of their love of reading.

It was Seylah's favorite room in the house. Her earliest memories were in this room, on her Papa's knee, as he read to her in front of the fireplace, or sitting with her mother while she read aloud from her newest purchase to Seylah and her sisters.

It was a good room, a homey room, and she naturally gravitated there when her work day was done. It was no surprise that Delilah should find her here, but what was surprising was the news the other woman brought with her upon her arrival.

"Everyone?"

Delilah nodded. "The entire town from the sound of it."

"The entire town?!"

"They were positively in a frenzy over the news that you have a courtship," her sister went on, crossing the room to a stack of well-worn books. She picked one up and held it up to her sister. "What do you think of gothic romances? I find that I am devouring them as of late."

"How on earth—" Seylah pinched the bridge of her nose, "a frenzy? How?"

Delilah bit her lip and put the book down in the stack. "Of that I have no knowledge. I heard about it in the mercantile, and by then it was well known around town, so it's hard to say where the news spread from."

Seylah groaned, slumping in her chair and landing face first into the book she had been reading. A lovely, dreamy novel about a woman's journey through Europe. She quite wished she was in a foreign land. Anything was preferable to the entirety of Gold Sky making up a reality in which she was being courted.

"This meddlesome town, it'll be the end of me, I swear it," she moaned from her place, lips and face pressed to the desk in front of her.

"You sound like papa," Delilah informed her.

"And he's not wrong. The whole lot of them are

73

meddlesome and eavesdropping, and entirely too dramatic for their own good and...and...well, I don't know what, but they are it," Seylah said, voice muffled by the pages at her lips.

"And they love you and support you at every turn. Accept you as you are no matter what," Delilah finished for her. "Respect you too, there isn't another place where you could bring a room of unruly men to heel like Gold Sky. They see you as an authority in town," Del tapped her chest where an imaginary deputy badge would be pinned, " badge or no badge you are respected here."

Seylah sighed heavily and pushed herself up from the books. "Yes, of course," she smiled at her sister's words, because they were just as much true as her own frustrated observation. "They are entirely too good and too damnable to be anything else, but what they are."

"And we love them for it," Delilah said, holding a finger up to make her point.

"Yes, we do." Seylah shut her book with a snap of her hand. There would be no reading now, or concentrating on plotlines, no matter how lovely or endearing they were. The people of Gold Sky had effectively stolen her attention, and when she turned to Delilah, she saw that her sister was smiling broadly.

"What is it?" Seylah asked.

"I saw the man in question. A mister Elliot Myers."

Seylah nodded. "That is he."

"He's a banker."

"He is, and it is not a courtship, it is simply a Sunday picnic at the church. I told August as much."

"August was not pleased by the flurry of interest your

new suitor caused in town, but I feel that the competition is quite good for him. He's had his time with you, and now could do with a bit of urgency," Delilah said as blithely as if she were commenting on the weather or the quality of cake offered that day at breakfast.

Cake, not her opinions on August and his need for, what was it? Urgency? Urgency for what? Seylah had no idea, but she had enough sanity to ask her sister.

"For what? Care to explain that bit on urgency once more for me?"

Delilah sat in the overstuffed armchair by the window and gave her sister a considering look. "Oh, sweet Seylah, you are the older of us but sometimes I wonder if you are willfully blind or just that naive."

Seylah chewed on her bottom lip. "Direct as ever, Del."

The other woman lifted a shoulder in a shrug and spread her hands over her skirts. "You know it's because I care, otherwise I'd tell you what I know you want to hear."

"Which would be?" Seylah wanted to know.

"That August has no feelings for you, and that he most definitely did not brood and stalk about when word of your impending outing with Mister Elliots Myers came about."

Seylah moaned and covered her face with her hands. "Oh dear. He was rather agitated when I left him at work today."

"That's putting it mildly," Delilah deadpanned, which earned her a withering look from Seylah. "What?" Her sister asked, sitting up in her chair and throwing her hands up. "The man is-is—"

"He's what?" Seylah sighed.

"I'm not quite sure yet, but I know it's with you, dear sister, and he has been since he clapped eyes on you in Mother's classroom."

Seylah shook her head and stood from her seat. "You are quite mistaken, Del. August and I—, well, we are friends."

"But Seylah—"

"No, Del. Listen to me." Seylah wrung her hands in front of her and cleared her throat against the rising lump she felt there. It was growing increasingly difficult to speak, to breathe, to do anything when the matter that Del was suddenly determined to drag out into the open.

Why would she do this now? After all this time.

"I almost lost him once, and I'll not risk it again."

Delilah's eyes widened. "What?" She asked, voice just loud enough for her sister to hear in the stillness of the library.

"When we were fourteen...that dance, August took me to that dance. The one that was just after school ended for the summer. Do you remember it?"

Her sister smiled fondly at the memory. "You were lovely, and you were, I mean, that was the last time that you dressed up. Of course I remember it. You were beautiful."

Seylah's eyes drifted closed. "I was not."

"Seylah, that's a lie. You were the most beautiful girl I had ever seen, you looked just like Mama in her wedding photos. Even Daddy and Papa said so."

Delilah's words poked at the sore spot Seylah kept covered for fear of someone finding it, of someone accidentally pressing upon that unhealed wound that would hurt her anew, fresh as the day it was wrought.

"No, I was not." She held up a hand when her sister made to protest and continued speaking. "That night I heard August speaking with a group of older girls, girls that had finally noticed him because August was far more dashing than the rest of the boys there. I had thought the night was the start of something bigger, of perhaps an *us*, because that was what I wanted so desperately as a girl. But, August told them he did not care for me like I did him."

Delilah shook her head, a frown on her face as she did so. "No, it can't be."

"He told them that he was only watching out for me as debt to our fathers for looking out for him. That," she swallowed hard, past the lump and forced the words out, "nothing was for free and that he owed them."

Delilah clapped a hand over her mouth and gasped. "Oh, Seylah, no."

"After that night, things were strained between us. I left the dance early and came home, I was so embarrassed. I felt like a fool and couldn't look at him for weeks. He started, ah seeing one of the girls from that night shortly after as well, so it was easier for us to avoid spending time."

Delilah nodded. "I remember that time. It was hard on you both."

Seylah cleared her throat and pushed past the bit where her sister said *both*, and continued on, "We didn't speak to each other like we did before—not as best

77

friends, until the night of my eighteenth birthday, when it was simply too much for us."

"What was?"

"The pain of missing one another. We reconciled, though I doubt he knows what our estrangement was ever over. August has no idea that I heard him that night. I never told him, or anyone until now, until I've told you. I kept it close."

"But why? Why would you not let us share that pain?" Delilah asked, her eyes shining with tears.

Seylah blinked back her own tears at the emotion she heard in her sister's voice. "I wanted it to be a memory. I wanted it to not have happened, so I pushed it aside and built a fortress around it so that it might never touch me again."

Delilah rose from her seat and embraced her, arms wrapped tightly around her sister as she squeezed her as hard as she could. "Oh, Seylah, I'm so sorry. I'm so so sorry."

Seylah hugged her back. The comfort from her sister's touch was enough for her to find the strength to keep talking even though the wound she had guarded so vigilantly was now stripped bare and left open for another to observe it.

It hurt, oh how it *ached*, but it also felt wildly liberating. To be able to speak her mind on her feelings, on what had transpired between she and August all those years ago. To be able to respond, honestly, now that they were adults, and the feeling of attraction she had felt for him at fourteen had only grown more intense and devout as she matured into a woman. She had always hoped that her feelings for her best friend would dim, simply vanish one day if she resisted the urge to be close to him like *that*.

Except that for all her efforts, her heart had only clung more desperately to the moments when August smiled at her, when he spoke to her as if she were the only person of import in his life, when it was just them.

Those were the moments she treasured. Her heart stuttered remembering his use of 'honey' just that afternoon. How was she to interpret this? And he had only used such a word when Elliot Myers had made his intentions known to take her to a picnic—had asked to call on her.

The timing of it was too neat. Seylah did not trust it, because as dumb as she played, Delilah was quite right in her estimation that August required urgency in his feelings. What if the man she had worked to stop herself from feeling as she did suddenly lost his interest in her when she turned away from Elliot?

She owed it to herself to follow through with the invite to the picnic. She owed it to her heart that she had carefully guarded to see what she might feel for Elliot. The leap to attraction was a small one as the man had thoroughly charmed her upon their first meeting, but even so...even so it was difficult to let go of August.

Try as she may. Her fragile heart would not listen.

But that did not mean that she would not do her utmost to keep to the line that she had drawn for herself wherever August Leclaire was concerned. She had worked valiantly to see him as her best friend, and her best friend the man would stay, no matter how much her sister said he brooded over the news of her picnic with Elliot.

She squeezed her sister tight and kissed her cheek. Delilah spoke plainly and honestly, which made the truth so much harder for Seylah to give voice to. She knew her sister saw something between them, that Delilah wouldn't have brought it up otherwise, but whatever it was, Seylah knew that it could not be. Not when it risked her losing August, not when it had nearly cost her their friendship already. She would never make that mistake again.

Seylah leaned her forehead against her sister's crown and smiled bitterly when Delilah whispered, "Please don't cry."

She hadn't even realized she had begun to cry, the tears had come so fiercely and suddenly that Seylah was left with wet cheeks and little recollection of when it began. Her heart ached, knowing the tears were for what never had been between she and August.

"Promise me that whatever brooding you see August doing, or saw him engaging in today, promise me that you will not make it out to be more than it is."

"But Seylah...it was something," Delilah insisted.

"No, it was not. It cannot be anything. It is August and I merely misunderstanding the other. There is a lapse in our communication, but it will all be laid to rights soon enough. I promise you. What you saw today was on no account of my having a scheduled outing with Elliot Myers," she finished, her throat burning by the time she was finished speaking. The tears were falling faster now, her chest constricting from the energy it took to hold back the sob that was rising up in her. She squeezed her eyes shut, willing them away, but even while she did, she knew the world did not operate in such a way that a woman was able to put aside life's hurts as if they never occurred.

A woman carried them with her for all of her days until she confronted them.

She prayed she would have the strength to carry hers with grace.

SEYLAH SQUINTED out at the horizon and frowned when the noonday sun made her yank the brim of her hat lower so that she could see anything of use.

"How far down the line are you wanting to go?" August asked her.

"About a mile or so," Seylah answered him, leaning back in her seat and pointing out towards the horizon. "Daddy said the fence was damaged out that way. Wanted us to take a look at it, maybe mend it while we were out on our ride."

August hummed in answer and nodded. "Sounds good."

Seylah waited for him to continue, but when her friend said nothing, she nudged her horse into motion. They were out for their weekly ride, a ride Seylah was quickly realizing would be a mostly one-sided affair in terms of conversation.

"How was your day?" She tried, but only received another grunt in place of words. Seylah blew out a deep breath, and the pair rode in silence for several minutes, until she tried again.

"Are you...upset?"

August frowned and looked at her. "Why would you think that?" His blue eyes were cool on her, and she hated how easy it was for the man to keep his emotions hidden. She was an open book, this she knew from the countless times August had teased her. Seylah was painfully aware that August could understand her by simply looking at her face, that her whole heart was to be found in her eyes when it came to him.

How was it so easily done by him when she couldn't manage it in the least?

"You're incredibly quiet," she told him.

He raised an eyebrow at her. "That's my way."

She nodded at him, flicking her reins and working to stay relaxed in her seat. It would do no good for her to become agitated on the off chance that her horse would pick up on it. "You're right. It is your way...when you're upset," she said, voice even and measured, but even so, August scoffed at her words.

"You seem to have something on your mind that you would like to discuss."

"What makes you say that?" Seylah was proud that her voice was still cool, there was no drama to her tone, only calmness. Perhaps she had been too hasty in her estimation of being an open book for August's perusal. It could be that she had grown some in her ability to conceal her emotions—

"It's plain as day, Seylah," August interrupted her, dashing any hopes that she had mastered the art of concealment, "you know I can tell what you're thinking by just one look." He gave her a smug smile that had her seeing red.

Just because the man could understand her easily did not mean he need be so assured in it, or at least not to her face.

"Plain as day is it?" She asked, flicking her reins again and urging her horse faster. "You say that as if I can't tell when you're upset from a mile off. Why I quite estimate that if I were standin' at the broken fence," she threw out her arm in front of them, and her horse sped up slightly as her speaking increased, "I could tell you're in a sour mood today."

"Oh, Seylah, don't get fussy."

"I am not fussy! You're fussy," she informed him, her horse now at a gallop. "And, you're smug too. A smug fussy man if I ever did see one!"

"Seylah, slow down."

"I'm fine with this speed thank you very much," Seylah tossed back, enjoying the way her horse was now moving. She could see the fence that needed mending just up ahead, and this horse did enjoy a sprint from time to time, so why not indulge the poor creature? She leaned over the pommel, the reins in one hand as she trailed the other out alongside her, catching the wind in her fingers.

Here, like this, nothing could touch her. Not anything, not her misunderstandings with August or the man's sour mood, nor her nervousness over her upcoming outing with Elliot, even the dramatics of her dress fittings could be left behind.

She was free like this. Her body relaxed and she

sighed, closing her eyes for a moment as the horse continued on towards their destination. She could hear August yelling at her to slow down, but she was of no mind to heed him. She was a seasoned horsewoman, she could handle herself, and he knew it.

She much expected August was only yelling at her on account of him no longer being able to tell her how easily she communicated her emotions or some other truth she wasn't keen on. On Seylah rode, the seconds passing to minutes before the site of their work was in front of them, and she pulled her horse to a stop.

When August arrived beside her, nearly a minute later, Seylah was happily unpacking the tools needed for the fence-mending. She cautioned a look up at him and saw that the man was glowering at her from where he was still astride.

"What?" She asked yanking her leather gloves on with a snap.

"You're goddamn infuriating," August bit out and swung down from his horse with another glare. "You'll be the death of me. I know it."

Seylah rolled her eyes at him. "Stop being so dramatic."

"Says the woman riding like the devil was chasing her. You need to take more care when you're out here."

Seylah approached the fence, the barbed wire at this point of the line had fallen, and clucked her tongue when she saw the braces responsible for holding the fence intact had been knocked loose. Most likely from the hard winds they'd had all summer. "Oh, I know the land like the back of my hand, you know that."

"Then you know to pay mind that we've been having a

rough storm season this summer. Plenty of the grounds have been washed out over the past few weeks, Seylah. Running your horse that fast without minding the new holes is foolish. The last thing any of us needs is for you to go breakin' your neck, because you were careless with your horse."

She froze at August's words and stared at the fallen fence. He was right, of course. There had been countless storms over the past weeks, more washouts than normal, and the land this way did have a tendency to be weak and sandy in some areas. She had closed her eyes, and he'd seen it, knew she hadn't been paying attention like she normally did because she was wound up.

Seylah grit her teeth. She was wound up, because of the same man that was right. She hated that he was right.

"I don't know what you're talking about," she replied stubbornly, because once Seylah had dug her heels in, she took great care to dig in doubly when August was involved.

"You damn well know what I'm talking about." He was at her side, then, and yanking on his own gloves with a snap of his hands. "You take any more chances like that and—"

"And what?" she interrupted, glaring up at him. She was mad at him, because she knew he was in a poor mood, and that he was unwilling to tell her why he was in such a poor mood, even though in her heart Seylah had a sinking suspicion what it was about.

Her scheduled outing with Elliot Meyers.

August raised one finger and pointed at her. "If you think for one second that I'm going to let you run wild and reckless you've got another thing coming, Seylah Wickes-Barnes. I'll not have it," he told her, his voice dropping an octave and filling the space between them with an air of authority she hadn't heard directed at her by August. She'd heard this voice, his no-nonsense, stern voice that commanded, left no room for arguments, but it had never been used on *her.*

She reared back on him, and slapped his finger away with an audible gasp. "You'll not have it? Who do you think you are to order me about?"

August avoided her hand when she made to slap at his pointed finger. Instead, he caught it and curled his hand around hers bringing it to his chest. "I'm your best friend, that's who I am. And I'll not see you hurt."

As if by magic, that simple touch, just the weight of his hand around hers, the steadiness of his chest against the back of her hand, served to leach all the anger and frustration right out of her.

"That's not fair," she whispered, and the stormy expression on August's face melted away to a reluctant smile.

"I know," he said, simply.

She wiggled her fingers slightly, the move working to press their fingers together. "Why won't you talk about what's put you in a mood?"

Again, the shutters came down over his eyes, and his smile vanished, as if it hadn't been there a moment before. Even though they were still so close, their hands curled around the other, she felt a gulf of distance descend them. "Nothin' to talk about, Seylah."

"That's not true. You know it," she insisted, but went

no further in her rebuke. There were limits. Boundaries to what she was able to say without fear.

August's lips pressed into a thin line, and he released her hand. "Let's mend the fence," he said, stepping away from her and walking towards the fence to busy himself with the fallen brace. "There's tools in the saddlebag."

She nodded, even though he wasn't looking her way, and turned away towards the horses. "Think we'll need the hand saw?" She asked, opening the saddlebag. She swallowed hard, as if the gesture could shove the words back down where they belonged. Far away from her heart and definitely not passing her lips.

An affirmative grunt from August had her in motion. The time for trying to clear the air was done.

There was work to be done, and at least in that endeavor, it allowed them the peace of being together.

"ell, it appears as if your fitting went well," Seylah's mother stood, staring at the stack of boxes and bags that had just been delivered from The Modern Dress. Seylah hadn't quite known what to do with the vast amount of bags, and dare she say she had spotted a trunk in the mix. There were far more in the lot than Seylah had remembered being fitted for—five in all, but if she were honest, it all became something of a blur past a certain point.

Somewhere between the third pin stick, and her nearly being run over by a coach, Seylah's memory had become spotty at best. She chewed on her bottom lip and nodded, considering the haul of new garments and accessories. She would sooner be tasked with bringing an entire unruly saloon to heel with naught, but a blunt kitchen knife than endure another fitting at Mrs. Rosemary's.

"It seems that Mrs. Rosemary was enthusiastic," Seylah

said, finally. She glanced at her mother to see that she was smiling, if albeit a slightly remorseful one.

"I may have had a thing or two to do with her zealousness," her mother said.

Seylah's hands went to her hips. "A thing or two, or the whole thing?"

Julie blew out a sigh and threw up her hands. "Oh, all right, I had everything to do with it, but what else was I to do? Your day dresses were positively threadbare, and your sleeves are entirely too short, sweetheart. You've outgrown the dresses you've been wearing. You're a woman now, proper and true. I don't care about the fashion, but there is something to be said for being properly attired for the elements and for your worth. You needed new things and you just hate fittings."

Seylah opened her mouth to protest, but she stopped short. Her mother was right, she did hate the fitting, avoided them at all costs, so much so that her mother was right. Her clothes were nearly threadbare, she had outgrown them by far, and then there was the bit about 'worth' that made her feel slightly abashed.

That was a matter Seylah had avoided for entirely too long, and she no longer was content to simply...*exist.* She wanted to thrive, she wanted to catch a man's eye. Elliot Myers was a man that she wouldn't mind starting with, and the new clothing from Mrs. Rosemary was just the thing to test the waters.

Julie came to stand beside the delivered clothing and picked up a hat box. "Not to mention that the fashion lately really is becoming for an active woman. Why, there are even pants now that are fashionable. You can go about your duties in town and still be feminine. Can you believe it?" And if you don't like it then we can--"

"Okay," Seylah said cutting her mother's words off.

"Okay?"

Seylah nodded and held out her hands for the hat box. "Yes, okay. You are right, Mama. I've neglected things like this," she nodded at the new clothing, "fashionable things, things that would make me truly shine. And the thing of it is, I can't even remember why I did it."

"Oh darling, that's wonderful news." Her mother rushed forward and hugged her, tightly, the hat box crushed between them. "I'm so happy for you. This year, this season will be absolutely lovely, you'll see it."

Seylah smiled and leaned into her mother. "I have a feeling you're quite right. Thank you for this."

Julie sighed and rested her chin on her daughter's head. "Oh, I had nothing to do with it."

"Don't lie. Mrs. Rosemary had an accomplice and I'm certain it was you."

Her mother laughed. "It was for a good cause, so I'm not too terribly sorry. And besides, what's this I hear about a man courting you?"

Seylah's eyes drifted closed in exasperation. "It's only a picnic," she said in what was fast becoming a well-versed mantra.

Over the past two days, Seylah had done nothing, but deflect the well-intentioned excitement and well wishes from the townsfolk who were pleased as punch to see Seylah on the receiving end of attention, and from such a handsome and well to-do man to boot.

"I heard he's a banker. That's a quite stable and profitable profession," Julie said, giving voice to the echoes of Gold Sky's townsfolk. There was no escaping it, not even when the horde of folk were absent they managed to worm their way into Seylah's ear.

She sighed heavily and pulled away, catching the hat box before it fell to the floor. "Already planning our engagement are you?"

Julie held up her hands. "All I am meaning to say is a man in possession of dependable work makes for an eligible suitor."

An eligible suitor.

Seylah raised the hat box accusingly at her mother. "I don't believe that's all you meant, Mama."

Her mother pursed her lips and brushed her hair away from her face. "Can a mother not be excited for her daughter to keep company with an eligible, and dare I say, handsome young man?"

Seylah blushed at the words. It was true that Elliot was handsome, she had seen him once in passing since he had asked to take her to the picnic, but she had scarcely managed a few mumbled words and a strained smile in his direction.

Who knew it was so difficult to keep one's composure when faced with an attractive man, an attractive man that had not only saved her but promptly asked her to a picnic. If only she'd had more practice in her formative years, she might be putting on a better showing now that she was presented with the opportunity to enjoy a man's company.

Seylah looked at her mother and saw that she was gleeful, her face shining with a bright smile. The urge to

keep it there seized her. The pair of them set about, trans-
porting Seylah's new wardrobe to her room, an endeavor
that was only made possible by the giddy energy of her
mother. In no time at all, Seylah found it had rubbed off
on her, and before long, she was in similar spirits. It was
difficult not to smile when her mother danced about with
each new day outfit, or riding jacket with a delighted
smile.

"You're going to look so lovely! And look, you can still
fit your single shot pistol here. There's room in this
jacket!"

"That color is perfectly suited to your complexion!"

"I've heard from *maman* this cut is all the rage in New
York!"

The time passed with such excited statements, and by
the end of it, Seylah found that she believed her mother's
words. She would be lovely, she would be intriguing, and
she would, above all things, carry herself as if she
deserved the world.

"Which will you choose to wear?" Julie asked, clasping
her hands in front of her and practically bouncing on her
toes.

"For the picnic?"

"Of course, for the picnic, you goose. What else?" She
turned to the wardrobe and ran a finger along the new
collection of sumptuous fabrics in all manner of cuts and
patterns.

Seylah tapped her chin and considered the assortment
of clothes. "I'm not quite sure," she said after a moment,
"it's all a bit overwhelming. Would you like to pick it out,
Mama?"

Julie clapped. "Oh, I thought you'd never ask. I know just the one!" She turned to the wardrobe and pulled out a dress of light blue silk and lace. Seylah's eyes widened at the sight of the piece and she cleared her throat.

"Don't you think that's a bit much for a picnic, mama? It's very casual, you know that."

Her mother waved a hand and strode forward with the dress in hand. "You can never be too overdressed, and this would look just lovely with the white parasol and those beautiful boots we bought you for Christmas." She pushed Seylah forward, depositing the dress into her hands. "Go on and get dressed while I pick out a few accessories. We will have just enough time to do your hair before the picnic. I think it should be left down, because the event is casual, as you said."

Seylah blinked, looking down at the dress that was suddenly in her hands and wondered if she had perhaps erred in her estimation of what getting ready for the picnic might entail. The lace of her dress felt dainty against her calloused hands, and she paused, looking down at the delicate threading for a moment.

Could she do this? Was this truly what she wanted?

Yes, she wanted to move forward. Yes, she wanted to enjoy her time with Elliot. But … that still didn't change the fact that she secretly wished for another to be arriving later that day to call on her.

August.

Her heart squeezed. Their interactions since Elliot had been … strained, to put it mildly, with her efforts to bring the issue to light failing spectacularly. The end result came to nothing more than a mended fence done in

93

silence. And now here it was, Sunday. The day of the picnic and she hadn't so much as spoken a word to him. It left an awful twisted feeling in her stomach that Seylah wouldn't wish on anyone.

"Seylah?" Her mother's voice roused her from her thoughts. "Are you all right?"

Seylah nodded and moved forward. "Yes, I'm quite fine. I'll just be a minute getting dressed."

Julie placed the accessories she had picked out on the dressing table. "I'll leave you to it, then." Her mother grinned at her over her shoulder as she bustled out the bedroom door. "Oh, I can't wait to do your hair. It's going to be so lovely! You're going to have such a wonderful time. Don't you think?"

Seylah clasped her hands in front of her, a tight smile on her face. "Of course, Mama," she whispered but the door had soundly shut by then. She sighed and turned to the dressing table. The glittering earrings and hair comb her mother had chosen for her glinted in the morning light. They would suit her perfectly, make the dress impeccable, and her footwear was at least conservative enough that she would feel secure on her feet---a blessing, indeed. With the right hair and makeup, her appearance would do, of that she was sure but still she hesitated in dressing.

She had not done such a thing for herself since that night all those years ago...

"You are not a child any more," she whispered, eyes squeezing shut for a moment before she sucked in a deep breath and moved forward. She could not wish to go on with her life, to prove that she was worthy of good, if she took two steps back for every one that she took forward.

She would never get anywhere like this. Nowhere at all, save for late to her picnic outing and disheveled looking. She began to work on the buttons at the front of her dress, her fingers blissfully moving by autopilot, and before long she was standing attired in picnic worthy attire. She had only just finished lacing her boots when her mother knocked on the door.

"Come in," Seylah called, smoothing her hands over her skirts and considering the hair comb. How was she meant to wear it, exactly? She was still looking at the accessory when her mother came to stand beside her. Seylah lifted her eyes and smiled at her mother in the dressing table mirror.

"How shall we do my hair?" She asked holding up the comb.

Julie met her daughter's eyes in the mirror and smiled at her, reaching out to lift a curl of hair up. "I think swept up will be chic and casual. It will showcase the comb perfectly, and keep your hair out of your face. It's a bit windy out today and we can't have you getting a mouthful of hair when you mean to take a bite of tuna sandwich."

Seylah cringed at the thought. "That would be a less than desirable first impression to make on Elliot," she said and Julie chuckled, pushing her down into the seat at the table.

"Oh, Elliot already, is it?"

Seylah ducked her head, a move that made her mother cluck her tongue at her. "He asked me to call him such."

"And does he refer to you as casually?"

"Well, yes," Seylah said, picking at her skirts. "It seemed the only polite thing to offer when he gave me his name."

Her mother hummed, but said nothing else. Her fingers moved lightly through the strands of Seylah's hair as she lifted the coils of hair to pin into an updo. Seylah bit her lip and said nothing, watching her mother as she worked.

"What?" Seylah asked when her mother remained silent.

A smile curved up her lips. "Nothing, nothing."

"It's not nothing, Mama."

The fingers in her hair stilled. "Well, I estimate that this Elliot is quite taken by you to ask for such an informal address so early, and then there's today to think of. No way that man hasn't taken a shine to you, sweetheart."

"He seems very nice," was all Seylah offered at the observation.

"And what else? You have to have some other thoughts on him than he is very nice. Pudding is very nice, cake for breakfast is very nice, but a man? A man should be so much more." The tone in her mother's voice was suggestive, alluring even, and Seylah blushed furiously at the unspoken intimacy she heard in it.

Storks did not bring children, after all.

"Mama..."

"Oh, humor me!"

Seylah dropped her eyes and looked down at her hands as she thought over her interaction with Elliot. He had been far better than nice.

Easily.

"He's, ah, very strong. Tall. I like his eyes very much."

"Go on…"

"And his voice is like warm chocolate or syrup. It just, well it warms me so, down to my toes. I've never heard another man like him."

Julie clasped a hand to her chest in a swoon. "Oh, this is wonderful! And now you have a picnic together. I cannot wait to hear all about it."

"I am…excited," Seylah said, choosing her words carefully. She smiled at her mother who was looking on in approval at her handiwork, the hair comb had been slid home and her earrings put on. The effect was transforming. She scarcely recognized herself, and there was still make up to come.

Julie plucked up a pot of rouge and grinned at her. "Are you ready for the finishing touch?"

Seylah leaned back in her seat, eyes wide as saucers and trained on the makeup her mother held. "I am, but I want it known that I am incredibly intimidated and uncertain of what to do with," she pointed a finger at the rouge, "that."

Julie lifted one shoulder in a shrug. "No one really does, not at first. I was very poor with it until I practiced, and I only did so because it was a prerequisite to graduate finishing school. Let me tell you, there is nothing more motivating at learning your way around beauty products than being threatened with expulsion or repeating a year of lessons."

Seylah laughed at her mother's reminiscing. "You almost were expelled?" It was surprising to think of her mother as anything but a master at the classroom, a studious woman who had made her way with books, and had always been a star pupil, but the exasperated look on her mother's face said otherwise.

"I was not the most motivated when it came to finishing school." She placed her hands on Seylah's chin and tilted her head to face her. "Purse your lips for me and hold still."

At those words, Seylah froze.

"Thank you," Julie murmured as she began to paint her lips. "Finishing school was not my element, you see? Not a lot of places in New York were. I wasn't like your uncle or *maman*. They thrived in the limelight, but I," she shook her head with a snort, "I was more suited to the frontier and life here with your fathers. It was terrifying to imagine such a life for myself, and it was difficult upon my arrival, but Gold Sky has proven to be a perfect fit for me."

Seylah repressed the urge to nod, her mother had told her to freeze and when the other woman was wielding makeup, Seylah knew better than to move. Who knew what kind of folly could arise from an errant gesture.

She glanced up at her mother and saw a look of concentration Seylah wasn't entirely sure stemmed from her focus at applying rouge.

"Do not be afraid if you don't fit the mold of what society expects you to be, sweetheart. You know that I love you, that your fathers and sisters adore you, for just who you are--who you choose to be. And I want you to have fun on your picnic outing, but please, do not change who you are for the sake of capturing a man's attention."

Since she was unable to speak, Seylah raised her eyebrows at that. Hadn't her mother just gushed over what fun she was going to have by dressing up?

"I know, I know what you're thinking." Julie paused and smiled ruefully at her daughter. "It was exciting today to do this for you, but you are already so lovely. Do not mistake my excitement at a new experience with you for anything else than simply that. I enjoy firsts with my daughters, and this was a first for us both. It makes my heart happy to see you this radiant. But know that you are perfect as you are every single day. I do not want you to forget that no matter what happens today."

Seylah fought the urge to nod when her mother continued applying the rouge to her lips.

Perfect as you are every single day.

If she could speak, or move for that matter, she would tell her mother just how much and how needed her words of affirmation were on this day, but as it was, Seylah was left looking up at her mother with shining eyes and a pursed mouth as Julie finished her work. She leaned back with a raised eyebrow, surveying her work before she nodded and tapped Seylah's cheek.

"Perfect. You look absolutely perfect, sweetheart. As you always do."

"Thank you, Mama."

❧

"SEYLAH, there's a dashing man here for you," Florence stage-whispered to Seylah from where she stood at the doorway. Seylah looked up from the book she had been pretending to read for the better part of the last half hour. Though she'd been studiously staring at the pages, flipping them as if she were engrossed in her story, in truth Seylah had been blindly staring at the pages until the ink on them had begun to swirl and swim before her.

"Hmm?" She asked feigning a calm, cool, and collected composure rather than admitting to the frazzled and frantic wreck she knew herself to be.

"A man," Florence hissed and crept into the room, but not before glancing behind her and back towards the entryway. "He says he's here to take you to a picnic, but that can't be true? Or is it? Because..." her voice trailed off and she hurried across the room until she was beside her sister. She dropped to her knees so that they were nearly eye-to-eye, "he looks like a dandy, but in the best ways. A man like that can get you in trouble."

Seylah rolled her eyes at her sister. "He is not a dandy," she said, but then paused and added, "at least I don't think he is." She didn't know Elliot Myers, hadn't the faintest idea about the man other than his profession and that he was able to pull a woman back from near death by an errant coach without so much as mussing his clothes, or missing the opportunity at making an introduction to a young woman...

She sat up straight when she thought about that. "Oh my word, what if he is?"

Florence clapped her hands and gave a delighted shimmy. "Then I am excited for you. You could use a bit of romantic drama." Her sister bobbed her head and looked towards the doorway. "I could be persuaded to take him off your hands if you find that we are right, and the man proves to be a dandy."

"And what exactly do you fancy you will be able to do with a dandy?" Seylah asked, crossing her arms.

Florence blew out an exasperated sigh. "Well, all sorts of things, that's *the point* of a dandy, sweet sister."

"Flo, no!"

"Flo, yes!"

Seylah set her book aside and stood quickly from her chair. If she did not make a hasty exit, then, there was no telling what might happen to Elliot. "I should be going, Florence."

Her sister pouted. "Oh, fine, keep him to yourself then."

"I'm not keeping him to myself. I hardly even know him."

"Well that's the point of a courtship, you goose. It's all outing and fine meals." She reached out and ran a finger along her sister's arm with a smile. "Pretty dresses and lovely lip paints. You look absolutely ravishing, I might add. The men of this town aren't going to know how to ride a horse when they catch sight of you, and all the ladies will faint with jealousy! How truly wonderful."

Seylah's palms began to sweat at the scene her sister was gleefully painting for her. "That sounds like a lot of attention…"

"Oh, it will be a wagonload of it! You'll have more than you know what to do with. Why, I suspect you'll come away with at least a handful of new offers at courtship as well. I have no idea how you'll manage all of it. Perhaps, you could even pick two?"

"Two?" Seylah squeaked.

Florence gave her a look that could only be vexation. "Of course, two. Two men is a fine number, just ask Mama." She clasped her hands with a sigh of longing. "I'd give anything for a marriage like our parents. Oh, how in love they are. Can you just imagine it?"

Seylah shook her head. "No, but only for the reason that I can't imagine how to even manage one, Flo."

Her sister's eyes moved over to the door and she grinned. "Well, use your imagination, Seylah because you have one fine specimen of a man awaiting you."

Seylah paled and glanced nervously at the door. "Perhaps, it isn't such a good idea that I go." She turned to her sister. "Perhaps it wouldn't be such a poor idea for you to go in my stead."

Florence blinked at her sister for a moment before she narrowed her eyes. "No, you are not getting out of this."

"But you just asked if you could have him."

"And it was a jest, you are going on this outing, or else."

"Or else what?" Seylah asked, arching an eyebrow at her sister who, to her credit, drew herself up until the two women were eye-to-eye.

"I know you can cuff me in a scrap, but that doesn't mean that I will make it easy for you," Florence told her, putting her hands on her hips and meeting her sister's gaze. "I wouldn't make it easy for you and I would hate to see your lovely dress ruined."

Seylah drew back in shock at her sister's meddle. She hadn't ever figured Florence one for fisticuffs, but she could see that Florence was willing to go the extra mile to ensure that she went through with the picnic with Elliot, and whatever else the outing brought with it—attention from the townsfolk included.

"Oh all right," Seylah huffed and walked towards the entryway where Elliot was waiting, and hopefully, had not over heard too much of their conversation. She paused in the threshold of the parlor and looked back at her sister. "Would you have really fought me to get me out the door?"

Florence smiled serenely at her sister. "Ah, now that is a mystery for you to contemplate on your wonderful outing with that fine looking man out there," she said with a jerk of her chin towards the door.

Seylah shook her head when her sister took to wiggling her eyebrows suggestively at her and opted for a hasty retreat as the best course of action given that Elliot was waiting on her. She turned on her heel and took a fortifying breath when the gesture brought her within sight of Elliot Myers. She gave him a tentative smile as she walked towards him, hands clasped in front of her as she went.

He was standing tall, broad shoulders filling out the charcoal colored suit he wore quite nicely, his hands were behind him and she forced her steps to remain unhurried.

"Hello," she greeted him. "I hope you haven't been waiting long."

Elliot smiled warmly at her. "No, not long at all. Your sister was gracious enough to give me entry." He brought his hands around and held out a bouquet of roses to her, "I saw these and thought of you."

"Oh!" Seylah took a step back in surprise at the sudden

appearance of roses. Outside of family, there had only been one other person who had gifted her flowers.

August.

She swallowed hard staring at the bouquet of roses as sumptuous as these. Crimson red with lush petals that had made her fingers itch to see if they were as velvety as they looked. But itchy fingers or not, Seylah still wondered if August would have chosen a different bloom for her. She gave herself a mental shake. It wouldn't do to think of him. Not with Elliot here with her. Not with these beautiful flowers. Flowers that were a far cry from the bullets and leather boots she was usually charged with keeping order of at the sheriff's office.

She raised the blooms and gave them a sniff. "These are lovely, Elliot. Thank you."

"They are not quite so lovely as you," Elliot told her and she once again was taken by that rich timbre that made her weak in the knees.

She blushed and held the roses closer to her chest. "You flatter me."

Elliot swallowed and took a step closer to her, offering her his arm. "I only speak the truth and may I say that you look stunning."

"I, ah,--" Seylah began, but Florence's voice rang through the hallway cutting her off.

"Those are beautiful!"

Seylah turned slightly to see her sister's head poking out from the doorway. "Hello, Florence."

Florence wiggled her fingers in hello and pointed at the flowers. "Shall I put those in water for you? Then you can be on your way to the festivities all the sooner? I'm sure you are both quite anxious to make your way to the picnic."

Seylah looked down at the flowers she was cradling. She hadn't thought of what to do with them now that she had them, but water did seem a prudent move. She held them out to her sister with a nod. "That's very thoughtful of you, Flo. Thank you."

Florence bustled forward and took the flowers from her with a wink. "What are sisters for? Now you two go on and shoo. You're missing all the fun in the square." Florence waved them forward and reached past them both to open the front door.

"Ah, thank you?" Elliot managed to get out before Florence practically shoved them both through the front door and onto the porch.

"Have a good time!" She waved at them, and in short order, slammed the door shut. The speedy manner in which they had been dispatched made Seylah suspect her sister worried that she might bolt from Elliot at any moment's notice.

She stifled the urge to roll her eyes and forced a smile onto her face. "She's just enthusiastic," she told Elliot when he glanced behind him, a perplexed look on his handsome face. "About picnics, I mean."

"She's a picnic enthusiast?" He asked, offering his arm again to her once more.

"Oh, she's the largest by far in the family. She just loves a good picnic and doesn't want us to miss out."

"Then, why is she not coming herself?"

Seylah pursed her lips at that question. She hadn't quite known where she was going when she opened her mouth, but now her rambling had seemed to put her into a corner with this observation. "She will be along shortly?" She tried and breathed a relieved sigh when Elliot nodded, accepting her comment.

The pair walked along in awkward silence for a few minutes, each step making Seylah more conscious that she had no words to offer. She glanced at Elliot and saw that he was looking off toward the mountains, his entire body relaxed, he didn't seem the least bit bothered by the silence.

Perhaps this was normal?

She did only have the one walk with August to compare it to, and they were just children. The words had flowed easily between them, but lack of conversation had never been a problem between the two long time friends. If anything, the pair of them had difficulties keeping themselves from too much chatter. Her mother could attest to their inability to stay quiet when near one another. Why, they had clapped more erasers after school, on opposite ends of the school house, to make amends for their constant whispering.

A smile pulled at her lips, remembering those afternoons with August. Things had been so simple then, so easily managed so long as August had been at her side and she at his.

"You have a lovely smile," Elliot told her, breaking the silence.

Seylah jerked, surprised by Elliot's words. "Sorry?"

He nodded at her, his free hand coming to rest where Seylah's touched the crook of his arm. "Your smile," he said again, "I couldn't help but admire it just now. I hope that our spending time with one another has put such a look on your face?"

If the world were perfect and good, if things were as simple as they had been in bygone days, and if life were neat, then Seylah would be able to say yes. Yes, it was he who had made her smile so, had made her eyes go soft and perhaps pulled a sigh from her. But, it hadn't been, because life was none of those things.

"Thank you," she told him, working to keep her smile in place as a realization took hold of her in the most uncomfortable way. If her smile became forced, Elliot did not notice because he was already looking ahead of them and talking of what they might enjoy at the picnic. Meanwhile, Seylah's heart thumped painfully in her chest. It was telling her one hard truth that she had willed herself to be blind to for years.

There was only one man that had ever made Seylah feel this way, had made her smile and forget herself.

And Elliot was not that man.

CHAPTER 6

"Now this is quite a spread," Elliot said, looking down the line of tables that had been assembled in the town square. Each and every surface was covered in dishes of every variety, and Seylah's mouth watered when she caught sent of the delicious offerings. Her stomach rumbled, and her hands flew to her stomach in shock.

"Oh, I-ah, well, yes?" She offered giving him a chagrined look. In all of her excitement over the picnic, she hadn't quite gotten around to eating breakfast that morning, and it seemed her appetite was making itself known now that food was readily available.

He laughed and patted his own midsection. "I'm hungry as well, so we don't have to hide our appetites then, hmm?"

"Hide our appetites?" She asked with a confused look.

"Yes, I once went to a similar function with a lady friend who refused to eat in mixed company, but you see it's quite rude to eat when your partner won't take a bite. I spent the entirety of our outing locked in a pitiful battle of wills with the young lady."

Seylah laughed at the anguished look on Elliot's face. She handed him a plate and asked, "Well, what happened? Did you get to eat?"

He sighed and took the plate from her with a chagrined look. "Yes, I broke not long into the outing. I know it is impolite, but I was left with no choice and she bested me that night. But, to be completely honest with you, I was glad to lose. I think I nearly fainted at some point on account of my healthy appetite. I hadn't eaten much before meeting the young lady, and it is a mistake I take pains not to repeat."

"So, then you've eaten already?" Seylah asked, dishing potatoes onto her plate. The humor in her voice was evident and Elliot chuckled, taking the serving spoon from her when she handed it to him.

"Oh, but of course. I wouldn't dream of ruining our first meal together." He flashed her a winning smile, and Seylah was unable to keep from being affected by the sunny expression Elliot directed at her. Though he was not the man that set her heart to racing, he was, so far as Seylah could see, a sweet, gentle, and funny man.

Perhaps they could be friends. True friends. Not the sort that she and August were … but proper friends with no blurry boundaries existing between them. She gave Elliot a genuine smile at the thought.

"I think I would very much enjoy having meals with you in the future," she told him, moving along the length of the table.

Elliot practically beamed at her. "That pleases me to

hear, Seylah." He served himself brisket and then leaned close to her. "Is it just me, or are we garnering a good deal of attention?"

"What?" Seylah asked, and at her confused expression, Elliot dropped his voice to nearly a murmur, the effect forced her to lean closer to him to hear what he said.

"Everyone is staring at us," he whispered in her ear.

She glanced around them and nearly swore when she saw that he was right. The townsfolk in attendance of the picnic, of which there were many given the allure free food had on a frontier town in possession of voracious appetites, was akin to moths and a flame. The town square was packed with people milling to and fro. Seylah could scarcely move without bumping into a neighbor, the effects of which she felt acutely when a passerby jostled her into Elliot's side.

Elliot reached out an arm to steady her. "Careful there," he said, still leaning close to her to speak.

"Thank you. It seems the picnic has robbed people of their manners," she muttered, giving the backside of the person, practically sprinting towards the cakes and pastries, a sour look.

"It would seem so, but I can't say that I do not find the outcome … agreeable."

There was no mistaking the flirtation in Elliot's voice, and it was enough to make Seylah stand up straight. There was no need to encourage his affections for her, not when her own heart was pulled in another direction, even if that direction led her right towards the one man she couldn't have.

It wouldn't do to have Elliot as a suitor when she could

not offer her entire heart. The effect would be spinster-hood, but Seylah would willingly welcome her status when the time came so long as she was able to keep August near. He would marry, of that she was sure.

August Leclaire was a desirable bachelor, even if they were always together. The women of Gold Sky knew better than to make anything of their propensity to be seen together. It had always been that way. Seylah was no threat, because there was nothing between them, or rather there was nothing of a romantic nature on August's side of their friendship.

Their young friendship had been the product of a debt. A debt Seylah refused to think too much on since they had reconciled.

She took comfort in the thought that August had taken to her and, debt or no debt, desired her company. It was easier to swallow than the possibility that August's honor-able nature had driven him to seek her out on her eigh-teenth birthday, had made him speak to her as he had, and she, a desperate fool, had taken the offering like a woman dying of thirst in the desert.

No, it couldn't be that. August cared for her, truly. She knew it even if it wasn't as she felt for him.

He had to.

"Are you not a fan of brussel sprouts, then?" Elliot asked, and Seylah nearly groaned at herself for not paying attention to the man. She gave him an apologetic smile.

"Brussel sprouts?" She asked, desperately trying to piece together the conversation Elliot had been having with her.

"Yes, I mentioned that there were some here and you got the strangest look on your face."

"I did?"

Elliot nodded, moving along the table and spooning more food on his plate. "Yes, you looked ... defeated."

She pulled a face. "Brussel sprouts do not suit my current appetite then it would seem."

"It would seem so," he said, reaching for a roll. "Isn't that gentleman your friend from the other day?" Elliot nodded across the square, and Seylah felt her heart leap into her throat.

It was August.

He was standing at the center of the excitement, citizens streaming around him as he stood still as a statue and looking ... straight at her.

"He's looking this way. I think he's noticed you."

"I can't possibly imagine that he has," Seylah said, dropping her eyes to the food in front of her. She began to blindly pile her plate and gave Elliot a tight smile. "But yes, you are quite right, that is my friend. His name is August Leclaire."

"Been friends for long?" Elliot asked, leading her towards the table where the punches and lemonades were housed.

"Yes, since we were children," she told him. "We are practically kin."

"Does he know that?"

Seylah jerked at the question and looked up at Elliot. "What?"

"I don't mean to pry, but does Mister Leclaire know that you think of him as family?"

"Yes," Seylah blurted out and then she winced, "I mean, I suspect so given that it is he who has the most..." her voice trailed off as she searched for the right words, "it is August who has the most familial feelings toward me."

Elliot handed her a glass of punch. "I am not sure you're correct in that estimation, Seylah."

"I don't understand what you're trying to say, Elliot."

"A man in possession of familial affection does not glare as Mister Leclaire does, and he certainly does not part the crowd like Moses on a mission to get here."

"What are you talking about?"

Elliot nodded over her shoulder. "See for yourself," he told her, taking a sip of his punch.

"I have no idea what you mean," Seylah protested, but even so, she turned in the direction he had pointed her in and felt a spike of adrenaline when she saw that Elliot's description was aptly used to describe August's current trajectory, which wasn't so much walking but marching across the square.

There was a determined set to August's shoulders and chin that she had only ever seen when he was preparing to confront a particularly unsavory individual. What on earth had gotten into him and why was he on his way over to them?

"He must have business this way," she finally concluded. "Beyond us, I mean."

"If you say so," Elliot said, and this time, there was no hiding the rueful smile. He took another sip of his drink and then said, "It's quite all right, Seylah. I see now you did not know."

"Know what?" She asked, her confusion mounting by

the moment. She wasn't sure what to make of Elliot's cryptic words or the fact that August was very nearly on them.

"Don't fret. It'll all become clear in a moment."

Her brow furrowed. "Elliot, I hope you don't think that anything is going on between August and myself. I assure you that is not the case. We are best friends, but nothing more."

"That's a right shame, Seylah," August said.

She whirled around to face August who was now only a few feet away. "August. What are you doing here?"

"Came to find you," he said, clasping his hands in front of him and then looked at Elliot. "I understand Seylah is here with you."

Elliot nodded. "That's right."

"I aim to have a moment alone with her," August continued on and then cleared his throat. "That moment will more than likely take her from you for the remainder of the picnic."

Elliot rubbed a hand along his jaw and then looked at Seylah who was gasping in shock at August's words.

"What are you doing?" She hissed at her friend, stepping in front of Elliot.

"'Takin' you on a much needed walk. We have a lot to talk about, Seylah and I'm not takin' no for an answer."

"You most certainly will take no for an answer, August Leclaire!"

He shook his head at her, the corner of his mouth lifting in a smile. "No, I don't think I will, honey."

Again, that word. *Honey.* Who knew one word could lay her low like a mortal wound. Seylah dropped back a step, her plate nearly falling from her hands as she did so. August looked over her shoulder at Elliot.

"Are we at an end, or shall we resort to other avenues of settling this?" August asked with flint in his tone that was unmistakable. Seylah blanched at the thought of them fighting on her account, but Elliot held up his hands, plate and cup in each.

"This is an affair that I do not see concerning me." He looked at Seylah then. "You do feel safe with Mister Leclaire, yes?"

She nodded dumbly at him and Elliot smiled. "Well then, I had best be off. It seems the pair of you have much to discuss."

"What?" How had her outing with Elliot been cut short by August? Why was a possible suitor giving ground to her best friend? And what precisely did August think he was doing barging in on her like this? She was fit to be tied, and she shook her head in disbelief when Elliot bid her adieu and even received a word of thanks from August.

"I'll owe you a whiskey next I see you," August told the other man as he moved away from them.

Elliot raised his punch glass in acknowledgement. "I'd like that."

"Excuse me!" Seylah raised her chin in defiance and pinned August with a glare. "I never said that I was amenable to speaking privately with you. How dare you barge in on my-my--"

"Your what?" August asked, stepping so close that she was forced to take a stutter step back from him.

"Well, I don't rightly know what to call it but I know

that it doesn't include you," she waved her punch glass, causing its contents to slosh over the rim and onto August's boots. He sighed and looked down at the mess for a moment before he lifted his eyes to hers.

"Couldn't have been much on account of how quickly he cleared out."

"That's because you came stomping over here and demanding time with me. What else is he to think? He mistook us for a couple only days before, and he seems quite sure something else is going on between us even though I have assured him that there is nothing of the kind."

August sucked in a breath at that. "Caught the tail end of that little discussion."

"Good! Then you know precisely what I'm talking about, so what is the meaning of this August?"

"The meaning," August said, taking her glass of punch out of her hand along with her plate of food, "is that we both know there is far more between us than friendship and I am damn tired of hiding it. I love you, Seylah."

Seylah was grateful he had taken her cup and plate because she was quite certain she was about to faint.

"I FEEL SICK," Seylah whispered leaning back in the chair she sat in.

"That's because you haven't eaten," August told her and nudged the plate of picnic food he had brought with them across the table towards her.

"No, I'm not hungry."

"You are, you're lyin.'"

She glared at him. "I am not. I feel sick on account of you fraying my last damn nerve, August, not for lack of food."

"Even so, you should eat. That's why I brought it," he said and she hated the absolute certainty she heard in August's voice.

"I should be at a picnic right now, not here," she muttered, gesturing around the familiar sight of the sheriff's office. After her near fainting spell at August's sudden declaration, Seylah's feet had set off on their own accord. She hadn't known where she was going but had within a few minutes found herself at the door of the place she went nearly every day. August had opened the door and followed her inside, wordlessly.

They had been sitting in silence ever since, the plate of picnic food on the desk in front of her while his words rang in her ears.

I love you, Seylah.

He couldn't mean romantically, not like she did him, how could he?

She raised her eyes from the floor to his and saw that he was watching her intently. "Why now?" She asked her voice a whisper.

"Why now, what?"

"You said," she paused and cleared her throat before continuing on, "your declaration. Why now?"

August crossed his arms and leaned against the wall at his back. "Because any longer and I was going to lose my mind over it." He looked away and out the window towards where the picnic festivities were still underway.

"Nearly did lose my mind when I saw you with him. I can't say that I'm not a jealous man, because I am when it comes to you. I want you, Seylah. Always have, always will, and I won't share you with another man so long as I breathe. Don't ask me to do it, because I can't."

"What on earth are you going on about?" Seylah asked, raising her hands to rub at her temples. Nothing made sense. Maybe this was all a dream, and she would soon awake to Rose shaking her and demanding to know when she would make breakfast.

"I don't understand," she said.

"I love you, Seylah. I'll keep saying it until you understand me." August pushed away from the wall, but then gestured at the food she still hadn't touched. "But I know well enough than to push the issue until you've eaten, so do us both a favor and eat."

"I'm not hungry," she muttered.

"Honey," he sighed and her traitorous heart set to thumping. Begrudgingly Seylah ate. It was only after she had finished half the plate that August spoke again. "Better?" he asked.

"Better," she said with a definite sullen downturn of her lips.

August chuckled and came to stand beside her. "Stop your pouting."

"I'm not pouting and if I were, I quite think I have the right to be as you barged in with such an unexpected declaration of affection," she informed him, putting down her fork with a thunk.

"It's not quite so unexpected as you have fooled yourself to believe, and we both know it."

Seylah reared back in her seat giving him a wild look. "Please tell me, how do we both know that? Because I, for one, was wholly unaware of your feelings."

"How could you be?" August asked, coming to stand beside her.

"How could I not be?" Seylah whispered, and she blinked against the sudden pin prick of tears that threatened to fall.

Hadn't she tried to broach this topic not only a day before? Where had his words been then?

And what of that fateful night?

She was so close to telling him she had heard him all those years ago when he had denied how he felt, had said she was a burden of debt, but she did not. Her lips would not form the words and she did not press the issue.

Instead, she asked, "After all these years...and then, *and then* there were those years when you were simply gone. Did you care for me then?"

"Do you mean did I love you then?" August asked, sinking to his knees in front of her. "Yes, honey, I did. I loved you then, every day, just as much as I do now."

She shook her head but didn't move away when he reached for her, his roughened hands skimming lightly against the backs of her hands. "What is this?" She finally asked when he laced their fingers together.

"This is me askin' you for the honor of courting you, Seylah Wickes-Barnes." He looked up at her from where he still knelt and asked, "Will you do me the honor of that?"

"You want to court me?"

"More than anything."

"But courtship is a road to marriage."

He nodded, his hand squeezing hers. "I know that. Aim to make it to the altar with you before long."

That knocked the air out of her lungs at August's words. "I quite feel as if though I'm dreaming."

"Do you mean that in a good way?"

"I don't rightly know," she confessed.

"Understandable." August gave her a chagrined smile and stood from where he was. "I know this is overwhelming. Let's get you back to the picnic if you like, or would you care to go home?"

"I think home would be best," Seylah said, following suit, and standing from her seat. Her limbs were shaky and the food she had eaten was like lead in her stomach. It was as if she had just worked the horses for hours on end, but she had done nothing more strenuous than paint her lips and dress prettily.

It boggled her mind that she was so weary after so little physical exertion, though she estimated her tiredness stemmed more from the wild swing of emotions that she had experienced in only a handful of hours. She smoothed her hands down her skirts and forced one foot in front of the other as she made her way to the door. She had very nearly calmed her nerves when she felt August's hand at her elbow.

She looked down and nearly tripped at the gentle touch. "What are you doing?"

"Keeping you from hitting the ground. Have you had any water today? Did you sleep at all?" August asked, opening the door. He paused and leaned close to peer curiously at her.

She batted him away. "Stop that."

He gave one shake of his head. "No."

Her eyes narrowed at him and she forced her way past him. Behind her August sighed heavily. "Where are you going?"

"Home," she told him without a look behind her.

"Not without me." The bang of the door sounded and then August was beside her, this time his hand was at the small of her back and Seylah's heart fluttered in her chest.

Seylah's steps quickened, and she suddenly wished her mother had chosen one of the outfits from her wardrobe that allowed for more freedom of movement. As it was, her attire kept her well within August's reach.

"Are you really so concerned about my welfare?" She asked him after a few minutes of walking. They were now in the square where the picnic was still going on. She bit her lip when she spied Elliot amongst the crowd, a group of women surrounded him and he had a smile on his face. At least he was enjoying the event despite how it had gone for them.

"Your welfare is of the utmost importance to me," August said without pause. The sincerity she heard in his voice struck her to her core. She looked up at him and saw that he was looking out at the horizon, his gaze sweeping to and fro as if he were scanning the distance for a threat.

"No one is going to attack us," she told him, unable to stop the words before they spilled forth.

He looked at her then. "I-well," August cleared his throat, and she felt him flatten his palm until the entirety of his hand was heavy against her back. "I don't think you understand how I feel right now."

"Then explain it to me."

He looked away, eyes moving back out towards the now thinning crowd. They were approaching the lane that led to her home, and it was significantly quieter here. It wasn't lost on Seylah how quickly things could change given enough time, why it had been only an hour or two at most since she had come this way, but with Elliot at her side, and now … now, she was with August.

The man her heart had whispered to her on this very lane that she wanted, and somehow inexplicably he had confessed himself to her, made his intentions known, asked for a chance at more with her.

For a future with her.

She blinked and shook her head. Life was peculiar, so much so that Seylah allowed herself a moment of peace. If she kept turning and twisting around the scene in the sheriff's office, she would be a wreck before they arrived home.

"Did you mean what you said?" She asked when August remained silent. His eyes moved back to her at her question.

"With all my heart," he replied, and this time where was a tremble in his voice that Seylah had never heard before. Her August was sure of himself, never doubted his words, and was steady in all things.

This, however, was new.

They were in front of her home now, the walkway to the front door before them. "And what will change if I say yes to your offer of courtship?"

August's hand left her then, and he turned to face her. "How do you mean?"

"We have been arguing as of late. There have been so many misunderstandings between us. For example, just yesterday things were tense and I was...not pleased with how it went. And yes," she held up a hand to stay his words when he opened his mouth to speak, "I am well aware that we have always bickered, but that was different. More natural, good natured, and...it is just our way to push the other, to poke sore spots for fun, because that's what friends do. But, our words have taken on barbs. It hurts. Yesterday I was so scared to lose you again that I did not press the issue that I knew had you in a foul mood. I let it lie to keep the peace, to keep you, and I will not continue to do so if we are to enter into a courtship."

August swallowed hard, his hand coming up to yank his hat off, and he squeezed it tightly in his hand. "I know. It hasn't set well with me. Kept me up thinking about how I said the wrong thing to you. I never picked the right words, not when it mattered."

"I don't want that anymore," Seylah said, reaching out to him. She touched his hand lightly as she spoke. "I want it to be like it was before between us. I want to speak my mind, to share my heart with you and know that you won't run from me."

His blue eyes met hers. "I would never run from you. Not again." He turned his hand up to hers, their fingers intertwining together.

"Then we are in agreement."

August raised her hand to his chest, pressing it close so that she was able to feel the steady beat of his heart beneath their clasped fingers. "You mean to say that you are open to that with me? To trying for more?"

Seylah looked at where they were touching, the thump of her own pulse matching August's heartbeat, both humming in tandem until they were in sync. She raised her eyes to the man she had called her friend since before she could remember, the man that had been there at every step, had been a steady presence, the one who she had feared losing the most and she nodded her head slowly.

Yes, she ventured she could try for more with August.

She flexed her fingers against his and leaned close. "Yes, I want that but there will be conditions," she told him.

"Conditions?" He tilted his head to the side. "What kind of conditions?"

"I haven't decided, yet. Give me two days time and I'll have them for you, if you agree to them, then we may proceed."

"To a courtship?"

"Yes, that's right." She nodded and moved back to take her hand away, but August caught it and raised it to his lips.

"Two days time then." August's lips brushed against the inside of her wrist before he let it go.

"Two days," Seylah said, her voice full of a confidence she didn't feel, the last of her sanity had been destroyed by August's last touch. She withdrew her hand, pressing it to her chest as she moved back from him. "Goodbye, August."

He raised his hand and tipped his hat to her. "Seylah."

She nearly stumbled, getting stuck in her hobble skirt

as she turned towards her house, but by the grace of God and more than likely a fair amount of luck she managed to make it inside without incident. Seylah paused on the porch, one hand on the door and cautioned a look behind her to see that August was still there watching her. He had always done this, since the time they had begun walking to and from school together as children. Rain or shine, August would wait for her to enter her home before he continued on his way to his homestead a few minutes journey down the lane.

She raised a hand in a quick wave, and she smiled when August returned the gesture with an easy smile. For all that had changed between them that afternoon, to see August standing there, dependable and reassuringly as ever, comforted her in a way she hadn't been aware she needed.

August Leclaire was her best friend, and Seylah aimed to keep it so come hell or high water.

CHAPTER 7

Seylah sighed staring at the blank piece of paper in front of her. It was just after lunch and she was woefully underprepared for the task set before her.

"What was I thinking?" She whispered, rubbing her temples and closing her eyes. When she had proposed a courtship with conditions, she hadn't quite considered that she would have to outline the conditions herself.

She bit her lip and tapped her pencil against the desk. Her conversation with August the previous day came to mind, and she supposed it was as good a starting point as any when it came to outlining her list. She was still in the quiet of the empty office, all the deputies and her fathers had cleared out for lunch, and given how much the town appreciated a good meal, the Sheriff's office was most likely the quietest place in town.

Seylah touched her pen to the paper and scrawled the following in quick succession.

No arguing.

Fancy Dancing.

A faint smile tugged at her lips at the second item she had written. The dances she had shared with August all those years ago had been some of the sweetest moments of her life, and if he thought to have a courtship without such activities, he was dead wrong.

Three outings a week.

She added the last half-heartedly when she realized that beyond no arguing or the necessity of fancy dancing, she had no firm conditions to entering a courtship with August. Seylah had hoped that she would have more, but her list, for as small as it was, was hers and she supposed it would have to do unless she thought of anything else. Expressing oneself in the written word was a difficult task when it...when it...

"Oh, that's it!" She snapped her fingers and hastily added.

Non negotiable: Communication.

Seylah nodded in satisfaction of the new addition. That was a perfect entry to her list of conditions. She would have to think carefully for more in the meantime. She did have twenty-four hours left at her disposal to do so, after all. She was about to put her list away when the door banged open and August ambled in, a pad of paper and a pencil in one hand, his head bowed over it as he scribbled away. He was so focused on his words that he hadn't taken notice of her, so when she cleared her throat, he jumped a mile.

"Seylah!" He gasped, a hand going to his chest as he stared at her in surprise. "You damn near gave me a heart attack."

"Sorry?" Seylah laughed, setting down her pencil and

pointing at the pad in his hand. "What are you working on?"

"Ah, it's a surprise."

"For?"

He rocked back on his heels with a chagrined look and then said, "You."

Seylah raised an eyebrow. "For me?"

August tucked his pencil behind his ear and walked forward until he was standing in front of her desk. "I mean, that given you've set your mind to come up with conditions for our courtship, I've decided to do the same."

"You have, have you?"

"Thought it might do to see if we had the same ideas of what this would be," he said and gave her a nervous look that she wasn't quite used to seeing on his face. "I know I'm not exactly the most talkative about this kind of thing."

"You mean your feelings."

August winced. "Yes, those. And this might help me remedy my shortcomings, because I--because you mean the world to me, Seylah."

Her face softened and she nodded at him. "You mean the same to me, August. I don't want this to change anything between us."

"But it will. It has to." His voice went hoarse and she paused, raising her eyes to his, trying to understand the emotion she was hearing. There was a multitude of things there. Desire, certainty, frustration, but most of all, Seylah heard need. It was so close to her own feelings that she wasn't quite sure what to say, so she proceeded as plainly as she was able.

"Why?" She whispered. "Why does it have to?"

"That's what happens when children grow up," he told her, rounding the desk until he was beside her. "We've grown up Selyah. We aren't children anymore, things have to change, but that doesn't mean we have to give the other up."

She swallowed hard at his words. "It just means that we have to change what we are, doesn't it?"

"That's about the measure of things. Yes, honey, there was never any world where we got to stay the same." He reached out, touching the cuff of the new lace button up she wore and smiled, "Can't say that I'm sorry about it."

"You aren't?" She asked, confused by his words.

August shook his head. "'Course not, Seylah. This way I get to keep you with me forever. This way, I get to be your man."

"My man?" His words made this real, struck her in a way that she hadn't let herself consider seriously, for fear that she might get too caught up in her daydreams when what was possible was so far removed from what August had just dropped on her.

Her man.

August nodded and set down the notebook he was carrying on top of her desk. "That's what I aim to be. There hasn't been a day between us that I haven't been yours, Seylah. Now is when I make you see it."

If Seylah had half a mind, or even possession of her arms and limbs to move, she would have flailed, but seeing as she was struck dumb, she did nothing and remained sitting.

"Oh," she managed with a slight nod. Blessedly the

door opened, saving her from doing or saying anything else that might result in her finding the motor skills required for a good and proper flail. They both turned to see Will enter the room wearing a look of annoyance.

"If those damned farmers that moved up the pass think I'm going to play servant to them, then they got another thing coming," he announced to the room. "If either of you get a telegram from them, you burn it, y'hear?"

Seylah nodded at her father. "Right in the fire, daddy," she swore, crossing her heart. The older man smiled at his daughter, the expression instantly making him look years younger.

Will nodded in her direction. "That's my girl." He turned to August and pointed at him. "Same goes for you, ignore those ranchers, or else."

August held up his hands in deference to Will. "I won't even so much as look at them on the street, but what's got you riled?"

"They've been cordoning off land that isn't theirs to begin with. Think just because they are up that way they own the whole pass. I've already told them that's not how homesteading works. There are rules in place for a reason," Will crossed the room to his desk and opened a drawer with a jerk of his hand, removing a firearm Seylah hadn't seen for quite some time—a Colt .44 revolver her father had used during the war.

She raised an eyebrow. "Daddy, why are you getting out your old .44?"

"Because I'm mad."

She steepled her hands and leaned forward, elbows on her desk. "What are you planning on doing? Going up there and running the homesteaders out? I thought you told us to ignore them, burn their messages?"

He scowled and looked down at the gun for a moment before he holstered and continued on rifling through his desk. Seylah groaned when she saw him pull the paper cartridges necessary to fire the gun. Her father's bringing out the Colt was by no means for nostalgia's sake. The man was intending to fire it.

"I'm not going to run them out…"

"Daddy. What are you going to do with that gun? Please be honest, because I can't have August running himself ragged while Papa and the other deputies are trying to hold you back. We all remember what happened the last time newcomers caused a fuss."

It was a not so well kept secret that William Barnes had single handedly sent more than one homesteader group packing from the area after they had, in her father's words, "caused more trouble than they were worth" and that the "U.S. government couldn't pay me to take them on, and besides the government still owes me wages from the war, they don't want me going down there myself or I'll get every last dollar. They won't challenge me if I say the homesteaders are out."

Coming to Montana was a dream for many, but it was known that the land around Gold Sky was a tad harder to get settled in on account of the locals who did things their own way. Seylah wondered if officials, or worse, U.S. Marshals would ever come to bring her fathers into line, but so far it seemed as though the government was inclined to allow her fathers leeway over who stayed and who went from the area. It still wouldn't do to have everyone racing to the pass trying to hold her father back when he was angry and motivated. She eyeballed the Colt warily as her father continued on, "Those honyockers deserved that beating and the whole town agrees with me."

August laughed, but the sound died on his lips when Will cut a look his way. "What's so funny, son?"

The smile faded from his face, and he stood up straighter, shoulders broadening. "Nothing, sir," he said, all hint of mirth gone from his face. Seylah rolled her eyes at the display and addressed her father once more.

"I mean it, Daddy. We already have Tom and Wallace out on the boundaries to the east of town, because of the trouble that new family's been having with bandits. That only leaves August and Liam to take your back if anything happens, which means it's just me and Papa in town."

"Oh, Forrest and you can handle things just fine here," Will grumbled, but he looked less inclined to storm off as he had a moment before.

"Can I help with the homesteaders?" August offered, stepping forward then. "I'm as fed up with all the newcomers' demands as anyone, but I'm not keen on Seylah getting involved. There's been far too many new people from the East coast coming to town these days. Feels like a powder keg around here, and I'd rather have you and Forrest managing the town if it comes down to it."

"And me," Seylah interjected, but August sighed and turned to her.

"I don't want you getting hurt."

"I'm just as good with a gun as you are. We had the

same teachers, or have you forgotten that now that you wear a badge?"

August crossed his arms and shook his head at her words. "Seylah, Gold Sky is home, but home is changing. It's getting bigger, people we don't know on the streets, it's not the kind of place that I want you enforcing the law."

Seylah's cheeks reddened at that. "I am not some sort of coddled lady. I am perfectly capable of taking care of myself *and this town.*"

"He's right, darlin'," Will said, and she stared at him in shock.

"You always said I can do anything a boy can; that I'm just as capable as any man I meet," she reminded him, not understanding his meaning. "Why would you say he's right?"

Will set the gun in his holster and glanced meaningfully at August who returned the look with a nod that had Seylah's hackles up. What were the two of them doing exchanging knowing looks as if she were daft enough not to notice.

"Don't think I didn't see that look," she told her father, who rubbed the bridge of his nose and exhaled at her words.

"Didn't mean for you not to see it, Seylah. August is right. That town is changing. Things are more dangerous now, we have to be vigilant, and that means you can't be going about as you did before."

"That's not fair."

"Life doesn't care about fair, sweetheart. And what I care about as your daddy is keeping you and the rest of my family safe. That means you don't patrol, not like before."

Seylah's face fell at her father's words. She had been raised to be as capable and outgoing as any boy, or man, never once had she been insecure of her abilities, but now her father was telling her it wasn't safe. Had things truly changed in Gold Sky that much? How had she not noticed it?

"Then what am I meant to do while the rest of you are out there keeping the peace?" She asked, hating how weak her voice sounded to her own ears.

Her father shifted uncomfortably, another shared look passing between the men that set her on edge. "We need you here," Will said finally, gesturing around the main office and looking back at her with gentle eyes, "For now I want you staying around the office, no runnin' off to give back up or responding to anything that needs a gun on it. This is non-negotiable, Seylah. For now you are a secretary in all sense of the word. Do you understand?"

Seylah's shoulders slumped. "Yes, Sheriff Barnes," she said, and her father's shoulders went rigid at her use of his title. He was all business now, they knew it and she could think of no other way to address him when he was like this.

"Good." He nodded and then cleared his throat giving her a pained look. "It's because I love you, you know that."

She nodded. "I do."

Will nodded again and then stepped back. "I'll be back after lunch. Tell your mama I'll be late on account of, well," he patted the gun at his hip and when she looked as though she might protest he held up a hand, "I'm not going to shoot 'em. Just talk."

August frowned and then said, "I'll go with you. Just in case they prove hard of hearing."

"Sounds good, son. Meet you out front." He walked to the door, but paused in the doorway, looking back at Seylah. "I love you, sweetheart. Don't forget that."

She gave him a watery smile. "Love you too, Daddy." Then her father was gone and out the door and she was left alone with August, an awkward silence settling between them in the wake of her father's departure.

"You know he's just concerned for your safety," he told her.

"I know but that doesn't mean I have to like it," she replied.

August hummed and rocked back on his heels. "True. You don't have to like a thing, but so long as that means you're safe I think we're all willing to risk you being upset at us."

Seylah crossed her arms and sighed. "I'm well aware of what the lot of you are willing to put up with to get your way. And what were those looks the pair of you were giving each other?"

He grinned at that and tucked the notebook he still carried in his back pocket. "That's about us knowing there's something we care enough about to put our foot down," he told her as he pulled on his duster and took a belt of ammunition with him. He slung the belt over his shoulder and looked at her. "That's you in case you don't know you infuriating woman."

She cracked a smile and leaned back in her chair. "I

wish the pair of you would care a little less about me so that I could be free to do as I pleased."

"There's not a chance of that, and this doesn't mean it's forever, just for now." August hesitated, looking at the door. "I'll have my list for you by tomorrow. Can I take you to Mrs. Lily's for dinner then?"

The question wasn't a new one as the pair had frequented Mrs. Lily's cafe since they were children, but this felt different, was different, and the invitation to dinner cheered her some after being banned from performing any duty more strenuous than office duties.

"Yes, I'd like that."

He smiled at her, the expression serving to lift her spirits, considerably. "Till then, Seylah," he tipped his hat in a move that Seylah considered particularly debonair and exited the office in short order, which was a blessing because a woman, whether or not she was barred from upholding the law with her own two hands, needed peace and quiet to swoon. And that is exactly what she aimed to do, and do so in spectacular fashion, in the solitude of the office.

CHAPTER 8

"*W*hat are you working on?" Rose asked, coming into the dining room and giving the sheet of paper Seylah was staring at a curious look.

"I have no idea," Seylah confessed, glaring at the half written list of rules for her courtship.

"What do you mean? Is it like a riddle?" Rose asked, sitting down with a carafe of coffee.

"I suppose you could call it a riddle. A very stupid, idiotic riddle that an imbecile is responsible for."

"You know how much Delilah loves a good puzzle. The more idiotic the better."

"Well, I mean, it's not actually a puzzle."

Rose gave her sister a confused look. "A riddle that isn't a puzzle?" She poured herself a cup of coffee and then snapped her fingers. "It's one of those puzzle problems that twists in on itself, like a two-in-one isn't it? Oh, we simply must tell Delilah. I bet even Florence is home to help!"

Seylah yanked the paper close when Rose tried to get a

look at it. "No!" She nearly yelled and then continued on in a slightly calmer voice when her sister looked at her in shock. "I mean, no, that's all right, I can solve this on my own."

"Don't be silly. We can all solve it in no time and what a fun activity with the rain driving us all crazy!" Rose turned in her seat and yelled, "Del! Flo! Are you home? We have a puzzle to do!"

Seylah winced and sank lower in her seat, paper clutched to her chest. "No, that isn't necessary, I'm quite tired of this puzzle."

"A puzzle? Just a moment!" Del's shout came with Florence's excited: "I cannot wait, I was positively dying of boredom!"

"Oh god," Seylah moaned, ready to bolt from the room before her sisters could appear, but unfortunately when the Wickes-Barnes women were motivated, they were quicker than the wind, and the pair of women appeared in the doorway before Seylah could so much as slid an inch on her seat.

"Hand over that puzzle," Flo demanded extending a hand.

"It's not a puzzle."

"Fine, is it a riddle?" Del asked, walking into the room and claiming the seat next to Seylah. "I'm an absolute wonder with them. Let me take a look at it." She held out her hand in a mirror gesture of her sister, and Seylah shrank back into her chair.

"It's not a riddle," she said, for what felt like the umpteenth time, and made to slide out of her chair. "I quite think I'm due for a nap as well, so I'll just be going..."

"Freeze!" Rose yelled, startling Seylah so abruptly that the sheet of paper she'd been clutching slipped from her hand and fluttered onto the floor in front of her sisters. Florence bent and snatched up the paper before Seylah could stop her, but it didn't stop her from rushing forward and making a wild grab at it nonetheless.

"Give it here!" Seylah demanded, swiping for the sheet of paper, but Florence danced away with it raised in triumph.

"Not before we get a good look at what you're trying to conceal."

"It's just a riddle, nothing special," Seylah insisted, but Delilah snorted, a hand on her hip.

"You've made it abundantly clear that it is indeed not a riddle, so now we know there's more to it."

"I told you that how many times and now you believe me?" Seylah asked, throwing her hands up.

"Oh, get the sour look off your face and explain this list to me," Florence said waving the paper. "No more fighting? Three outings a week?" She raised an eyebrow and looked at Seylah with a smirk. "Is this what I think it is?"

"That depends on what you think it is, and the answer is most assuredly no," Seylah replied, lunging for the paper with a growl escaping her as Florence danced out of reach once more. Florence twirled and gave the paper to Rose who had joined the fray.

"Rose, I am not inclined to see this continue. Give me

that paper," Seylah grit out, but Rose was too busy reading to pay her sister much mind.

"This is a list of curious demands, sweet sister." Rose raised her eyes to her and pointed an accusing finger at Seylah, "This is a list for a suitor!"

"No, it is not, it's a-a puzzle?"

"A suitor?" Delilah asked, giving Seylah a smirk. "I think we all know that means August."

"How do we all know that?" Seylah demanded. "I was out at a picnic with another man. A new man, freshly arrived to town. Perhaps this list is for him?"

"We might believe that if we all hadn't heard of how August dragged you away from that nice new man," Delilah replied.

"Absolutely barbaric," Rose said and then let out a dreamy sigh. "I adore it. Being fought over by two men!"

"No one is fighting over me. There are no men fighting over me."

"Then they mean to share?" Florence asked, perking up. "How lovely. A fine idea if you ever had one, Seylah."

Seylah rubbed her temples in exasperation. "There will be no sharing, Florence. There are not two men in this story."

Rose's face fell. "Oh, how boring. I was so hopeful."

Delilah jabbed her sister with her elbow. "Florence, stop foisting your own desires on Seylah," she said and turned towards Seylah. "If there are not two men, then is there even one? Tell us yes."

Seylah swallowed hard and then turned away from three pairs of eyes that were firmly trained on her. "Yes, there is one man," she finally said, voice barely above a whisper.

A collective shriek arose from the women, and Seylah leapt back in shock. She glanced around and assessed the distance between herself and the dining room exits.

"Please tell me that is a good sound...it is, a good sound, right?" She asked, edging towards the window at her back.

Rose nodded. "A very good sound indeed!" She reached out and caught her sister by her hand, pulling her away from the window. "Don't you even think of making a run for it."

"I knew this day would come eventually," Delilah told Seylah, who was now struggling to free herself from Rose's grip.

"How on earth are you this strong?" Seylah asked, trying to yank her arm free. "You're like a Vaudeville act."

"Stop struggling," Rose ordered, dragging Seylah closer to their sisters and what Seylah was now forever thinking as 'that damnable list.'

"I for one," Florence held up her hand as she spoke, "think you can add more demands to this list," she said, pointing at the list in earnest.

"They are not demands," Seylah protested, still struggling against Rose who only seemed to be growing stronger by the second.

Florence scoffed. "Then, what, dear sister, are they?"

"They are--they are guidelines," Seylah finally managed to spit out.

"Guidelines for what exactly?" Rose asked, throwing

both arms around Seylah's waist and dragging her forward.

"Guidelines for amorous situations with a suitor, that's what," Florence crowed, and then directed a hopeful smile at Seylah, "or two? Are there two suitors?"

"There are *not two suitors*. For the absolute last time, Florence." Seylah grit her teeth and struggled for breath beneath her sister's ever-tightening embrace.

Her sister rolled her eyes. "How positively droll."

"Stop being salacious. Let's take a look at these guidelines, shall we?" Delilah held out her hand in a perfect impersonation of their mother when she was at the head of a classroom of unruly school children.

Florence handed over the paper, and Seylah muffled a curse when Delilah began to read aloud from the list.

"No arguing. Fancy Dancing?" Delilah smiled at the paper and raised her eyes to Seylah. "I know who this list is for."

Seylah sighed, eyes closing in resignation at the knowing tone in her sister's voice. "I suppose you do."

"Tell us who it is," Florence clasped her hands in front of her and gave Delilah a pleading look.

"Oh, it's August, stop being obtuse," Rose growled from where she was still wrapped around her sister. "It's always been August."

Florence snapped her fingers. "That does make sense when you say it as such," she nodded approvingly at Seylah before she pursed her lips. "And I was not being obtuse. Seylah was at a picnic with a very handsome banker just today, which is why I was praying for two suitors."

Seylah sagged in Rose's arms. "I can barely manage the suitor that I do have. That's what the list was for," she explained with a sigh and pointed at the list in Delilah's hand, "that was my attempt at managing my relationship with August."

"Which is?" Delilah asked.

Seylah raised a shoulder in a shrug. "A courtship?" It was true that they had agreed to begin a courtship, had decided to take a new direction together, but what that meant for their friendship was unknown to her. Her eyes lit on the list in Delilah's hand and she swallowed hard against the rising lump in her throat.

She did not understand this.

This was not her element, not that she particularly knew what *this* was.

"I, ah, need some air," Seylah choked out, looking down at Rose's grip assessing how to best break her sister's hold.

Delilah stood up straight and flicked the paper at her. "You're not to go anywhere until we figure out this list," she paused and cleared her throat, "as crude as it is, and we all ensure that your courtship with August gets off to a wonderful start."

Selyah reached down, gripping her sister's wrists and shook her head. "It's quite all right. Everything is fine." She thrust down on her sister's wrists, breaking the grip and stepped away from Rose quickly before she managed to grab her once more. "August and I will manage. I am confident things will return to normal before long."

"But why?" All three of her sister's cried out, making Seylah jump.

"Well, because, well…" her voice trailed off when she couldn't much think of any reason why she wanted it to go back as it was, especially when returning to life as they had known it was at the bottom of Seylah's to-do list. "It just will," she finished lamely.

"I refuse to accept that," Florence declared, moving to block the window when Seylah darted that way.

"And I am of the same opinion," Delilah informed her when Seylah looked in her direction, pleadingly. It seemed there would be no help coming to her from that corner. "And that is why we are going to add an addendum or two to this list."

"Addendum?" Seylah paled and wrung her hands in front of her. "Is this now a legal document?"

"Perhaps it should be," Rose interjected. "To add an air of legitimacy to the whole affair."

"It does not need an air of legitimacy. It is a lover's pact," Florence replied, rolling her eyes. "You are the youngest of us and it is showing, sister."

Rose narrowed her eyes. "No one likes a know-it-all, Flo," she replied, and in quick order, the two sisters descended into bickering that only siblings were capable of. Seylah let out a breath of relief when the two women's focus was pulled off of her, and in their lapse of attention, Seylah turned to make for the door, but was stopped in her tracks when Delilah stepped in front of her.

"It's normal to be scared," Delilah said.

"I don't want anything to change," Seylah admitted, giving her a rueful smile.

"I know, but it must. You aren't children anymore," she paused and glanced at their still arguing sisters, "even if we forget from time-to-time. Things have to change eventually, but we can all embrace the change together if we keep an open mind."

Seylah turned over her sister's words, words that were an echo of August's words to her, and she looked away. "What am I supposed to do? I tried to write down what I wanted."

Delilah held up the paper. "Your list."

"Crude as it may be?"

Her sister stepped closer and pressed the paper into Seylah's hand. "Take the list. It's a good list."

Seylah took the piece of paper and frowned. "It's a short list. I thought things would be grander if this were to ever happen."

"I think so long as you have August you will be happy. You've always been your happiest when you were with him. You both are. Anyone can see it even if you've both been trying to close your eyes to it for years."

Delilah's words struck her wordless for a moment, and not for the first time, did Seylah wish to be anywhere but in the room, but now it was a different purpose. It was not to escape embarrassment and meddling by her sisters, but because Delilah had spoken so plainly about the entire matter between herself and August.

For years, she said. *Years.*

How much longer would she go on denying what was between them, what apparently was no secret at all despite Seylah's best efforts. Working to keep needless distance between them would only frustrate the pair of them, and that was no way to begin a courtship. No way at all.

"I think you're right." Seylah looked down at the paper and ran her fingers along the lines of pencil. "If you'll excuse me, I think I have someone to find."

Her sister hummed, but said nothing else, already turning towards where Rose was now exerting her strength on Florence, who was, for all intents and purposes, putting up quite a fight when confronted by such a test of endurance. The last she saw of them they were naught but a heap of skirts on the floor with Delilah standing by as if to referee.

No one could ever accuse the women in her family of being dainty or unlively.

She left the room, her feet carrying her away from the bickering of her sisters and towards the makeshift shooting range her fathers had created for their leisure. Of course, Seylah was the only one of the girls to make use of it. Save for her and her fathers, August was the only other person to visit it. She had an inkling she would find him there, which suited her perfectly. There was no need to wait for the next day, not when she had the clarity that only words from a sibling could bring.

Delilah was right in her estimation of Seylah's happiness. August had always been instrumental to Seylah's joy. Since they were children, and now again as adults, their lives were ever changing. But that did not mean they could not repurpose change to create something anew, weave it into their every day until the pair of them had become different.

Her feet hit the wood of the back porch and she paused in the late afternoon light. Fall was here, her favorite season, and the crisp air made her palms tingle.

The season never failed to make her feel like she was waking up, even as it put the Montana scenery around her to sleep, these few precious weeks heralding the coming cold and bitter snowstorms.

She crossed the yard and made for the barn in the distance; the shooting range was just beyond it. All around her, the vibrant golds of fall were flashing in the afternoon light. She smiled, watching the larch tree boughs sway. The cool fall breeze blew her hair into her face. Seylah briefly closed her eyes, inhaling deeply. The faint sound of a gunshot floated to her and she opened her eyes with a smile.

Yes, change was scary, as Delilah had said, but that did not mean it could not also be good. Seylah tucked the paper into her pocket, her heart feeling lighter at the thought of what precisely different could mean.

By her estimation, different could be perfect when it came to courtship and August.

CHAPTER 9

*W*hen Seylah rounded the corner, her eyes caught sight of August walking along the target stands at the far end of the open space.

The range was a luxury, considering her hobby of target shooting, and she was thankful her fathers had seen fit to create it for her. The target stands were at varying heights, allowing for variety in terms of target practice. Raised earth created a protective barrier for when shots went wild, which though a rare occurrence given the household's affinity for firearms, but one could never be too careful with live ammunition. A partially covered firing point afforded Seylah the choice of practicing during the more severe seasons of Montana. She continued forward to the enclosure and leaned her elbows on the high tabletop of the firing point.

Seylah glanced at the guns and smiled when she saw the revolvers August favored. She reached out and touched one of them, thoughts straying to the day he had been given this particular pair. She had given them to him the year they had made up with one another.

Her fingers traced the curve of the *A* that was etched into the handle of the gun and her eyes moved to the next in the set, her eyes landing on the *S* the gunsmith had engraved. When Seylah had presented the guns to August, the look of awe on his face had filled her heart to capacity and she'd made a quick study of how to set the look on the man's face as often as she could. She hoped she would see such a smile from their encounter today.

Seylah raised her eyes and pushed herself up to her full height as she watched August approach. August liked it out here on her family's property, and she knew why. It was easy to relax when there was no one to see their every move. The town of Gold Sky meant well, but at times it was overwhelming to have so many invested in the comings-and-goings of your every day.

He raised a hand in greeting when he saw her. A thrill went through her, watching August approach. His broad shoulders stretched the flannel pleasingly, and Seylah's earlier infatuation with a man in fine attire, a man built like a house, vanished.

If Elliot were a house, then August was a mountain. Raw and powerful, steady in his everlasting presence with roots far beyond what anyone could ever hope to witness. The man cut a fine figure in his denim and plaid. His golden hair gleamed in the afternoon light, the reddish hue of it akin to the larch boughs, and she suddenly wondered if the reason she adored fall so much was for the way that the season and this man resembled the other.

He wasn't on duty today, and the casual attire softened

him enough that Seylah was able to imagine what he might look like when they were alone, when work and the eyes of the town were nowhere to be seen.

"Hi," he said, coming to a stop on the other side of the table top.

"Hi," she answered and pointed out at the targets behind him. "Still shooting?"

He hooked his fingers into his belt loops, and Seylah struggled not to let her eyes stray to where his exposed forearms bunched. Who knew a pair of rolled up shirt-sleeves would be her undoing?

"Was planning on it, but it wasn't too enjoyable alone."

"May I stay a while?"

He flashed her a smile, his blue eyes warm on her. "I'd like nothing more than your company, Seylah. You can use one of our guns if you don't want to go back to the house for yours."

Her heart fluttered when he said *our guns.* "Do you mean that?" She asked.

August ducked under the tabletop and came to stand beside her. "Mean what?" He asked, placing ammunition on the table between them.

"Our guns," she said, nodding at the revolvers. "Do you really think of them as ours?"

"Of course I think of them as ours. They have our initials on them and everythin'," he said tapping the handle of the revolver with the engraved S. "I'd say that's pretty official. Don't you think?"

"I'll agree with you on that one."

"Do you like that, I--ah, think of them as ours?" He asked, his voice soft. The change in tone pulled at her. It was tender and searching, so achingly new and full of the fright Delilah had assured her was entirely normal.

She cleared her throat and pushed forward. She had come this far and could manage to continue on. August was worth it, *they were worth it.*

"I do," she told him and bit her lip, and continued on, "I've always thought of them as ours."

His hand found hers and she swayed in her boots at the touch, the warmth of him drew her close like a moth to a flame. "That makes me happy, honey. Real happy. Only one thing that could make me happier."

"What's what?" Her breath was coming faster now, the rise and fall of her chest forcing her breasts to graze his bicep ever so slightly, the teasing touch of it nearly setting her aflame but she managed to stay whole, if only just.

"That someday, these guns won't be the only thing you think of as ours."

Her eyes widened and her feet faltered though the misstep only worked to thrust her forward, the movement causing August to reach for her, his arm catching her around her waist and steadying her against him.

"Yes, Seylah May?" His eyes dropped to her mouth and the span of another shared heart beat passed between them.

"Nothing," Seylah whispered. Though the words she wanted to speak were caught in her throat her hand reached up, tentatively, until she was cupping his jaw. She nibbled her lip, watching the storm of emotions that seemed at war in August's eyes. He was wrestling with something, back and forth like a pendulum. He wanted to touch her, like she was touching him, she knew it but for some reason he was holding himself back from doing so.

"August," she tried. If he knew how much she wanted him, that she desired his touch, ached for it. Perhaps then the pendulum would swing in the direction she desperately wished for, and he would close the few inches that separated them. She was leaning against the tabletop with the span of it against her back and August in front of her. There was precious little room for her to move, though she could think of no other place she wished to be than exactly as she was.

"You can touch me," she told him, a note of neediness she had never let slip into her voice said everything she hadn't voiced. It was there if only he chose to listen. She wanted him to touch her, willed it more than anything else at that moment, had dreamed of it for as long as she understood what it was that she wanted.

"Honey."

That one word that filled the air with such potential, so much confusion for Seylah before she allowed what she wanted to root down and make a home was now a source of excitement that set her to trembling with want. Seylah felt the air leave her lungs when the moment his decision was made registered. August Leclaire had made up his mind, it was written all over him, plain as day, easily seen in his eyes.

He reached for her, the pads of his thumbs running along the line of her jaw before moving up to brush against her ears as the man cradled her face in his hands.

"Honey, come here," he murmured, stepping into the

space between them and leaning down until his mouth was pressing against hers.

She had waited years for this kiss. Written it off as impossible, the stuff of fanciful girlish daydreams, but it was here and it was as beautiful as she had always imagined.

August kissed her gently, tentatively, as if he were acquainting himself with a landscape at twilight. He moved closer still, slanting his mouth to herself and Seylah parted her lips eagerly with a moan when she felt him deepening the kiss. The answering groan her invitation for more elicited set her into motion and she wrapped her arms around his neck eager for more, to feel the muscle of August against her more, in as many places as she was able to manage. She kissed him hungrily. She had wanted this for so long and would take her fill from it before it was done. August, it seemed was of the same mind and she scarcely noticed when he swept her up against him setting her on the table behind her. He stepped into the space between her legs and threaded his fingers through her curly hair with one hand while the other dropped to the nape of her neck, the strength of his fingers there as reassuring weigh as they continued to kiss.

Lips and tongue moving together without any hint of tentativeness, this was no longer an exploration but a conquest conducted by the pair of them in perfect tandem.

August and she had always given and taken from the other in equal measure and they were no different in this aspect of their relationship. Kissing, was it seemed, no different to them than verbal sparring or shared laughter, and in this endeavor like the rest they participated in enthusiastically and without censor. It was only when they were left gasping that they parted and Seylah blinked at the stars that swam before her.

"August..." Her chest was heaving, heart thumping like a runaway horse from what they had just done. The fear she'd almost let hold her back was gone, in its place was exhilaration.

This was right. This was true.

This should have always been.

August pulled back and looked up at Seylah. Her seat on the table top boosted her above the big man between her thighs and he shook his head. He dropped his hands from her face to her shoulders, and Seylah leaned into his touch.

"I shouldn't have waited all those years. We missed this for no reason but fear," he murmured. His fingers moved lower and he flattened his hands until they molded to her sides, the heat of his palms seared her through the fabric of her dress.

Seylah reached for him, her fingers burying themselves in his hair. Her fingernails scraped his scalp and she arched closer until they were pushed close once more, bodies flush to the other. August's head tilted back, his chin grazing against her and making her breath come short from the slight touch. Already her body was on fire, her hands greedy for another touch, her mouth desperate for another taste.

"Are you still scared?" she asked tugging on his golden strands between her fingers.

He gave a slight shake of his head. "No," he whispered, eyes drifting closed. "Are you?" He asked her, leaning his forehead against her breastbone.

Seylah wrapped her arms around him, pulling him tight against her. "No." She smiled and squeezed him tighter. "No, I'm not."

There was no going back to the way it had been. It was not an option, not when she knew what his lips tasted like or how it felt to have him pressed close, the feel of him between her thighs would never leave her as one of her most treasured remembrances.

She had never been happier.

CHAPTER 10

*S*eylah was busy, resetting the firing pin of her revolver the next morning. Her hands were busy, but her mind was busier, thoughts of the previous day and her time with August had turned her mind into a whirlwind of memories. The way his hands had felt on her, the heat of his body against hers, the way he'd felt between her thighs, the taste of him.

A sigh escaped Seylah and she grinned, looking down at her work. She was nearly done with her task, and if she were lucky today would be full of her indulging in one of her favorite past times with one of her favorite people.

Target shooting and August Leclaire.

Hours alone with August, hours alone where they were free to relax, to talk, to...revisit the previous day's encounter. Seylah was not opposed to such a proclivity.

"What's put such a smile on your face?" Florence asked, sailing into the room with all the pomp of a queen. She was dressed in an extravagant gown of crimson silk and velvet. Her hair was done up with flowers and ribbons, the effect was lovely, if out of place for day-to-day affairs in Gold Sky.

Seylah picked up a rag and wiped her hands clean of the oil her work had left on them. "Where are you going in that outfit?"

Florence stopped pinching her cheeks in the mirror. "Out."

"Yes, but where and with whom?"

Flo held up a finger, eyes still on her reflection and said, "That still remains a mystery, but I know they will be lovely."

"They?" Seylah asked, cocking her head to the side. "What are you going on about, Florence?"

Her sister turned to look at Seylah over her shoulder. "Oh, just a little hopeful planning, but for now I'd rather discuss what's put such a smile on your face."

Seylah forced her lips to not erupt into a wide smile and she began to collect her tools together into her leather tool kit. "I think you might have an inclination as to who it's about."

"And it's not a Mister Elliot Myers, now is it?"

Seylah rolled the toolkit up and tossed the small hand towel over her shoulder as she stood. "No, it's not."

Florence swayed on her feet, her hands throwing her skirts out in excitement. "Why I never thought I'd live to see the day. Did your little list help refine everything?"

"I, ah, actually never used the list."

Florence pursed her lips. "But it was a good list. Why didn't you share it?"

Selyah cleared her throat and picked up her shotgun. "I had meant to, but things became busy."

"Busy?"

She nodded, pocketing her tool kit. "Yes, busy."

"Does busy pertain to the passionate embrace I glimpsed?" Florence asked, coming forward in a rustling cloud of silk. "Because from my observation, I quite envy your type of busy."

Seylah froze and swallowed hard. She hadn't thought they'd had an audience when she'd given herself over to her desires. "You saw that?"

"We did."

"We?"

"Yes, well, all of us."

Seylah's eyes widened. She prayed that did not mean the entirety of their family. If her fathers caught wind of what they'd shared, she couldn't say how they might react. "Who is we?" She asked, playing for nonchalance and tapped her palm on the butt of her gun.

Florence circled a finger around the room. "Oh, get that look off your face. I only meant that Rose and Delilah were with me. We all ran after you when the dust from my little spat with Rose finally died down."

Seylah let out a relieved breath and she doubled over, cradling her shotgun close. "Oh, thank god."

"You thought I meant Papa and Daddy?" Florence pulled a face and waved her hands. "I would have given a warning shout if they had been with us." She shook her head and gave a shudder. "They might have drawn and quartered August right then and there, especially the part where he picked you up? That was unbelievably passionate."

158

Seylah lifted her head. "Unbelievably passionate?" she murmured weakly.

"Yes, but unbelievably passionate means utterly necessary and satisfyingly wanton. And get that look off your face, you look as though you might be sick, we didn't stay long after that little move. Delilah marched us inside."

Seylah straightened. "Praise the Lord."

"Delilah is entirely too much a mother hen. She never allows any of us to have any fun."

Seylah uttered a silent prayer of thanks for her sister. She would have to remember to make only the finest cake for Delilah's breakfast tomorrow. August and Seylah had spent the better part of an hour together and there was no telling how much they would have seen if Deillah hadn't taken her sisters away.

She cleared her throat, fingers tightening on her shotgun. "Flo, I need you to be a little less enthusiastic about yesterday."

"But why? I think it's so wonderfully romantic and passionate of you two to have a clandestine meeting."

"Exactly," Seylah said with a sigh and set her gun down on the table beside them, "clandestine is the perfect word for describing what it was. And do you know the definition of clandestine, dear sister?" she asked, gesturing her sister forward with a tired hand.

Florence rushed forward and lowered her voice to a hush. "It is a deed done in secret."

"Exactly," Seylah said, leaning forward and giving her sister a serious look. "But rushing in here and talking about it where anyone can hear is not clandestine. I need

159

you to keep yesterday's events away from our fathers' ears. Can you do that for me?"

"You can count on me," Florence pledged, holding up her hand in oath, "In the spirit of clandestine trysts, the region over!"

Seylah winced ,and held up a hand, silencing her sister. "Shhhh! Flo, please!"

"Right, right." Florence held up her hands and gave Seylah an apologetic smile. "My apologies. I saw nothing, and neither did either of our sisters. I can assure you of that."

"Assure her of what?"

They both turned toward the door to see their fathers standing in the doorway. They looked as if they had just entered the house and were still wearing their dusters, a fine coating of dirt and grime covering them from head-to-toe. Seylah prayed the homesteaders hadn't been causing her fathers to run themselves ragged policing their penchant for redrawing land boundaries.

"Nothing," Seylah said quickly.

"It's private," Florence blurted out at the same moment.

Will raised an eyebrow, his gray eyes moving from woman to woman. "Well, now that doesn't sound like nothing."

Forrest sucked on his teeth and crossed his arms. "Better we not pry. You know how it is in a house full of women. Nothing and private, well that's a fine line into territory we have no business venturing."

Seylah breathed a sigh of relief when Will nodded in agreement. "You're not wrong on that. Make a note of that, August," he said turning to the man that was walking into the room after them.

August froze when he caught sight of Seylah. He opened his mouth to say something, but then snapped it shut and looked at Will. "Sorry, sir?"

"When a woman says it's nothing, it's most assuredly something and sometimes it's best not to pry," Forrest supplied, clapping August on the shoulder. He turned to Florence and gestured to her attire. "Are you off to a ball, sweetheart?"

Florence shook her head and gave them a proprietary spin. "A singles soiree, and isn't my dress lovely?"

Both of her fathers hummed in approval and told her just how lovely it was while Flo preened for them, eagerly. Seylah took advantage of her sister showing them the ribbons in her hair to walk over to August.

"Hi," she said with a nervous smile. She glanced over at her fathers and sister and pointed to the door. "Should we escape now?"

He smiled at her and reached for her, catching her hand. "Why? We just got in from a long ride."

She looked down at their hands in shock before she leaned close to him. "What are you doing?" She whispered. They hadn't told her fathers, but here he was, holding her hand as if it were the most natural thing in the world. Seylah's eyes slid to the side nervously while she tugged on her hand.

"August we--"

He tightened his grip, refusing to let go. "I talked to them."

"You did?"

"'Course I did. We had a long ride, seemed like as good a time as any."

"And they were accepting?"

He reached out and touched her cheek. "If they weren't I suspect I'd be walking back to town barefoot, but seeing as they let me ride back and keep my boots, yes, they were very accepting."

"Doesn't mean we didn't think about shooting him." Will's voice pulled Seylah's attention away from August and to her fathers.

Forrest lifted a shoulder in a shrug. "I know that I am usually the cooler of the two of us, but Daddy is right. Thought about leaving August out there."

August cleared his throat when Seylah rolled her eyes at them. "Thought I'd leave that version of the conversation out of it, but it was tense there for a few minutes. I meant what I told the both of you," he nodded at the men and then looked at Seylah. "I aim to court you properly, Seylah May. Let the whole town know how I feel about you, and what I want for the two of us."

"Which is?" Seylah asked before she could stop herself.

"For you to be my wife," August said as if it were the easiest thing in the world.

Her heart leaped at his admission and she felt her knees go weak at the soft-eyed look he aimed her way. "Do you mean that?"

"With all my heart."

"Oh, August."

"Shoulda shot him," Will grit out, watching as his daughter threw her arms around August. The pair embraced each other and his cheek set to twitching when he saw them share a chaste kiss. He could scarcely stand the thought of his girls marrying, but it seemed that day was bearing down on the Wilkes-Barnes household with all the force and speed of a steam engine. "Why did you stop me?" He asked Forrest with a glare.

"He's a good man," Forrest replied, undeterred by the narrow-eyed look his husband was shooting his way. "You know it, I know it. We damn near raised him, raised him to be a good man. He will take good care of Seylah."

Will sighed, rocking back on his heels, but he was still frowning at the sight of his first born in the arms of a man. "Oh, all right but I want you to know I don't like it."

Forrest watched the scene in front of him. Seylah was happy, August was a good man, and Florence was practically weeping with joy. He wondered why she was dressed so fine, but knew the women of his house enough to know it would all come out soon enough.

"You don't like much," he reminded Will, fighting a smile at the sour look on his husband's handsome face.

Will's lips pursed. "I like you."

"That'll do just fine then."

∽

"Can I see your list?"

Seylah looked away from the stars in front of her and to the side where August was sitting beside her. Not wanting to test Will's self-control, they had set out for Gold Sky proper and enjoyed dinner together. If any of the Gold Sky citizens observed a change in their demeanor, none of them commented on it and Seylah wondered if that had been the town busybodies' intentions all along. She shook her head, thinking of the attention and how it might have all stopped years ago if they had only confessed their feelings sooner. Now they were in the town square, enjoying the evening air, the briskness of fall was giving way to the chill of winter and she knew that it was only a matter of days before snowfall would blanket the town.

The night had passed, enjoyably. Knowing that her fathers knew took a weight off her shoulders Seylah hadn't been aware she'd been carrying. She let out a happy sigh, her shoulders drooping slightly at the thought that she and August were now publicly a couple, even if they hadn't chosen to verbalize it quite yet to the town.

The townspeople would, as they always had, ask if they had questions. The people of Gold Sky were not known for their shyness, and Seylah was sure word of their changed relationship would soon be common knowledge. A passing couple gave them a knowing smile as they exchanged "good evenings" and Seylah wondered if maybe the reason no one had commented was for the very fact that, well, perhaps the town already knew.

She was staring after the couple and turning this thought over in her head when August touched her shoulder gently. "Seylah?"

She blinked and looked at him. "Pardon?"

"Your list," he tried again and held up a folded piece of paper. "I have mine if you'd like to see it."

"My list, right, right," she murmured, hands going to pat at her coat pockets. "It's not a long list, or a very detailed one," she said, retrieving the piece of paper and hesitating before she held it out to him. "My sisters had ideas for it but…" her voice trailed off when he took the piece of paper and passed her his own, "it was determined it was, ah, fine as it was." She looked away and took August's list into her lap.

Why she was suddenly nervous to share with him, she didn't know. It was a basic checklist of requirements that were, at their core, mundane and simple. There was nothing to worry with in sharing with him except that… except that Selyah knew there was one fear that she hadn't quite let herself think, dreading that it would then take shape and become undeniably true.

It was true that her list was mundane and simple. It was also true that Seylah worried the same could be said for her relationship with August.

For all their bickering and banter, for all their tendency to push the other, to get beneath one another's skin, she worried that their friendship, their fledgling romance, could and would be termed as mundane and simple. Her heart hurt at the thought. It was not mundane to her to be with August, to sit with him as she was now. It was the most exciting part of her day, the best part of it even.

But what if he came to see them, her, as simple? What if he tired of their time together after it had become expected? The uncertainty and self-conscious nature of her early years came flooding back to her so quickly that Seylah could scarcely breathe. August was like the sun to her, warm and pulling her close no matter what transpired, but what if she were not that to him?

Could she be able to go back to the way things were?

"Seylah."

How would it be possible?

"Seylah."

She jumped with a start, the paper in her hands wrinkling beneath her now clenched fist. "What?" She asked, blinking in confusion.

"Are you all right?"

August was looking at her with concern now, his blue eyes filled with question. He leaned closer to her and touched her arm. "I was calling to you, but you were somewhere else."

"I was thinking," she supplied, quickly unfolding the paper in her hands, but she was still unable to focus on the script it held.

He nodded. "I could tell as much. Was my list too…" his voice trailed off and she looked at him then, the uncertainty in his voice drawing her out of her storm of thoughts.

"Too what?"

August looked uncomfortable and swallowed hard. He leaned forward, elbows braced on his knees, body folded close in on itself. The posture was so reminiscent of childhood that she smiled at seeing it. August was a big man, but to see him now like this was reassuring in a way she hadn't been aware that she needed.

He was a man, her new romantic interest, but most of all he was still August.

"Demanding," he finally said and Seylah sat up straight, her back coming off the bench with all the posture of a ramrod.

"What?"

He sighed and rubbed at his temples, his head hanging low between his hands. "It is, isn't it?"

Seylah's smile vanished and she frowned in confusion and turned towards him then. "What is?"

"My list," he said gesturing at the paper she held. "I knew it would be. We don't have to--"

"August, wait, I haven't--" Seylah held up her hand and took in a deep breath, "no, it's not the list. This list is..." She dropped her eyes to the paper, eyes skimming over the words to see what August had written. What could have brought him to such worry?

Fighting not allowed.

Allowed to escort to work and home after work.

Allowed to take to lunch every work day.

Weekly horse rides following church.

Courtship with intention to marry.

She looked up at him to see that August was watching her intently. The man was bracing himself, scarcely breathing, and Seylah gave him a rueful smile when she saw the uncertainty in his eyes.

"The list is what?" He asked.

"Not demanding."

"It's not?"

"Not at all." She smiled at him and held the paper close to her chest. "I like it very much."

August's body relaxed. "Truly?"

Seylah nodded her head. "Truly. I like your list," she told him. Seeing the words August had written assured Seylah that he wanted what she did, their lists were normal and in step with who and what they were, and had been to one another.

"I was worried that you might think my list was too simple," she admitted, "but seeing your list makes me feel better about all of this. I was quite worried earlier."

"Why?" August asked. He moved closer until they were sitting in a mirror image of the other, papers in hand, bodies angled towards the other, knees touching slightly, earnest looks trained on the other.

"Old insecurities," Seylah said quietly. "There's no other reason for it. I thought you would find my list simple. Something that would bore you once the novelty of us wore thin."

"Novel or not, a life with you would never bore me"

"What people desire changes."

August shook his head. "A life in Gold Sky is what I've always wanted." He reached for her. "You are all I have ever wanted."

Seylah sucked in a breath at the heartfelt words and she looked down at the paper she had been clutching.

Courtship with intention to marry.

It struck her then, staring down at those five words that this was not a passing fancy for August.

"You would want to marry me?" She asked. "I mean to say, if we suited."

He nodded, dropping a hand to hers that rested beside them on the back of the bench. "I do. And I am quite confident we will suit. We already do."

"When we aren't bickering."

He nodded and settled back in his seat. "Yes, when we aren't bickering, but seeing as that problem appears on both of our lists I think we can manage to come to an understanding."

"That means you would be my husband," she informed him helpfully, and he grinned at her.

"I am well aware of what titles we would be awarded if we were to marry."

"You want a family," she told him. It was no secret that August wanted to be a father, that he had always envisioned a home full of laughter and closeness, a house that was so very much like her own. If August intended to marry her, meant to have her as a wife, wanted a home with her, a place where the two of them would be together, where they could start a family. Her cheeks reddened when she thought of how one went about starting a family, and she cleared her throat.

"You do too. One like your own," August said watching her carefully. "We could have that."

Seylah forced herself not to think of their stolen moments at the gun range with him and nodded. "We could."

"It would be good." He held out his hand to her, palm up and fingers outstretched in a gesture that Seylah was quickly becoming familiar with. She placed her hand in his and threaded their fingers together.

"It would be," she replied, following August as he stood from the bench and set off in the direction of her home. They walked hand-in-hand down the boulevard, eyes only for each other in the fading twilight, the lights that had once illuminated her feelings for him now lighting the path ahead of them in the darkening night.

"It would be ours," she added and August drew her closer still against him until she was leaning against his side. The pose attracted a fair share of attention from the others out that night but Seylah had no eyes for them, and August seemed content to hold his tongue when he heard a chuckle from a passerby.

"I like the sound of ours," he told her and they walked out onto the lane. "Ours sounds mighty good to me."

Seylah nodded and rested her head against his shoulder. "It sounds perfect."

August hummed in agreement and they walked in companionable silence. She relaxed then, August's steady presence beside her making her feel at home. This was her place, right here beside August like she'd always been, and she smiled at the thought that it was precisely where he wished to be as well.

"I just have one question," August said, breaking the quiet.

"What is it?"

"What exactly is fancy dancing?"

Seylah laughed and looked up at him. "I can tell you, or shall I show you?"

August tilted his head to the side and thought it over. "I've always been a man of action, and you are a woman cut from the same cloth."

She nodded knowing what he was going to choose.

"Show me then, honey."

She grinned at him and stepped away holding out a hand. "I was hoping you would choose thusly."

"And now that I have, what follows?"

"Take my hand." She wiggled her fingers at him excitedly and he chuckled at the gesture.

"Now what?" He asked when he was holding her hand.

"Put your hand on my waist," she said, reaching for his other hand and placing it at her side.

"Ah, I think I understand your intentions now." August's hand slid lower until his big hand was splayed across her lower back, the warmth and weight of his palm made her shiver as he stepped closer still. "But we have no music."

"We don't need it. The demand was for fancy dancing, not music," she reminded him.

"Very true." August looked down at her then and Seylah was struck with how large he was. She knew that August was not a small man, she had compared him to a mountain with deep roots, had she not? But knowing and understanding, experiencing something, was vastly different. She was now intimately familiar with the feel of August's hands, the warmth and touch of him against her that could set her body singing, how her head barely came to his lips, and the way his broad shoulders felt beneath her hands.

"I imagine it goes something like this?" August began to step through the paces of a waltz and she smiled up at him when he maneuvered her through the silent dance with a light touch.

"You're a master of fancy dancing," she told him, a note of surprise in her voice.

He raised an eyebrow at her. "Why do you sound so surprised?"

She shrugged. "We've never done this. For all I knew you were bound to step on me."

"We've danced before," he said with a frown. "When I escorted you to the dance."

Her heart squeezed, remembering the night that had changed so much between them. "Ah, yes, that night."

"We danced plenty then."

"So we did."

She turned away from him then, her eyes trained on the faint lines of the lane ahead of them, the light of the moon was now overhead and she wondered what someone would think if they happened upon the two of them dancing in the middle of the lane with no music.

"We should go home," she told him, giving his hand a tug.

"Are you tired of fancy dancing already?"

Seylah hesitated at the question because she was not ready to leave August's arms, but being with him like this and talking of that night made her feel anxious, as if the past would suddenly appear in front of them and drag them back as they had been.

"Yes," she lied. She was not ready, but nor was she willing to take chances with what they had only begun to explore.

August scoffed. "Liar."

"I am not!"

"You are biting your lip. You're lying."

"You can't even see me in the dark. How do you know what I'm doing with my teeth."

"Because I know you," August replied as he stopped moving them, leaning down to peer at her in the moonlight and laughing when he saw her bottom lip between her teeth. "And there you have it. Just because it's dark, does not mean I cannot see you, Seylah May."

She let her bottom lip go with an audible sound and

leaned away from him. "I was not biting my lip," she insisted, but August was already moving them again in the steps of the waltz.

"You were," he said as he spun her around. "Why you are lying to me, I don't know, but now that we are clear you were lying--"

"Bending the truth."

"We can keep at this fancy dancing, and--"

"Anyone that comes up the lane will think we've gone mad."

"Ensure that your demands are being met. If I've learned anything from your fathers it's that a happy home is built on a happy woman, and that is a rule I plan on implementing in my own home."

She pursed her lips at that. It was true that her fathers doted on her mother, that her happiness was their utmost priority, because yes, when her mother was unhappy they all felt it. It appeared as if August had done his fair share of observing like she had and was finely in tune with the rhythms of the Wickes-Barnes household.

"Your home?"

"Hopefully your home." He brought them closer together then and Seylah would have tripped if not for his sure hand guiding her. "Our home," he added as they continued to move together, "Humor me and fancy dance with me a few more moments. At least until you stop biting your lip, hmm?"

"What if someone sees?"

"Let them see."

"They'll think us mad dancing out here with no music in the dark."

"They wouldn't if they felt what I feel for you now. And if they think us crazy, then they'll leave us alone then, won't they?"

He did have a point, but Seylah wasn't of the mind to tell him such. Instead, she rolled her eyes at him and settled once more into his arms. It was lovely to be with him this way, without a care of hiding from anyone that might see them, of knowing that he wanted this as much as she. They danced on, the sound of their feet on the graveled road serving as their music.

"Very well," she said trying for unaffected but failing miserably, and this time, the smile on her face rendered it impossible for Seylah to bite her lip.

CHAPTER 11

"We might have to do it."

"I don't like it."

"Never said I didn't, but that doesn't change the fact that we are being ordered to Butte City."

"Goddamn Summit." Will grumbled, leaning back in his chair, he turned and met the eyes of his husband. "If we leave, we're leavin' the town exposed."

Forrest shook his head. "We've got three deputies here, plus Seylah."

"Seylah isn't getting involved in this. I thought we were clear on it."

Seylah looked up from the paperwork she had been filing and sighed. "I'm sitting right here," she reminded her fathers with a frown.

Will's eyes slid over to her. "We know, sweetheart."

"Then perhaps it would be best if you both stopped speaking as if I wasn't present?"

"Sorry, sweetheart," Forrest sighed and ran a hand through his hair that was now more silver than blond.

"I'm not." Will crossed his arms over his chest and leveled a hard look at his daughter. "You know it's been dangerous lately on account of the newcomers."

Seylah deflated at her father's words. He was right. She knew it. There was no way to argue around it, no matter how it stung her to hear.

It wasn't safe for her to patrol.

Her hands clenched at the thought and she dropped her gaze to the papers in front of her. There was no weight of a badge behind her, not like her fathers, not like August and the other deputies. Even if she was a crack shot, even if she had been raised to run towards a conflict, to have a cool head no matter the circumstances, or risk.

She had pushed to become deputized at one time, thought her fathers would welcome her with open arms but they had always put her off claiming that she was not ready, that she could learn more, or that the timing wasn't right. Seylah hadn't given up on her desire to wear a badge, to lend a hand in an official capacity, but as it stood things were not in her favor to win her fathers over.

She was not the law. She was a secretary.

Paperwork was all that was in Selyah's foreseeable future given the conflict with the homesteaders. There was no changing. Not the way it was, not without something big. What that was, she didn't know, but now was not the time to push. She could see it in the set of her fathers' shoulders. They were not inclined to listen to her protests, this was a matter the two men had already made their minds up on.

She sucked in a deep breath. "I know, Daddy," she murmured, picking up another sheaf of paper and filing it away with a sure hand. The only thing she would be doing was sorting through paperwork, even if she knew she was up to the task of putting homesteaders in line, or keeping the peace.

"It's not forever," Will said, coming to stand beside her desk. He put a hand on the papers she was filing, stopping her from continuing on with her work. "Sweetheart, look at me. Please."

Seylah let out a shuddering breath and raised her eyes to her father's. "I know," she lied.

His mouth pressed into a thin line. "Seylah, if it were different, we would not stop you."

"When will things change then? When will it be perfect?" She asked, crossing her arms over her chest. "The answer is that it won't ever be safe enough for me if I'm ever to come out from behind this desk."

Forrest watched them with a frown. "We just want you to be safe. It's our job to protect you, your mother and your sisters. That's what we were put here to do."

"You raised us to be strong. You should know that we can handle what life brings our way. You told us that we could do whatever we put our mind to, and sometimes that puts us into uncomfortable or imperfect situations."

Will sighed. "Seylah, this is not just uncomfortable. This is dangerous."

"Then let me handle the danger."

"If you were hurt," Forrest shook his head. "We would never survive it if anything happened--" he continued after a moment, but he stopped speaking, rubbing a hand across his jaw and took in a shaky breath.

Will went to him, a comforting arm wrapping around

his husband. Forrest turned into him with a shake of his head. "I can't even say it," Forrest mumbled into Will's shoulder.

Seylah looked away, hating the fear rolling off her fathers. She knew their worries, how they wanted her and her sisters to be happy and healthy, and most of all safe. If her dreams could be safer life would be far simpler, but she was her fathers' daughter and all that she wished for in her life was to wear a badge on her chest as they did.

"Now is not the time, Seylah. But soon," Will told her, rubbing Forrest's back.

"I know," Seylah said quietly. Now was not the time for pressing her hand, now was the time to simply be with her family as their daughter. She went to them and held her arms out and immediately the men drew her close into a hug that had her sandwiched between them, smothered in paternal love so fierce she could scarcely breathe.

Secretary or not, badge or not, Seylah knew one thing would never change, and that was the unwavering love of her fathers. That would be constant, true, and strong no matter her profession.

SEYLAH WAS WALKING through town when she caught sight of August. He was at the end of the avenue, his back to her but she would recognize the set of his shoulders anywhere. The earlier disappointment of the day faded away with the prospect of seeing August.

She quickened her steps and made to lift a hand in greeting but her limb froze when she saw that August was not alone. There was a woman at his side, a pretty auburn haired woman that was clothed in a dress so fine it looked like the images in the fashion periodicals Rose loved so much. It wasn't that August was speaking with another woman, that he had a smile on his handsome face, or that she was beautiful.

It was that she was touching him, her hand resting on his chest in a possessive manner Seylah hadn't ever managed to do in public. Seylah swallowed past the lump in her throat and tucked her hand close to her side.

"It does not matter that she's touching him," she told herself, forcing her feet to carry her forward once more. She knew how August felt about her, for her, and a hand on his chest was not enough to make her waver in her affection and trust. But even still, she heard the whispers of doubt that told her to be wary, to know that all was not as it seemed. A peal of laughter from the woman rose above the din of the busy avenue and Seylah's step faltered.

Should she approach him? What would she say, did he want her to interrupt, or was he happier as he was?

"You're staring," her mother's voice sounded without warning and Seylah jerked to a stop.

"Mother!" A hand went to her chest. "Where did you--"

"Why are you standing here, gawking?"

"I'm not gawking."

Her mother's mouth turned up in a smile and she tilted her head to the side looking at August and his companion. "You are, but I ask again, daughter. Why are you gawking?"

Seylah shifted uncomfortably under her mother's shrewd gaze. "August," she said finally.

"And?"

"And nothing."

"I think you meant to say, August and his lady friend?"

Seylah made a face. "Who says they are friends?"

Julie grinned and threaded her arm through her daughter's, pulling her forward with her. "There is no need to turn taciturn."

"I am not taciturn...merely, concerned."

Her mother nodded, but kept walking forward. "Why?"

Seylah sighed and leaned into her mother's side. "I don't know."

"That's odd, because I have an inkling that tells me you do know why, and that the center of your emotions is the woman?"

"I am not jealous of a woman I do not know," Seylah insisted, but her voice sounded thin and tinny to even herself. She closed her eyes and turned her face into her mother's shoulder. "I'm not," she said, again.

"Darling, it's all right to feel like this."

Seylah opened her eyes and looked up at her mother. "Is it? I find it irritating," she confessed.

"Irritating? I thought you were unaffected," her mother said, full lips turning up into a smirk that set Seylah's face aflame. Seylah was glad her mother's eyes were still trained ahead of them and not on her. If she had been looking at her daughter, she would have witnessed the mix of embarrassment and ire that was at war on Seylah's features.

"I was--ah, I am unaffected." Seylah scrambled to recover from her misstep and she cleared her throat. "What I mean to say is that I assumed I would be irritated if I were jealous."

Julie patted her hand consolingly. "Right you are in your estimation of the scenarios. Hypothetically speaking, of course."

"Of course." They walked on in silence, Seylah willing herself not to look at August where he was now crossing the street with the auburn haired beauty on his arm.

"But if I could offer you a bit of advice from personal experience?" Her mother asked.

"Yes!" Seylah nearly tripped over her feet in her haste to face her mother. "I mean, if you would care to share, that would be welcome. As a mental exercise, of course."

"Of course." Julie nodded patting her hand again with a knowing smile, "A mental exercise, nothing else. Though…"

"Though what?"

"I will be offering you my thoughts as a woman once in these hypothetical shoes, and all I can advise you on is to communicate. Jealousy becomes no one, and you will find that many problems can be avoided with a simple conversation, as uncomfortable as they may be to have."

"Communication?"

"Always communicate. It's been your fathers' and my golden rule throughout all our years of marriage. We have a happy home, but it has not been without its ups and downs. Relationships are hard work and when," her mother looked across the street to where August and the woman were standing in conversation, "an unknown variable is introduced to a relationship whether it be seasoned or just beginning."

"That makes sense." Seylah cleared her throat when her mother hummed knowingly. "I mean to say that it would make sense if I were in such a situation." She paused and looked at her mother who was still mercifully looking ahead and not at her. "What was the...variable for you?"

Her mother smiled ruefully. "Rosemary."

Seylah's eyebrows shot up. "Mrs. Rosemary? How is that possible?" The woman had been a family friend, a dear one, since Seylah's birth. There had been no holidays spent in Gold Sky where Mrs. Rosemary was not present, bustling about and ordering a touch more drama to each festivity. Seylah thought of the woman as family, she knew her sisters did too, her mother considered her a close friend, but she had once been a variable?

"People change," Julie looked at her, leaned close bumping her daughter's shoulder with her own, "though you may see us as old, we were not always so, and young hearts are full of passion. There was a time when Rosemary was moved in such a way that she was directly in my path, and in those moments I did not communicate. Your fathers failed to communicate, which made everything harder than it needed to be. I do not want that for you now."

"Hypothetically speaking."

Julie chuckled and shook her head. "Yes, but that doesn't mean you should leave it as such."

"Meaning?"

"Meaning that you should speak with August. Your

fathers told me the good news," she held up a finger when Seylah went to protest, "and do not think I will forget your lack of forgetfulness in telling me of your change in relationship with August."

Seylah rocked back on her heels and gave her mother a chagrined smile. "I meant to tell you."

"I know."

"So you know this hypothetical is-"

"Happening in front of me?" Julie nodded. "Absolutely, daughter." Seylah winced and looked away, eyes sliding to August's form. "Talk to him," her mother told her and gave her a gentle push in his direction. "Now," she said giving Seylah a stern look. "Do not repeat my mistakes."

"Very well," Seylah conceded and moved reluctantly off the boardwalk and into the avenue. She glanced back at her mother who gave her a shooing motion.

"Now, Seylah May." Her mother's voice was stern, it was the voice reserved for wayward school children and her fathers when they were prone to drama, this was not a request but a command. Seylah's feet carried her forward.

"Yes, ma'am," she called over her shoulder, making her mother's eyes dance with merriment though she kept a stern look on her face as her daughter continued towards August and his female companion.

Seylah was scarcely breathing as the walked forward purposefully. Her mind was not on her words, or what she would do when she was in front of August, simply that she must go there. If she thought too carefully on the particulars she would surely lose her nerve. She was still walking forward, legs blessedly carrying out the action with little input from her and if Seylah could have continued walking she would have done it, she might have done it, if August hadn't caught sight of her.

"Seylah?" He asked, stepping away from the woman who was still holding onto his arm.

Seylah nodded. "Yes." She stepped up onto the board-walk and came to a stop beside him. "Yes," she said again earning a puzzled look from the woman and August alike.

"Are you all right?" August's voice was concerned and he was tilting his head to the side, eyes sweeping up the length of her and back down again before they came to rest on her face.

"Of course." She drew herself up to her full height and cleared her throat. "I'm well, just...ah, I needed to speak with you." Seylah turned towards the woman and gave her a tight smile. "But if you are busy..." her voice trailed off and she swore she could feel her mother's glare burning into her back. She would not be pleased with Seylah's sudden reluctance to speak now that she was with August, but it was more than uncomfortable, it was daunting with an audience to pull August away from. She hadn't considered this when she had dutifully approached August on her mother's order.

"No, I'm not busy," August told her breaking into her thoughts before he turned back to the woman and gave her a quick nod. "It was a pleasure to meet you Elizabeth. I hope your time in Gold Sky is enjoyable."

Elizabeth returned his nod with a smile. "I am sure the town will be to my liking if the people I meet are anything like you, kind sir."

August tipped his hat to her and made to turn towards Seylah but Elizabeth reached out a hand and touched his

184

arm, it was just a brush of her fingers, August most likely barely felt it but even so, Seylah felt her blood boil at the sight.

"If you're amenable, I would greatly appreciate you taking the time to escort me through town." She flashed him a smile and took another step but August was clearing his throat and stepping away from her. Seylah did her utmost to not take offense at the fact that Elizabeth hadn't so much as glanced her way. If she did, it would cause Seylah to give in to her baser urges and insecurities, and that was not something she was content to do any longer.

"I apologize, Elizabeth. I'm not free to take you on a tour of the town, but I am more than happy to have another of the deputies take on the duty of a tour."

Elizabeth's frowned. "A tour?"

August nodded. "That is what you wanted, isn't it?" This was not a simple question or clarification, there was more in August's tone than that. They all heard the unasked question concerning her request, it was a request for more, it was the woman expressing her interest. And August was declining the offer in the gentlest way possible. Seylah felt a swell of pride for him. The man was kind, if anything, and she was happy to be in a courtship with him.

Perhaps this conversation would not be as painful as she had anticipated.

Elizabeth cleared her throat. "Yes, it is. I would love an appointed escort for a town tour. I'll be staying at the Ms. Alice Stanton's boarding house if you would send them that way?"

"I'll be sure to send them along. It was a pleasure meeting you, Elizabeth."

The woman smiled warmly at him, and then she was turning away and making her way towards the boarding house. The pair of them watched Elizabeth walk away in silence, Seylah so intently and entirely unsure of what to say or do next that she jumped when she felt August's hand brush hers.

"Follow me," he said, gesturing at her. Wordlessly, Seylah fell into step behind him, her eyes landing on the spot in front of her, the space between his shoulders and she had the urge to reach out and touch him, to let her palm smooth itself over his muscled back. She would wrap her arms around him, chest pressed flush to him, her cheek against his back, hands exploring his body as she slid them across his sides and chest. August would not let her touch him in peace, not for long, she knew that. He would turn towards her, his own hands warming the curves of her body before he would claim her mouth in a heated kiss that would leave her gasping.

It would be so easy to do, to be close to him, but that was not what she had been sent to do.

She had been sent to talk, not touch.

And there was also the matter of their being out in the open with what seemed to be the entire town bustling by. Such intimacies as she was suddenly imagining had no place on the avenue in broad daylight, especially not if she wished for her fathers to let August see another day. What was the use in a courtship if her actions resulted in an outright duel. The town had not witnessed one in fifteen years, and she would not help revive the practice.

On they walked until they were standing at the stables housed beside the sheriff's building. She gave him an inquisitive look.

"What are we doing?"

"Talking," he answered, walking into the stable and towards his horse. A well-tempered cream mare. He paused in front of her, reaching out run a hand over the animal's velvety muzzle. "Well, for now, then a ride. Does that appeal to you?"

She nodded, walking into the quiet of the stables and suddenly felt nervous. "It does." She crossed her arms and made to go for the horse but August stopped her with a gentle hand on her arm.

"But first, you wanted to talk," he reminded her and Seylah nearly swore at nearly forgetting the sole reason she had asked him to be alone.

"That's right," she nodded, tucking a lock of her hair behind her ear and giving him a weak smile. "I did." She wasn't thrilled about the prospect of talking, even with his show of support and interest in her. Seylah could already tell she'd been wrong in her estimation of how easy talking to August might be.

This would still not be easy, necessary but not easy. Not in the slightest.

"Well, the matter at hand is simply this," she began, choosing a direct approach rather than continuing to procrastinate in her reluctance. Fortune favored the bold, or so Virgil touted. Seylah would rather just survive the conversation intact and move on to enjoying her horse ride. She gave the horse a longing look and rubbed its forehead affectionately before she continued on, "I was jealous today."

"Were you?"

"Horribly so," she told him with a frown.

"I know."

She froze, her hand pressed close to the mare's forehead. "Pardon?" What did August mean he knew? She had collected herself before hand, she had been slighted by the woman at his side but maintained her civility. How had he known?

"Honey." August reached out taking her hand in his. "Your face tells your secrets. Always has and I suspect it always will."

Her hands went to her hips in frustration. He was right, she knew it, her parents knew it, why the whole town knew it. When Seylah was troubled or glad of something, there wasn't a person who didn't know it.

"Damned thing," she muttered.

He laughed at her annoyed expression. "I wouldn't call it a damned thing, but rather one of my favorite things."

"You what?"

"Your face," he said reaching out to rub a thumb against her cheekbone, "is easily one of my favorite things."

"Why?"

"Because you are one of my favorite people."

"I see."

August hummed and raised her hand to his lips brushing a kiss against her skin. "You were jealous today, and?" He prompted.

"I didn't care for it much."

"I wouldn't expect anyone would," August replied. "I hated it when I saw you with that banker," he said, spitting the last word out as if it were a curse.

"Elliot," she corrected.

His eyes narrowed. "Yes, Elliot."

"Do not tell me you are still jealous."

He kissed her knuckles again, this time with more force. "And what if I am?"

"But I am in a courtship with you. Not him. How can you still be jealous?"

"Logic has no place in jealousy or matters of the heart, Seylah," he said and August rolled his shoulders, blond hair catching in the light as he stepped closer to her. "I know he isn't a threat now, but I didn't then."

She raised her eyebrows at that. "A threat? A threat to what?"

"To you. To us." Blue eyes met brown in an earnest gaze that pierced her to her core. There was something vulnerable in his gaze that hadn't been there before, not fully anyhow. "I knew when I saw you look at him that for the first time I might lose you to another. I couldn't bear it."

"I wouldn't go anywhere."

"Not physically, but in your heart?" He reached up again, big hand cradling her jaw. "In your heart you would have been a million miles from me. As untouchable as the moon."

Her breath caught in her throat. "August..."

"So, I understand jealousy. How it feels like a hot coal in your hand, tastes like bitter cold coffee you're forced to drink. It's a dirty thing."

"But it has no place between us."

He smiled at her then, thumb caressing her lips. "No, it doesn't. Not if we talk like this. Even if it is hard. I aim to share my heart with you."

"I would like that very much. I won't keep my mind from you." She leaned into his touch with a barely restrained sigh, her hands reaching for him. "My mother told me it was essential, if difficult to a happy home."

"I intend to have a happy home with you, Seylah." He touched his forehead to hers and looked her in the eyes, the effort it took for him to lower himself to her eye level was not lost on her. She was not a small woman, but August was, by and large, a tall man. Seylah smiled, lips parting against his thumb before she moved forward, tilting her face up to meet his, her fingers pulling at the material of his shirt.

"I know," she said, kissing him soundly, if far more slowly than the kisses they had shared the previous day. Those had been born of passion, a thing of unrestrained desire and want that bore the brunt of years of quiet longing only to riotously bloom in a single moment. Seylah treasured those first intimate touches, but now she was learning the difference between lust and desire.

One was rushed in its hunger, starved and grasping for any morsels it could steal while allowed, while the other understood there was a table set for each of them with plenty to feast from. She found she much preferred the latter and slanted her mouth to August's once more in a sensual and thorough kiss.

When they parted, Selyah's breath had not been stolen, but her heart? Her heart had been filled with more affection and tenderness than she knew was possible, and it overflowed running over and filling up the spaces between them like water until they were both soaked through and left clinging to one another for fear of drowning. She opened her eyes and looked at him, fingers curled tight in the material of his shirt.

"I know," she said again. They stared at one another in silence, the silence transforming the stables from ordinary to a peaceful respite for the couple. Their affection had grown that day, the trust of speaking freely nourishing their hearts in a way that neither could have anticipated.

Some said love was pain, that it was hard, a thing to be cultivated with a careful hand and Seylah estimated they were not wrong in their assessment, but she knew it to be another thing: Magical. There was no way to explain the beauty of this moment, the mundane became extraordinary and she swore there was no place finer than the straw and sawdust covered floors of the stables of this frontier town. There couldn't be when August was holding her this closely or looking at her with such open affection in his eyes that she was speechless.

No, this, this was pure magic.

Love was magic.

"Ready for our ride?" He asked her, kissing her again, the quick press of his lips both chaste and intimate in the casualness of his touch. She nodded in agreement and in short order August had them both up, she in front of him in the saddle, his arms sturdy and strong on either side of her. She leaned her head against his chest and smiled at the feel of him at her back. Oft she had wondered what it would be like to ride like this, in August's arms in a display of intimacy their friendship would never allow to happen.

She had thought it would be exciting, perhaps a bit scandalous, but now she saw that it was neither of those. Instead her place in August's arms was comforting, it was safe, and most of all it was hers.

And that was perhaps the most magical thing of all.

CHAPTER 12

"There's a caller here for you," Rose's singsong voice reached Seylah's ears. She was sitting in the parlor a book in hand when her sister had entered the room with her announcement.

"What?" she looked up from her reading and took care to mark the page. It would not do to find herself lost when she returned to her novel.

Florence waved a hand, her head still bent over the adverts she was reading. "She means to say that August Leclaire is here for you."

"As usual," Delilah added from where she was doing her needlework beside the fireplace. The days were growing chilly with the onset of autumn. Thunderstorms were sweeping through the area regularly leaving the ground wet and muddy. It was these awkward days between fall and winter that Seylah longed for winter. She did not love the snow so much as wish for the rain to end. Rain was always more trouble than it was worth where they lived, and at least they would be able to settle in for the winter once the snow arrived. Settling in meant an end to the local cattle drives and it also meant an end to the homesteaders pushing their luck by way of expanding their holdings with illegal claims.

Their fathers had been tense and tight lipped on the matter which meant only one thing: things were getting worse. It was no secret that the men of the Wickes-Barnes household were prone to keeping their troubles close to themselves. It was made easier when the men shared their concerns with each other rather than burden the women in their lives with worry, and the touching, if misguided sentiment never failed to inspire the ire of said women.

Seylah wished they would learn but every year her fathers did the same thing. This year it appeared the homesteaders would be the conflict her fathers kept close, but with winter on the horizon they would all be able to breathe a sigh of relief that all would be calm and content until the spring thaw.

She looked towards Rose who was practically skipping back and forth in excitement. "Is it August?"

"Yes!" Rose clapped her hands.

"Then why not just announce him as such rather than as a caller?"

Rose rolled her eyes, her hands dropping to her sides. "Because there is positively no drama in such an entry."

Seyah rose from her seat, tucking her book under her arm and gave her sister a confused look. "Who requires drama for an introduction?"

Rose's hands shot out to the side and she groaned. "Us. Him. The world over and this quiet little town, that's who. My efforts go wholly unappreciated here."

"What a hardship you carry," Delilah said eyes still on the needlework in her lap.

Rose pointed a finger at her sister. "Though I know perfectly well that you are mocking me, you have no idea how close you are to the truth. I am indeed taken for granted here. And that is why I have plans to make my move to New York as soon as I am able."

Delilah raised her eyes to rose. "You'll never convince our fathers."

"We'll see about that."

Rose's threats to leave Gold Sky for the big city were not new, and so Seylah slipped out of the room content to leave her sisters bickering behind. After all, she did have "a caller", as Rose had put it, to greet. She smiled when she caught sight of August's familiar form. He was standing on the front porch with his hands behind him, his back to her as he stared out towards the horizon.

She stepped out onto the porch and sighed in relief when she shut the door behind her leaving her sister and their bickering behind.

"August."

He turned his head looking at her over his shoulder and smiled. "Honey."

Seylah's skin flushed at the simple endearment and she did her best to keep from running to him. She wanted to throw her arms around him and kiss his handsome face but she didn't risk it, not with Rose inside going on about drama. If Rose caught one look at them kissing, then she would never hear the end of it.

"What do I owe the pleasure of your visit?"

"Wanted to see you."

She hummed and walked forward to the outstretched hand August was holding out to her. "That right?"

He nodded and brought her hand up to his lips, pressing a kiss to her knuckles. "That's about the measure of things."

She grinned at him and reached out to wrap an arm around his waist. All of her earlier resolve about not giving her sisters the opportunity for drama slipping away. In her defense, it was entirely unrealistic for her not to give in to her wants when it came to August.

They had spent so many years apart. She hated to play at it any longer.

August moved to touch her face, but the sound of approaching horse hooves made them spring apart. She bit back a wince at seeing that it was her fathers on horseback. She cleared her throat and smoothed her hands over her skirts while August blew out a heavy sigh.

"Do you think they saw?" He asked, pulling at the collar of his shirt. Seylah rolled her eyes at him.

"You're scared of them."

He laughed and gave her look. "Of course, I am. Your pas are frightening. You forget they raised me. I know exactly what they would do if they caught me pawing at you."

She scoffed. "You weren't pawing at me," she told him giving his arm a swat.

August grinned and caught her hand in his. "No, but I was plannin' on it if they hadn't arrived."

"August!" She cried, a blush creeping over her cheeks as he laughed at her shocked expression. He winked at her and Seylah couldn't help the laughter that bubbled out of her. She relished the lighthearted moment. It had been like this between them when they were children, and now the easiness she had grown up with had returned.

But now they were no longer children. They were adults. Adults that were in a courtship. What that meant, Seylah was still trying to understand, and for all her inexperience she was delighted that it so far encompassed being pawed at and stolen kisses.

Kissing, Seylah found, agreed with her very much.

The pair had just settled down when her fathers dismounted and joined them on the porch. It only took a few seconds for Seylah to know that something was wrong.

"What happened?" she asked seeing the strained look on the men's faces. They exchanged a look and then sighed in tandem.

"Big commotion outside of town, down by Butte. We have to go lend a hand," Forrest answered her.

"When are you leaving?" Seylah asked. She was already going through the mental calculations associated with what would be needed in town and at the office with her fathers gone.

"Now," Will said his face grim. "They sent two telegrams about it. Train was hit at the depot last two days runnin'. We're going to be leaving Tom and Wallace behind with you, August. You'll look after things here until we get back from this."

August nodded. "Understood."

"Why do they need the both of you? Can't Wallace or Tom go?"

"Those boys are boys. Too young. Besides, it's the

McCarron Gang we're hunting," Will answered, gruffly. Seylah's heart sank at that news. The McCarron Gang were among the roughest outlaws in the state. The Frontier was home to its fair share of law breakers, but the McCarron Gang was in an entirely different class of outlaw. The men would be hard to find and even harder to subdue. The Wickes-Barnes men were in for a battle and they all knew it.

"We're going on as trackers. This gang isn't taking kindly to being told what to do. They've holed up somewhere nearby, but authorities aren't sure where."

Seylah's face fell. "Let me go with you."

Both of her fathers blanched at her request. "Sweetheart, it's not safe. You have to stay here where things are looked after. We can't take you with us."

"You have a job to do here in town, Seylah," Forrest told her gently, but she shook her head.

"As what? A secretary? I'm a sure shot, you made sure of that. You need me to watch your back while you work," she insisted. She didn't know why they needed her fathers but the familiar pang of fear and anxiety associated with them leaving town on the trail of criminals had her feeling faint. This time she wouldn't be able to go with them. There would be no one to watch their back, not if she was to stay here in her role as secretary.

"I'm more useful to you as a deputy, as a gun and a pair of eyes. Not filing papers and taking messages!"

Forrest held up a hand. "Seylah, no."

She threw out her hands in frustration. "Make me a deputy. I'm trained for it. We need the extra people and times like this when they call the both of you away show it. What happens when you're gone? Who is going to make sure Gold Sky keeps on being Gold Sky."

The men were silent, they moved back and looked at each other. Even though no words were exchanged she knew they were communicating. They had always been like this. Silent but speaking to the other. How they did, she didn't know. She had always found it endearing but now? Now it was acutely frustrating. She scowled at them.

"I'm better with a gun than a pen. Admit it." She had never missed a target, was as disciplined as any man on the job, and understood the land and the people she had grown up with. It was only her gender, the fact that she was a woman that swayed her fathers' idea of what her "safety" encompassed. Her family was progressive in their living, and encouraged each of them to be their own person, but she was under no illusions that what she was allowed would be vastly different if she were a man.

The men nodded, the gesture so slight it might have gone unnoticed except for the fact that it was their daughter and the man they had raised who watched them. Both August and Seylah stepped closer together, his hand brushing hers lightly giving her comfort.

"You're trained. We know it, but it isn't safe," Forrest began. "The life of a deputy isn't the one meant for you, sweetheart."

She flinched at his words. "But Papa--"

Will gave a shake of his head. "Seylah, you can't come. We'd spend more time worrying over you than looking for the gang." Forrest nodded along with his words and Seylah felt her heart sink. How she wished she'd been born a man. In that moment, she would have given anything to change places with August. To have a spot beside her fathers in their job. To be able to actively protect those she loved from harm. "Your place is here in the office. They'll need you making sure it all runs smoothly with us being away."

"No one knows this land like us. We'll find them and it will be quicker if we go it just the two of us," Forrest said. "Need you here with August keeping an eye on things for us. Do you understand?"

"Yes, Papa," she murmured and gave them a weary smile. She didn't like it one bit, but there was nothing she could do without going against her fathers' wishes, even at the expense of hers.

"You'll see it's for the best," Forrest told her. He came forward, pressing a kiss to her cheek. "We love you."

Seylah blinked back tears and nodded at him. "I know, papa." Will came close and kissed her other cheek. She knew her fathers only wanted to protect her, their kisses a reminder of their love for her but even their gentle touches weren't enough of a balm to her wounded spirit.

"Love you, sweetheart," he told her. "Goin' on in to tell your mama." Will nodded at August. "You come with us on our way out. Forrest and I will give you the rundown on what the towns gonna need with us gone."

"Understood." August's shoulders broadened and he crossed his arms. "I'll be here. No rush."

Seylah knew that stance, the one that was said August was no nonsense, that he was on the job and focused. There was a certain look to the men that patrolled, the ones that were enforcers of the law, that came about when there was a job to be completed. August had it now, the flinty eyes, the impersonal mask the same that had settled over her fathers' faces.

There was no talking them out of their decision, and now August was gone, lost to her because of his duty. A job that she could not follow him into, and that was, Seylah realized, the hardest part of all. They had always followed each other, found a way to intertwine their paths, but this was one place Seylah could not go.

Seylah turned to look at August with the door firmly shutting behind her fathers. "You know this isn't right," she said. He sighed, his shoulders dropping slightly, and he gave her a pained look.

"Honey. It's not ideal but it's for your safety."

She glared at him. "My safety? As if I were a hapless waif unable to care for myself?"

He held up both of his hands and moved to take a step towards her, but Seylah pointed a finger at him. "You stay put. Right there. You could have spoken up for me but you didn't. How could you let them decide that I was to stay behind."

"Now wait one second, Seylah. No one thinks that but it's dangerous out there!"

"Danger or not. I should be out *there*."

"You're better here with me. I'm not going either, an--"

"Fine then let me come with you on patrol."

He gave a shake of his head. "Seylah, you have to be at the office."

"You're just like them. You expect me to stay behind a desk, too!"

"Seylah, we need you to help handle the paperwork and—"

"You mean the paperwork we can all complete? This isn't about paperwork, this is about you and my fathers not trusting me to decide what I can and cannot do with my life." She backed away from him and shook her head. Anger and hurt were coursing through her at lightning speed, and she could not remain where she was for one more second. Seylah needed to move, and immediately so.

"I have to go," she told him.

"Seylah, wait--" August made to follow her but the turning of the door knob made him pause, he looked over his shoulder at the opening door.

Seylah took the opportunity to put said need for motion into action. "Stay for your orders, deputy," she tossed bitterly over her shoulder as she stormed up the pathway. She heard August groan but the man was stuck, and for the first time she was grateful for August's loyalty to her fathers. He would not move to follow her, not when there were orders to be issued and followed.

It took everything in her not to turn around but somehow, she managed. She was well into town by the time her anger abated enough for her to realize that she had stormed off with her fathers' departure on the horizon. She faltered then, her steps slowing as she hit the main avenue. She had to go back, but even if she did what would she say?

She didn't trust herself to say the right thing. Not with how she had just exploded at August. Seylah winced and ran a hand over her face.

"What have I done?" she whispered. She bit her lip and

looked back towards the lane that led to her home. Yes, she had been upset at the situation but her words had been too harsh. August hadn't meant to hurt her. She knew it was a difficult place to be, between her and her fathers. Her ire was with her fathers' decision, and that was a matter left for her to discuss with them, not August.

She made to walk back towards her home, but the sight of her fathers astride stopped her in her footsteps. They were not the men who had raised her, not now. Now they were lawmen, they were soldiers on a mission, she could tell by the rigid lines of their bodies and their narrowed eyes. Seylah couldn't approach them. It would take them out of their current mindset, and that would not do. That would put them at risk.

Seylah stayed silent and watched her fathers ride out of town. The people in their way cleared the path, each one knowing the look of the sheriffs when they were on the job. Everyone seemed to quiet down sensing the intensity of her fathers' focus and Seylah counted herself one of them.

She like everyone else continued to watch them with bated breath, her hands clasped together until they were out of sight. The townsfolk around them slowly came back to life, the scene springing into action until Seylah was the only one among them not moving. She bit her lip and turned away, the fire that had propelled her snuffed out under the weight of knowing her fathers had left while she had been upset with them. She blinked back the tears that threatened to fall and trudged forward towards the Sheriff's station.

If she could not take back her goodbye to her fathers,

then she could, at the very least carry out the duty they had given her.

And all the while she would pray that nothing happened to them. She entered the office and sat down, her hands already working on filing the papers that awaited her. Her fathers would return, there would be a tomorrow with them, a day where she would finally have the words to make them understand her.

But for now there was paperwork, and she would not fail them in that.

CHAPTER 13

"*Y*ou're moping."

Seylah kept her eyes trained on the mail she was sorting through. "I am doing nothing of the kind. My family does not mope."

August snorted and leaned against the wall beside her. "Your family most certainly does."

"Does not."

"Then someone ought to tell your sisters, because they've made a business of it."

Seylah pursed her lips, but said nothing. It was nearly quitting time and she hadn't been able to shake the previous day's events from her mind. The fact that word from her fathers was woefully absent did not help the matter. She slapped down a letter with far too much force and August came forward to put a hand over hers.

"Seylah," he said, but she refused to stop in her sorting which made for an awkward arrangement, but she somehow managed to carry on one-handedly sorting mail around the hulking man. "Seylah stop," he tried again.

"Stop what?"

"The mail."

"It's my job. That's my duty, hmm? Let me do it."

August sighed and pried her hand away from the letter she was clutching. "Honey, look at me," he said touching her shoulder gently.

She wanted to refuse but it was difficult to when he used that soft voice with her. Seylah pursed her lips but did as he asked and looked at him.

"What?"

"You're still upset about yesterday. What can I do?"

Seylah bit her lip and sagged forward. It was easier to be mad, mad at herself, at him, anything. But it was impossible to maintain it when August had a knack for cracking her shell. "Nothing short of taking us back there. If anything happens to them I'll never forgive myself," she whispered.

"What do you mean?"

"I left and I was angry with them," she said voice shaky. "If they don't come back the last thing I would have felt was anger, the last real conversation with them would have been an argument."

"That's not going to happen." August dropped down to his knees until he was level with her and pulled her chair around so that she was facing him. "You are going to see them again. Trust me."

"But what if I don't?" She asked, covering her face with her hands. "What if that was it?" Her shoulders shook with unshed tears. August gathered her close to him and smoothed her hair back from her forehead.

"Seylah, it's going to be all right. Do not put this stress on yourself. It isn't good for you."

She lifted her head to look at him. "I'm scared, August."

"I know, honey. I know." He wiped away her tears and gave her a sad smile. "This will sort itself out. I promise. They will come home and you will have that conversation with them. The one that you didn't have yesterday, and I will support you in it."

Her eyes widened. "What?"

"You're right. You're better suited to being out with me in town. The desk isn't for you. We will find a replacement for you when they understand that."

"You-you're going to side with me?" She asked, still not believing his words.

He nodded at her and rubbed his thumb along her cheek. "I should have done it then, but I just…" he dropped his eyes and frowned, "it's hard to go against your Pas. You know that."

"I do."

"And I don't know how to do it, but it's something I have to learn if I'm going to be good to you. Good for you. What kind of husband would I be if I didn't know how to do that?"

Her mouth dropped open at his declaration. "August what are you saying?"

"I'm saying that you're the woman for me, Seylah. We both know it. I've loved you since I clapped eyes on you. I intend to make you my wife and there's no tiptoeing around it. I can't do it. I tried with my list, but I was never any good at lists or writing things down. Neither of us were," he said gesturing at the desk she sat at that was, as always, in a slight state of disarray.

"I want you to marry me. And I will spend every day putting in the time to make sure that happens."

"I want to marry you," Seylah blurted out. It felt good to admit it, even after the short time they had agreed to enter a courtship, an affair that she knew normally took months, not weeks, or in their case, days to arrive at a conclusion. But August and Seylah had something most courtships didn't have.

They had years of friendship, of being best friends, to know that the other was undoubtedly the soul for them. They had spent years fighting it, and Seylah was tired of fighting. When August looked shocked she laughed nervously.

"You're right, we really are no good at tiptoeing around things."

He leaned his forehead against hers. "No point in it. Life's too short for pretending." Seylah's eyes drifted closed at the gentle brush of his thumb across her cheek. The warmth of him was comforting and she relaxed into August. He was right, she would get to speak with her fathers, there would be another day to remedy it all, but first securing word of her fathers' arrival in Butte City would be a start. They were meant to meet the rest of the lawmen on the case there before continuing on to track the McCarron Gang. She opened her eyes and sat back in her seat.

"I'm going to check the telegram messages. See if they've sent word from Butte City." The men should have gotten in the previous night and surely there must be word from them, but when Seylah went to check the messages, there was nothing of her fathers' whereabouts. She frowned and looked back at August.

"There's nothing here," she said, gesturing to the woefully silent machine. August joined her and frowned.

"Odd. Let's send word to them. Maybe they've jumped right in."

Seylah nodded, fingers already working out a message. Once it was sent she gave August a tight smile. "It'll be alright, honey." He hugged her to him and ducked her head leaning into his side.

"I'm sure they're just busy and that you're right. Daddy gets forgetful when--"

The clicking of the telegram as it sprang to life cut Seylah off and the couple rushed over to the telegraph. Seylah could scarcely contain herself as the message came through and she yanked the paper to her with eager fingers only to have her momentary excitement morph into confusion, and then fear.

"They never arrived," she whispered, holding the paper out to August who gave her a perplexed look.

"This makes no sense. It says they've no word of them. Assumed they were coming in today."

"This isn't good, August." Seylah's heart was thumping wildly in her chest. The force of it making it difficult to breath, to think, to do anything other than worry herself over where her fathers had vanished to. The Frontier was a wild place, a hard one, but the men that had raised her had mastered it.

If they had not arrived in Butte City as scheduled then something else had befallen them. *Someone else.*

"Don't get that look on your face, Seylah." August held out a hand to her and hurriedly shoved the missive into his pocket when he saw the resigned look settling over her features. "I know what you're thinking and the answer is no."

"Ha! You think a 'no' is going to stop me?" She asked, already storming across the office to where the guns were kept. "Then you don't know me, which gives me concern as to our pending nuptials, darling."

August nearly tripped over his feet at the endearment. "Darling?" He asked with equal parts awe and confusion.

"That's right," she hummed giving him as saccharine a smile as she was able to. The big man looked like he'd been punched in the stomach and would fall at the barest touch, which Seylah fully intended to exploit to carry out her plan.

"I aim to go after my fathers and you are welcome to accompany me, but whether you decide to or not, I will not be stopped. Do you understand me, August?"

Her voice was stern enough to snap August out of his love addled stupor and he snapped to attention. "Now, Seylah. Patience might serve us well in this.

She yanked down a shotgun and turned to him. "Patience? Will patience be there to comfort me when my daddy and papa are put in the ground?"

August's brows drew together at that. If he was right then they were simply engaging on an overzealous outing, but if she were right then the entire world as they knew it was in jeopardy of being destroyed. He rocked back on his heels and then nodded to himself.

"Oh, all right, get the spare ammunition from the back and I'll get to saddling the horses up."

Seylah's mouth dropped open. She had thought she would be embarking alone, but August's presence was a godsend.

"Truly? You mean to come with me?" she asked unable to keep the shock out of her voice. When August raised an eyebrow at her surprise she schooled her features into one of confidence, or rather what she assumed passed as confident in such a moment. "I mean, of course, you are. I'm glad to have you as a companion for the journey.

August scoffed but kept moving towards the door. "Make sure you grab an extra duster for yourself. Your clothing as of late isn't right for this sort of undertaking."

"My clothing is just fine!"

He dropped his eyes to look over the verdant green skirts, and lace white blouse she wore courtesy of Rose and Mrs. Rosemary's fitting all those days ago. She pursed her lips when she saw that he was right. She would have to change immediately if they were to be on their way before nightfall.

"Fine, you do have a point there. I've got a set of clothes here I can change into so we can leave immediately."

August gestured to the back store rooms. "There's supplies ready for us to take as well. No sense in wasting time if we can help it. I'll send word to your ma and sisters that we mean to track Forrest and Will. Do what I can to let Wallace and Tom know what we mean to do."

Seylah's heart sank. Her mother would be devastated

at the news. "Please, let her know that things will...they will be okay."

"I'll keep her spirits up. You focus on getting ready for the trip." He turned then and left the room. Seylah sprang into action the second the door slammed shut, and she rushed to the backroom. She needed to get changed into more appropriate clothing if she hoped to find her fathers. Never in all her life did Seylah get changed as quickly as she did now and the familiar feel of the worn cotton and denim beneath her fingers was reassuring to her.

She paused when it came time to pull on her gun holsters, the thick supple leather of it in her hands a reminder of her fathers. They had given her this gun belt when she was sixteen, her mother had been concerned but supportive. Her sisters over the moon to see her following in the footsteps of their fathers. Seylah closed her eyes, briefly, fingers splayed across the leather of the holster as memories of her family danced before her.

Her Daddy grinning at her as he showed her how to ride. Her Papa's sky blue eyes while he showed her how to sight a target. The proud look in her mother's eyes when she won the town's annual sure shot competition. The encouragement of her sisters when she'd fallen from her horse during it's breaking in period, but with them in her corner she hadn't given up and now her dappled mare was one of the swiftest in the county.

Seylah opened her eyes and buckled the gun belt. She would not let her family down, even if she was going on a fool's errand and her fathers were safe, she had a duty to make sure of it. She hadn't counted on August coming with her, but she supposed she should have. If the man meant to marry her as he declared, she didn't think there was a power in existence that would keep him from accompanying her. She yanked on her leather gloves and pulled on the worn hat she hadn't touched as of late.

She didn't much think she looked the part of the simpering lady Mrs. Rosemary had hoped she would, but this was her. Seylah stepped out of the office, leather saddle bags thrown over her shoulders, guns on her hips and boots on her feet. No, she wasn't the lady one would take to picnics, or make gallant overtures to, but that was all right. If the wide smile on her intended's face at the sight of her was anything to go by, August wasn't scared off from her less than fragile appearance.

He never had been.

The couple readied themselves to leave and it was only when they were astride that Seylah let herself think of what her mother and sisters must be feeling. She turned to August trying to gauge his expression but the man gave nothing away.

"What is it?" He asked as they set off for the outskirts of town. They would be traveling down the same avenue her fathers had the previous day albeit with less intensity and acknowledgement from the townsfolk, but that suited Seylah just fine. She didn't want the entire town to know that she'd taken off after her fathers. Tom and Wallace would already have enough of a job on their hands keeping order in Gold Sky without everyone knowing the remaining deputies were woefully shorthanded.

"How was she?" She asked. "My mother, I mean."

"Not happy, but she understands." August shook his

head and looked out ahead of them. They were now free from most of the bustle of Gold Sky and Seylah could see the empty horizon ahead of them. "This isn't new to her. She's been the wife of lawmen for over twenty years. She understands why you're going even if she doesn't like it much."

"And my sisters?"

"You know how they are," August told her dryly and Seylah laughed.

"Yes, I do." She much suspected Rose had taken to dramatics with Florence encouraging her and Delilah tired of it all while trying to keep her younger sisters in line.

"We'll be home before you know it," August told her, urging his horse to a trot now that town was behind them. "Keep an eye for tracks. We don't have much light left but if we ride at this pace we'll make it to Butte City before nightfall. We can make contact with the posse there and make a plan for the morning."

"Understood." Seylah nodded, her eyes already moving over the ground for anything out of the ordinary. She wasn't the best tracker but she was decent. Thankfully between them pair of them they should be able to catch anything of use.

They set off at a decent pace and after an hour of straining her eyes for anything amiss, Seylah began to wonder if she had somehow missed an important detail related to her fathers' journey. It was only when she was about to give in to her worry that a clue so large and obvious that even the blind would find it appeared in front of her like a heaven sent gift.

A gift that was simultaneously able to make her tremble with excitement and want to vomit from fear. Said gift was an overturned wagon. The overturned wagon was at the juncture of the main road they traveled and one that veered to the right.

There was no way her fathers would have passed this up. They would have tracked it, found out why this had happened. She dismounted and took in the scene from a closer vantage point, the proof of her fathers' footsteps around the wreck was obvious, but it was when she rounded the wagon that Seylah considered the wagon more terrible than helpful.

Her daddy's horse lay on it's side. The poor thing had been shot, but she couldn't say if it had been done by her parents or someone else. She forced herself to stay strong, she would not be helpful to their cause if she broke now.

"Seylah, what is it?" August asked, but he froze when he came around the wagon and saw her standing in front of the prone horse.

"Will's mount," he breathed, coming forward on unsteady legs. "Oh hell, I'm sorry, Seylah."

She held up a hand. "This doesn't mean anything. There's no blood, and no sign of anyone. That means they rode out, which they could have done if Papa's horse was fine."

August sucked in a breath. "That's right, that's right, I just…" his hands went to his hips and he shook his head, "that's just shocking. You're right. And the trail leads that way." He pointed in the direction of the less traveled road.

"If they went east, then there's no wonder they didn't make it to Butte."

"There's a town about an hour's ride from here."

A rumble of thunder caught their attention and Seylah swore. "Goddammit. This isn't the time." She turned to see a dark cloud line sweeping towards them. A big enough storm would cross the plains to them in half an hour, an hour if their luck held but that did them no favors considering the town was well beyond that time frame.

August put a hand on her elbow. "We need to move. Get mounted. I'll do a once over here and see if I find anything we can use."

He urged her back towards the horses and for a moment Seylah almost did not go. She knew what he was doing, he was sending her away in case he found anything grisly. She knew she could chafe at that, but it was a kindness. Whatever it was that August found or saw, he would not be able to forget it.

"Thank you." She caught his hand and August's squeezed her fingers tightly before he let her go.

"Of course. I'll be along in a minute. The sooner we move, the better."

Seylah made for her horse and was careful to keep her eyes open for anything of use, but there was nothing. She was just beginning to fidget when August came out from behind the wagon, a grim look on his handsome face.

"Nothing. There was nothing, but it was definitely them, definitely Will's horse. There are tracks leading to the town, Franklinsburg. We'll make it after the storm hits, but it shouldn't be anything we can't manage. Let's head out. When we're closer to town we'll make a plan. I want to get as far ahead of the storm as we can before it hits."

Seylah fell in behind August. Normally, a plan would be best from the start, but he was right. There was no time for it if they meant to make any progress before they were caught in the rain. When the first drops hit them, Seylah was glad they had decided to forgo the plan. The town was nowhere in sight and it was nearly nightfall. Pulling the brim of her hat lower, Seylah leaned over her horse, the move allowing for her to escape the worst of the rain but even still there was no way to avoid the downpour.

It was only when the dim sight of lights in the distance appeared that they slowed and stopped. August turned towards her and leaned as closed as he was able to, but even still he had to shout to be heard over the roar of the falling rain.

"I was here on patrol, but it was well over a year ago. The town is odd, Seylah. You need to be on your guard!"

"What do you mean by odd?" she shouted back.

"It isn't Gold Sky and I don't want people getting the wrong idea about us."

"And what idea is that?" She turned her face away from the gust of wind that was now kicking rain into their faces.

"That you're a loose woman. We'll be staying the night when we get there."

She shook her head trying to wipe the rain out of her eyes. "No, we have to keep looking for my fathers! We can't stop now."

"It's a downpour, Seylah! We won't find them in this

storm and that means we stay the night. I am telling you this now because I won't argue with you when we are in Franklinsburg. We have to stay collected in front of strangers if we want them to talk."

She squinted towards the lights of Franklinsburg. There was too much rain to see, and even if there wasn't, nightfall made seeing any tracks impossible. He was right. They both knew it.

Seylah pursed her lips. "I don't like it," she said.

"I know."

"All right then. We have to look unified if we want information." She looked at him expectantly. "Then what is our story?"

"That we are married. We will share one room."

Her eyebrows shot up. "One room? But that means one bed?"

August cleared his throat. "I'll sleep on the floor of course."

"Of course," Seylah replied, but she would be lying if she wasn't disappointed at August's words, thankfully the lack of light meant August wasn't able to see it.

"Follow my lead when we get to the saloon. It's the only place to stay for the night."

She squinted towards the town lights. "She didn't like it, but there wasn't much to do, not when there was no other option when it came to finding her parents. They would have to stay somewhere for the night and the saloon would be a vast improvement to making camp in the rain. It was also infinitely easier for patrons to solicit information from loose lipped barkeeps than a deputy and…well, whatever it was that she was.

"Their daughter," Seylah whispered to herself falling into line behind August. She wasn't a deputy and she didn't much think her profession as a secretary would motivate the locals to speak to her.

She wasn't a deputy like August, but she was Will and Forrest's daughter and she would get the answers she needed. They dismounted and tied their horses to the posts in front of the saloon, which from the sound of it was the site of a raucous evening. Shouts and laughter mingled with music, the sound of merriment floating to them despite the roaring downpour. August caught her arm when they hit the steps of the saloon and pulled her behind him.

"Stay close," he told her. "Remember, you're my wife. One room."

Seylah nodded. "Understood...*dear*," she drew out the last word, unable to keep the smile off her lips at the pinched look on August's face.

"Wish the first time you talked sweet to me wasn't in this place." He pushed open the saloon door and the scent of spilled ale and whiskey assaulted her senses like a runaway horse.

"Oh, it looks all right," Seylah lied as a man crashed to the floor beside them.

A game of poker was underway at a table in the far corner, billiards in the other, there was a pianist hard at work entertaining the bar patrons. A number of tables dotted the available space, each one filled to capacity as men and women wove through them in both dance and play, and then there was the bar, a long stretch of polished oak with silver dusted glass shining behind it. Patrons were at every bar seat, and a bartender worked to keep a glass in every hand.

Spilled drink and food crumbs crunched underfoot, but Seylah supposed it could have been worse. She could be here soaking wet and searching for her fathers, and alone, rather than with August at her side.

She glanced at him and saw that August was regarding the saloon with distaste. That wouldn't do. The people here wouldn't speak to them if they thought August considered himself their better. She moved forward, a sharp but swift kick to the back of his heel had him glancing at her over his shoulder.

"Smile, sweetheart," she crooned when August's brows furrowed. "We are in a fine establishment and sour looks are unbecoming." She crossed her arms over her chest and aimed a pointed look his way. Realization dawned on August's face and he sighed heavily.

"'Course, darling." He pulled his hat off and turned back to the bar, a fake smile plastered to his face. He couldn't help reaching back and taking her hand in his when a man came too close. A sharp look from August sent the man scurrying away and Seylah did her best to play the part of simpering wife as they neared the bar.

"Barkeep, we need lodging," August barked when he was at the bar top. Seylah's sharp elbow ensured the quick addition of, "Please."

The barkeep, a man with graying hair and a neat beard gave them a considering look and tossed a towel over his shoulder with a raised eyebrow. "We've only got one room."

August nodded and reached for his billfold. "That'll suit me and the missus just fine."

"You're married?" The man ran a hand over his jaw, eyes moving between the two of them. Seylah beamed at him, and leaned into August's side.

"We are, and happily so, sir! Why we've just celebrated our month anniversary and I must say we are so very lucky to happen upon your fine establishment."

A glass shattered across the room and a fight broke out. The barkeep let out an aggrieved sigh before reaching under the bar and pulling out a pistol. He fired a shot into the fray and the entire saloon fell silent.

"I said no more fights, goddammit! Next one of ya that fights gets the next shot 'tween the eyes." He waved the pistol at the bar and then pointed a finger at a woman with unruly black hair. "See them out, Ruth." She nodded and marched to the door, a group of chastised men sheepishly following her.

The barkeep turned back to Seylah and August, the gun coming down to rest on the counter between them. "Names Maurice, ma'am. You and your man need a room for the night?"

She nodded, the smile on her face slightly less fake than it had been before. She could respect a man that took no grief. He reminded her of her Daddy. Will Barnes stood for no unruliness, but he was still a reasonable man and she suspected Maurice was well.

"That's right, sir."

"I'm no sir, ma'am. Just a barkeep in a cow shit town but this is my place. It's anything but fine, but it's warm and dry." He moved to snatch a key from the wall behind him. "Room is five dollars a night."

August spluttered. "Five dollars for a room in this place? That's robbery."

Maurice crossed his arms and cocked his head to the side considering August. "It's called supply and demand, son."

Seylah laughed. She was charmed by the gruff barkeep even while August looked fit to be tied. "We'll take it."

August's jaw clenched. "I don't like it," he told her.

She smiled broadly. "I know."

"Wives are like that. Get used to it now and you'll save yourself some grief." Maurice held out his hand for the bill August slapped into it.

"Forgive me if I don't take marital advice from you, Maurice."

"Stop being sour," Seylah said hopping up onto the barstool that became vacant to her left. "I happen to find Maurice charming."

"All the ladies do," the older man told her matter-of-factly. Seylah was delighted. August was anything but.

"I'd like a drink, Maurice."

He nodded and poured her a measure of amber liquid in a glass. "Whiskey for the lady then. You drinking, son?"

"Whatever she's drinking is fine."

Maurice snorted. "She's drinking the good stuff. You haven't earned that yet." He made a show of picking up a different bottle and pouring a scant amount of liquid into August's glass. Seylah giggled while August raised an eyebrow.

Maurice slid the glass and a key towards August.

"What are a pair of newlyweds doin' here? This isn't exactly Paris."

"Traveling to meet my family," Seylah offered. "We've been away since the wedding and my mama's awfully sick over me not being home for so long." The lies were coming to Seylah easily now, but it wasn't so hard if she managed to keep a kernel of truth in her words. August leaned against the bar beside her and eyeballed the glass he had been offered.

"Y'know how ma's are," he said joining in Seylah's story, "knew I had to get her home sooner or later."

"You always have your woman dressed like a man?" Maurice asked, giving Seylah a once over.

She sipped delicately at her glass. "That's quite intrusive, Maurice."

The corner of Maurice's mouth turned up in a smirk and he winked at her. "My apologies, ma'am. Didn't mean to overstep."

"No offense taken, sir." She set down her glass and leaned forward on her elbows. "The frontier is a very dangerous place and my husband has graciously provided me with this sturdy attire for my safety."

"That account for the gun on your hip too?"

She smiled at him. "You like my gun, do you? Why didn't you just say so?"

"It's a fine piece. Much too fine for a newlywed." The meaning of Maurice's words was plain. He knew they were lying but for all that the man hadn't sounded the alarm to the locals. All around them the bar was full of activity, all except for the woman named Ruth who was still as a statue and watching them intently. Seylah was sure that at Maurice's signal, Ruth would spring into action, what that meant she didn't know---she also didn't aim to find out.

"And yet you remained silent and serve me the smoothest whiskey I have ever enjoyed." She tapped a finger against the rim of her glass.

Maurice shrugged. "I have a soft place in my heart for dark haired women. My first wife made me partial."

"What's your game, Maurice?"

"Tell me why you're here, ma'am."

A tense moment passed between them, Seylah and the barkeep locked in a stare, while the crowd continued to enjoy themselves. "Seylah…" August put a hand on her shoulder but she didn't break eye contact with the barkeep.

She had her fathers to find. She would not lose now. Whatever she said next was paramount to them finding her parents. She knew it.

"I'm here for my fathers."

Maurice sucked in a breath and chuckled reaching for a glass. "So the men are yours then?"

"What men?"

"Two men, outsiders came through here the day before. Law men or soldiers from the look of them."

"Where did they go?" Her fingers tightened on the glass so tightly that she was surprised it didn't break under the pressure. "Tell me."

"Please goes a long way, missy."

August growled and moved his hand from her shoulder to the bar. "Listen here--"

"Please, tell me," Seylah interrupted him. She had no

hesitation when it came to her family. She would do what she needed and one small nicety was a bargain for their safety. "Please, help me find my fathers, Maurice."

"Curious thing, the plural on the end of that word." He took the rag from his shoulder and cleaned the glass in his hand. "But I've never been one to shame how folk live. That's why we came out here, hmm? Even shithole towns have their appeal."

"That's true. Family came out here to live their lives. Part of that was being law men. They were on their way to Butte to track the McCarron gang."

Maurice's hands froze. August hissed out a breath. "Seylah, stop talking."

"Let your woman talk. I'm interested and if I'm interested then that means Ruthie over there doesn't put an end to ya."

Seylah grinned. "I knew she was important."

"She's everything. She's my daughter, and I know if I was missin' she wouldn't hesitate to walk into a place like this lookin' for me. Now why did your pas go looking for the McCarrons?"

"They're sheriffs. It's their job."

"They're no spring chickens to be takin' on that job."

Seylah hummed and sipped her whiskey. "That's what my mama tells them. They went missing on the way to Butte City and we came upon a wagon wreck with my Daddy's horse shot dead, but you say the pair of them came through here yesterday?"

Maurice nodded set the glass he was cleaning down. "They did. Lookin' a little banged up, but fine. They were going north."

August cleared his throat and looked towards where Ruth was still watching them. Save for her eyes the woman hadn't moved from her post by the door. "What's north?" he asked.

"The McCarron hideout, that's what. If your pas went that way then that's where they'll be. It's a homestead, few buildings aside from the main house, a barn and stables, one building for storage, all of it south facing. If you approach from the east you'll be able to take them from a hilltop. Good vantage for shooting."

"Why are you telling me this?"

Maurice's eyes moved to where his daughter stood and he gave her a slight nod. The small gesture relaxed the woman instantly and she turned then moving to the side and towards the poker table. Whatever possible threat associated with Seylah and August had been dismissed.

"Few summers back the younger McCarron's took a shine to Ruthie. Caught her alone when I was in Butte. Never forgave myself for it. If you aim to make them pay, I'll help you."

She reached out, putting her hand on the bar in front of Maurice. "I'm sorry about your daughter."

The man smiled bitterly and Seylah saw plainly that Maurice for all his liveliness was a man with weight on his shoulders. "Don't be sorry, get even for her, hmm?"

Seylah nodded an accepted the top off he gave her. Maurice even poured a finger more of liquid in August's glass. "Go on then to your room. No one will trouble the pair of you. I'll see to it. Need you in fighting shape if you plan on making the McCarron's pay. I'll get your horses stabled, make sure they're rested too."

Seylah raised her glass to Maurice. "Thank you, sir." The man took a swig from the bottle he was holding and gave her a gruff, "Ma'am."

And then he was moving on to the next patron as if the conversation had never happened.

"Let's go." August put a hand on her arm and guided her towards the stairs. Neither of them spoke a word until they were standing in front of the door marked with a 4, same as the number carved into the small leather thong tied to the key. Seylah slid the key home and opened the door, August at her back and watching the hallway until she was safely inside. He followed her inside and only when the door was latched did he relax.

"What the hell was that?" He asked, pointing at the door.

"A father's love." She pulled off her leather duster and dropped it over the back of a chair. The room was what Maurice had said, dry, warm, a little sparse but comfort wasn't the reason for their stay. It was tidy which was a pleasant surprise. She turned towards the fireplace and sighed tossing her hat on top of her coat as she considered the dark fireplace.

"You think he was telling us the truth?" August asked, walking past her and working on lighting the fireplace.

"Of course, he was." There was no doubt in her mind that Maruice had been anything but truthful. The way he looked at his daughter, the heavy look in his eyes at confessing his reason for helping. This was no trap.

"Even so, I'll go first. You stay behind tomorrow."

Seylah's mouth dropped open. "What? August, no! I have to go with you."

He rose from the fireplace and frowned. "Seylah, it isn't safe for you."

"And neither was this, remember? My pas thought I couldn't do it, and yet here I am getting information to get them back." She tapped a finger against her chest. "I did that, not you," she reminded him. "I thought you were on my side. Taking my back if we were to marry."

August sighed and scrubbed a hand over his face. "Honey, it ain't like that. We don't know that barkeep. You saw the saloon. It's not safe here."

"That man down there was telling the truth. We have the directions to the McCarrons and I am going to be there with you when we find it. I can do this and you need me watching your back if we are going to get my parents back!"

August held up a hand. "Seylah, I have to protect you. I can't have you walking into an ambush with me."

"I can protect myself. I can protect the people I love."

"You heard that man down there. How he never forgave himself? How do you think I'll be if anything happened to you?" He gave her a pained look. His eyes showing her a vulnerability she still wasn't accustomed to seeing when August looked at her, when it came to her. "Seylah, it would be the end of me. You're everything."

He stood still, his broad shoulders slumping, yet another sight Seylah was unfamiliar with. She had never seen August like this. He looked fragile, his large frame lent him no strength and she suspected he would crumble like dust at the slightest bump. She came forward reaching for him, fingertips cautious and gentle as she touched him.

She looked up at him. "You can't protect me from everything, August." Her palm flattened on his chest.

"That doesn't mean I can stand by idly while we walk into what might be a trap."

"It's not," she told him, "but I need you to trust me, August. That man was not lying to us. We will find the hilltop and the buildings exactly where he said." She reached up to cup his jaw and came closer still until the were standing toe-to-toe, their chest brushing with each and every breath.

"Trust me," she whispered. August took in a deep breath and then gave a nod, his hand coming up to cover the one cupping his face.

"I do, honey." He smiled at her and pulled her hand to his lips. "I do trust you."

"Then you understand why I'm coming tomorrow. I have to."

August cupped her hand with both of his and kissed her knuckles. "I understand. Whatever happens tomorrow is your choice. I'm with you till the end of it." His words touched her, the thick emotion in his voice wrapping itself around her like a homespun sweater. She believed in her heart that Maurice had been truthful in his information, she knew that her skills as a sharpshooter were unparalleled, and that she had the training to save her fathers. With August with her there was no way they would fail.

So long as they had trust. This would not be the end of it. She knew it.

CHAPTER 14

*I*f Seylah closed her eyes she could pretend that tonight was like any other. If she didn't open her eyes then the fire crackling merrily away, and the comforting roar of the storm overhead created the perfect backdrop for a cozy evening. That is until she remembered what awaited her the next morning.

There was nothing but danger in her future.

Seylah crossed her arms over her chest and stared into the flames. It was hard to think about what might happen in the morning, what could be lost, what could already be lost. She gave a quick shake of her head and shut her eyes again. She wouldn't think on that, not about how she could already be too late to save her fathers.

About what might befall herself and August. No, it was far easier to pretend that today was nothing more than stolen night between the two of them. A night when they pretended to be exactly as they had claimed to be.

Husband and Wife.

"Seylah." August was beside her now, his hands gentle

on her shoulders. His fingers caught in the strands of her braid and he came closer as he curled a lock of hair around his finger.

"Mmm?" She turned to glance at him over her shoulder and smiled when he kissed her shoulder.

"You should get some rest."

"I'm not tired."

August cleared his throat and looked towards the bed. "Be that as it may, you need rest, honey." He moved away from her then and began to work on pulled his suspenders off his shoulders with a jerk. "I'll sleep by the door. Make sure Maurice keeps good on his word."

She reached out, catching his arm before he could move away from her. "August, wait." When he looked at her she bit her lip and then said, "I don't want to be alone."

"You won't be. I'm just going to be there." He motioned towards the door but Seylah's hand tightened on his.

"I don't want you to sleep on the floor."

"Seylah, I don't--"

"I want you to sleep with me. In the bed."

August's mouth opened and then shut, a motion that he repeated several times before he responded. "Oh," he husked out, his blue eyes dawning with understanding. The expression had the ability to make August looked infinitely younger, less hardened. Suddenly she could see the boy she had fallen in love with all those years ago and she squeezed his hand again.

"Tomorrow isn't the end, but…" her voice trailed off and she sucked in a breath before continuing, "tonight I want us to be together. Please don't sleep on the floor."

"Oh, honey." He brought his hands up to cup her face

and shook his head, the look in his eyes fading from awe and confusion to lust and desire. No trace of the boy she loved lingered, August was a man now, the man she loved---the man she would love for the rest of her days. His eyes dropped to her lips and he drew her closer still to kiss her. His mouth slanted to hers, lips gentle on hers as his hands moved to trail gently down from her face to her sides and then back up again.

He drew back to look at her and carded his fingers through her hair. "Tell me to stop if this is not what you want."

"This is what I want. You are what I want," she whispered and reached for him. "Now take me to bed."

August chuckled and gave her a mock salute. "Yes, ma'am." He reached for her, sweeping her up into his arms bridal style. He turned towards the bed and Seylah threw her arms around August's neck. She wanted to touch every part of him, kiss and feel the man holding her.

"August." She kissed him then, claiming his lips for herself and arched up against him as he settled her back against the mattress. "August," she breathed again and fumbled with the buttons of his shirt. In her opinion, there were entirely too many clothes between her hands and August's body, and the sooner she fixed that the better.

A button went flying, skittering across the floor as it popped free in her haste. August caught her wrist and pinned it to the bed.

"My sweet Seylah." He was above her now, a leg on either side of her as he worked on removing her blouse, albeit with far more finesse than she had displayed. When the last button was undone and her skin exposed to the cool air of the room, August went still, his hands hovering an inch above her skin. Anticipation mixed with chill and Seylah shivered. She raised her hands laying them atop August's where his still poised above her.

"Touch me," she murmured. "August, please."

"Oh, honey," August sighed, his hands dropping down to her skin. Seylah arched into his touch, the drag of his palms on her skin sent her heart to skipping. She closed her eyes and sucked in a deep breath. She had to get a hold of herself, she was a frontierswoman, she could not swoon from the first touch of his hands.

"Seylah, I love you," he told her, leaning over to pepper kisses across her collarbones and across the tops of her breasts. All the while he continued to touch her, fingers ghosting over her skin, slipping her blouse from her shoulders, helping her with her undergarments.

"I've always loved you," Seylah whispered, her hands just as busy as August's. She pulled his belt free and had his denims open in short order. "I've waited far too long to touch you," she confessed.

August kissed her then. "Whatever happens tomorrow this is not the end," he said, echoing her earlier words.

Seylah gave a quick shake of her head. "No, it's not." And then she reached for him determined not to speak a word more without touching and kissing her fill of the man she loved. August seemed to be of the same mind, his lips exploring her slowly. Seylah raised her hands to rake through his hair, the blond strands gleaming in the fire-light. His lips brushed across her nipple and she gasped in pleasure, the touch of his tongue on the sensitive flesh had her crying out. August turned his attention to her other breast while he cradled her close, his palm teasing her nipple as he continued to lave attention on her breasts. Seylah whimpered when August moved farther down her body until he settled between her legs.

"These are to come off at once," he said, already yanking at the soaked denim molded to her thighs.

She laughed and raised her hips, helping him pull her pants off. "Only if you return the favor."

"Oh, woman, if I had three hands I would already have them off." He tossed her pants to the side and then slipped from the bed to yank his own off. He turned towards the bed and Seylah sat up, the sight of him striking her as both beautiful and raw.

"Wait," she said, holding a hand out to him.

"What?" he asked raising an eyebrow.

"You're beautiful," she breathed and rose up to her knees to look at him. Her eyes moving slowly over August's body.

The flickering light from the fireplace softened the hard planes and edges of August's body. He was a big man, a powerfully built man whose body was honed to protect, to defend those weaker than him. That had for a time been her, but Seylah now was different, stronger than she had been---they were equals now and the sight of him set her alight with a fire she had never known. She was sure it would consume her whole if August did not touch her but that would have to wait, because for now she was content to look her fill.

The man was far from unblemished, scars and the marks of hard work that went hand-in-hand with life on the frontier, but to Seylah he was perfect. Her eyes moves lower and she bit her lip at seeing his thick cock heavy and proud against his thigh.

Save for August, no man had ever caught her eye, nor had they touched her like he had, like he would. Another soul had never set her heart to racing or made her blood sing with desire. There had only ever been August in her heart and in her mind. The male figure was far too handsome to keep clothed, or at least it was when it came to August.

"I want to look at you," she told him. Her dark eyes sweeping over him again eagerly. He was such a beautiful man, and he wanted her just as much as she did him.

August scoffed. "Not much to see."

"You don't understand women, August." Seylah held a hand out to him. "Because there is entirely too much to look at when it comes to you." She smirked at him when a blush colored his cheeks.

He ducked his head and cleared his throat. "Aw, hell, Seylah."

She held out her hands to him. "Come here, August. I'm done looking."

"Thank god," he muttered coming to her then. "Because there's only so much a man can take." He swept her up against him, the sudden movement stealing her breath away as he claimed her mouth in a hungry kiss. He drew back and when she raised a questioning eyebrow he said, "Fair is fair. I like lookin' at you too."

She blushed and felt a wave of pleasure bloom in her chest at his words. "Then by all means, sir."

August groaned shoving her back on the bed. "You're

perfect." She gasped, her back hitting the mattress as she bounced slightly from the momentum. August pulled her towards him then, but this time he was between her legs, his hands on her hips pressing her down to the bed as he began to lick and kiss her thighs. A warm breath against her inner thighs was the only warning she received before she felt the first brush of August's lips against the now throbbing bundle of nerves that was suddenly the center of her world.

"August!" She cried out as he continued to lick and kiss her. His mouth and tongue showing her a pleasure she hadn't thought possible. Kissing August was wonderful, being in his arms made her feel complete, but this?

This was utter *bliss.*

"Take your pleasure, honey. Take it." August's fingers tightened on her hips as he moved them, encouraging her until she felt bold enough to chase her own gratification. Seylah raised her head and gasped at the sight of August between her legs. He was focused wholly on her, and she knew what she felt in this moment was just as rapturous for him. She shivered, hands tightening in the bed sheets as a wave of pleasure began to sweep up her body. From her toes to the ends of her fingertips--her body was singing with ecstasy.

On and on, that wave moved over her until it was a tide that was overflowing and crashing over her.

"August!" His name escaped her lips in a cry, and Seylah lost herself to her pleasure. She sagged against the bed for a moment but opened her eyes and reached for him. She could feel August pulling away and she would not have him leaving her, not so soon.

Not ever.

"I need you," she told him. There was a heat in his eyes and August came forward with the barest touch of her hands.

"We don't have to, Seylah."

"I want to. I need you, August. Love me."

He smiled down at her and raised a hand to brush her hair back from her face. "I already do." He pushed her thighs apart and guided himself to her entrance. "Always have." August's hips moved forward, the head of his manhood thrusting into her and making Seylah gasp.

He kissed her softly, one hand going to catch her leg and lifting it to his side. August rocked into her once more, the gentle rhythm making her moan and move to mimic August's movements. Sex was not a topic discussed or taught in polite company, but Seylah had been gifted with a mother who prided herself on ensuring her daughters were not confused and ill-prepared upon their first sexual intimacies.

But what her mother had not stressed enough was how enjoyable it was. Sexual intimacy with August was a gift, one that made her feel as if she were flying. Seylah hooked her leg around August and kissed him deeply, the kiss stealing their shared noises of bliss. August and Seylah moved together, their bodies fitting perfectly into one, until their movements lost the rhythm they had built and the couple found their release in the other.

"Seylah!" August's held her tight against him, his body tensing as he climaxed. He continued to move in her, thrusting until Seylah was sobbing out her release against his chest, fingernails digging into his shoulders. August moved to the side and he gathered Seylah close to his side.

"August, what--" she began, but he hushed her with a gentle kiss.

"Shh, honey." He kissed her and smoothed a hand over her hair. "I love you."

She smiled laying back on the bed. August pulled the quilt over her body and settled against her side, his body curling around hers. Seylah smiled when she felt August's lips brushing against the nape of her neck. The fire crackled away, the flickering flames lulling her to relax, and later to sleep.

Tomorrow was unknown, but for now Seylah's world was perfect and right.

"I love you, too."

CHAPTER 15

Seylah and August left their room before dawn. The saloon was empty and quiet, the revelry from the previous night long over. Their footsteps echoed in the silent bar of the saloon. It was neat and tidy, every chair and table set to rights as well as the floor which looked clean enough to eat on. How anyone had managed such an undertaking in a few hours was nothing short of a miracle.

It was only when they were leaving the saloon that it dawned on her that they hadn't a clue where their horses had been stabled. She frowned, steps faltering and slowing. It wouldn't do for them to approach the McCarron's on foot and she didn't much like the thought of losing time on their hunt for their horses.

"The horses. Where do you think they are?" She said and glanced over at August to see that he was looking beyond her.

"There," he said nodding past her.

Seylah turned in confusion. It was still dark out, the

sun had not yet risen and she could not see anything beyond darkness and the vague shape of what could be a water barrel. Except that the water barrel was moving and growing until there were two.

"Oh," she said when she realized their horses were staring back at them. She moved towards them and held out a hand to her mare. "But how--"

"Papa needs his sleep," a voice said from the dark and Seylah did her very best not to scream bloody murder. She was lucky that she only jumped about a half foot rather than screech like a mad woman as instinct demanded of her. Seylah steadied herself with a hand against her chest and gave the woman now standing in front of her a tight smile.

"Ruth."

The dark haired woman crossed her arms and gave what she supposed was a scrutinizing look. "Is it true?" she asked.

"Is what true?"

"That you're after the McCarron's?"

"We are," August said coming forward to take he leads from Ruth.

"My pa said you'd make them pay and I quite like the idea of that. I wish you speed and that your aim is true." She turned then and made to move away into the darkness but she stopped and added, "And that your pas are unharmed."

Then Ruth was gone. Melting away as if she had never been there and Seylah was left staring after her with an open mouth.

"That was interesting," she said taking her horse's reins from August.

"I'll say," he replied and swung up onto his mount. "I don't expect that's the last we'll see of her. Woman like that has a way of reappearing."

Seylah shrugged pulling herself into her saddle. "I think I'd like that. She seems like the sort of woman you want on your side."

August hummed and urged his horse forward. "S'long as you don't cross her I think you're right."

They moved then, their horses taking them towards the road that would, as Maurice had told them, take them to the hilltop above the McCarron's hideout. Neither of them spoke again and only the noise of their horses broke up the silence of the early morning. Dawn's light was only beginning to appear on the horizon when they reached an incline.

"This must be it," August said leaning back in his saddle. "I know the maps of this area well enough that this would be the only hilltop that barkeep could have meant."

"Maruice," Seylah corrected sliding down from her seat.

"Yes, Maurice," August drawled. He reached out a hand for her reins and took them. "Wait here. I'm going to hide these two. Won't do for us to get spotted from the road before we've had a chance to light a fire on the McCarron's."

Seylah nodded and watched as he turned and made for the gulch to the left of them. He vanished out of sight with the horses and after a few minutes reappeared, one of their saddle bags slung over his shoulder.

"We'll take the hilltop and assess. I suspect I'll have to go down and investigate the buildings." He started up the hill and Seylah fell into step beside him. "You'll keep watch from the hilltop, make sure my back isn't taken while I take a look around. Hopefully, I'll get eyes on Will and Forrest. Once I do, I'll come back to you and we can plan how to take the McCarron's off guard."

"What if you don't make it back to me?" Seylah asked, trying to keep the waver from her voice. It was difficult but she managed it. The prickly feeling of fear was like ice water on her skin.

"I will make it back," he assured her.

"But-"

"But if I don't," he said, cutting her off and for once Seylah was glad to be interrupted, "you are to report to Butte and tell them where we were, what has happened and bring them here immediately."

She balked. "You can't expect me to leave you. To leave my family."

"I can and I do, Seylah. If you mean to claim that you are suited to the job of deputy then you have to remain above what your heart tells you. If you do not bring the authorities here then the McCarron's will go free. You cannot take them all on your own. If I cannot return to you then you must take care to get word out about what has happened."

She flinched from his words. He was right, they both knew it but that didn't mean she was apt to like it.

She shook her head, shifting the rifle she was carrying. "Fine."

August snorted and put a hand on her arm. "I know it's

hard but we are a team in this, Seylah. Promise me you'll do as I ask."

She nodded, his touch making the truth easier to swallow. "I will. I promise." Seylah glanced towards the ridge in front of them now. The buildings Maurice had told them of were below, just as the man predicted. The barkeep had been right, the hilltop was the perfect vantage point for keeping watch, and sharpshooting, of those below, and August crouched down gesturing for her to do the same beside him.

"You'll be safe here. Use this boulder for cover," he put a hand on the rock beside them and then nodded down at the scattering of buildings below them. "I'll come back as fast as I can, cut down that side of the hill so I can use the outcropping for cover." He pointed to the side of the hill and gave her a reassuring smile.

"This will work," he said."

Seylah nodded. "Yes, of course." She lowered herself down into position and made a show of getting her rifle's sites set.

"Seylah, look at me." August crouched down beside her, and put a hand on her shoulder. When she didn't immediately look at him, he sighed. "Honey, please."

She looked up at him then. That voice, that sweet endearment could make her agree to damn near anything and she suspected he knew it.

"This will work." He squeezed her shoulder. "I love you, Seylah."

She blinked back the tears that burned her eyes. "I love you too," she replied. Seylah reached for him then and pulled him close. She kissed him as if it were the last thing she might ever do, as if the very air in her lungs demanded it because for all she knew it would be the last time she kissed him. He cupped her face, hand gentle on her skin as he returned her kiss. August took freely of the love and need Seylah offered him, drank of it like a dying man in the desert.

They parted, foreheads touching as they looked at each other in the ever growing light of the morning.

"I love you," he said.

"Come back to me," she whispered.

August kissed her once more before he was gone, moving away from her and down the hillside before Seylah could think too much on what would happen next. Drawing out their goodbye wouldn't do. It would only make it harder for them to focus. She knew that but it didn't mean it was any easier to watch him go.

"Focus," she whispered forcing her attention away from August and towards the McCarron's buildings. She scanned the area taking special care to do a sweep of the surrounding area. Even if she had the high ground, it wouldn't do for them to be spotted by a lookout who would alert the rest of the McCarron gang to their whereabouts.

Seylah blew out a steadying sigh when she spotted no movement from the buildings or the surrounding land. August had reached the base of the hill and was making his way to the first building.

Seylah bit her lip. "So far, so good." She blew out a heavy sigh, the sight glass on her gun was useful for allowing her to focus but it was still an exercise in patience not to abandon it. Both a blessing and a curse it was to be able to see so clearly within the sight glass's narrow scope when there was so much ground to watch.

She continued to watch as August peered into a building, she could scarcely breathe when he vanished from sight. Seylah cocked the gun in anticipation. Each second mattered when it came to matters of life and death.

August came back out of the building and continued on his trek between the buildings. Around the corner of the building he went and again Seylah tensed as she waited for him to come back into view. This time it wasn't seconds before August was back in sight, but minutes, long, terrible minutes that stretched on. It seemed like an eternity until August emerged. Seylah breathed out a deep sigh, but her momentary relief vanished when movement at the corner of her eye caught her attention.

It was a man.

"Damn," she whispered. It was a man, a very armed man, a man that she was certain was responsible for her fathers disappearance. And that man was on a collision course with August who was continuing on around the building. They would meet in just a few more seconds when the stranger crossed the open space to the right of the building August was currently behind. Seylah had no way to alert August, not from where she was, not if she wanted to maintain her cover.

But that didn't mean that she couldn't take him out.

She bit her lip and continued to watch. August had not yet heard the man, had no prayer of doing so if he hadn't done it by now. She would have to act. She would have to do it now.

"Hell, hell, hell," she chanted as she made her decision. It was only meant to be an information gathering excursion, but now here they were. There would be no helping it, not with her hand forced by fate.

Seylah was going to have to shoot the McCarron.

She focused on the man and breathed out steadily. Her body going at once tense and relaxing as she lined up the sight. She would not miss, not if she was going to risk firing a shot. Forward he walked and still August kept on. They were nearly face to face now.

And finally, Seylah fired. The gunshot cracked across the open air like a whiplash. August went tense dropping to the ground immediately just as the man slid around the corner. He did not move and she knew her shot had been true.

"Get out of there," she urged August even if he could not hear her. She continued to watch as August took shelter beside the building. The door to the building swung open and two men came rushing out, guns in hand and looking in either direction in bewilderment. They gave a shout when the dead man's body came into sight and ran towards him. It was then that Seylah knew August heard them and knew just how close he had come to being discovered. He hurried to the right, avoiding the men as they began to comb the area. By now four other men had joined the searching pair and Seylah toyed with the idea of picking them off one-by-one, but she knew it wasn't prudent to do so.

August was gone again, vanishing behind the cover of the building and Seylah was left with the sight of the searching half dozen men. Maurice's words came to her mind, the hurt the men had inflicted, the impact they'd had on her world and countless others made her finger press tight to the trigger but she held herself from firing. She shook her head and forced herself not to shoot.

She watched as the men split and divided to go separate directions. Just as half of them went one way, August and Will came into view. She let out a startled cry at their sudden appearance. Will rushed forward, taking out one of the men closest to them and August fired, injuring one of the two remaining, but the shot did not take the man down.

"Oh lord," Seylah groaned, settling back down and lining up take aim. At her shot, the man August injured dropped. She would have liked nothing more than to move on to the next of the three, but the rest of the McCarron men plus her father Forrest in tow rushed onto the scene making it impossible to discern which man was friendly and which was not.

She grit her teeth in frustration as every shot available became a risk to the men now engaging in fisticuffs. Each time, just as she meant to fire, one her fathers or August was thrown into her sights and that would not do.

She had to get closer. This was getting them nowhere.

Seylah pushed herself up from her hiding spot and hurried forward following the same path August had taken on his journey down. Rocks slid loose under foot due to her lack of care. Seylah didn't much care where she stepped or how much noise she made so long as she reached the bottom in time to be helpful.

She skidded to a stop at the bottom before she took off at a sprint towards the fray that she could hear now.

Shouts and swearing, cries of pain reached her ears. She dropped to a knee when she came around the corner and lined up a sight, firing upon the first of the gang that came into view. The man went down instantly, arms flying out as he fell forward.

A man with dark hair and a bloody nose whirled towards her. "They've got a shooter! Get her!"

Seylah fought the urge to recoil and fired again, this time at the man who was sprinting towards her. The shot went wide and she swore under her breath. Now was not the time for nerves. If he reached her, he would kill her, she knew it. Could see the murder in his eyes and Seylah fired, this time her bullet flew true and he fell in a heap a few feet away from her. She looked back to the men who were still fighting and her blood ran cold at the sight of Forrest pinned to the ground, a man on his chest, hands reaching for the gun at his hip. It all happened in a flash and Seylah shot again knocking the man off of her father.

A wave of relief hit her when Forrest sat up and looked towards her with a bewildered look on his face. "Seylah?"

She gave him a quick nod and rose to her feet stalking forward to where August and Will were wrestling with the remaining three men. Their guns had been knocked free she saw and she kicked a pistol to Forrest.

"Freeze!" she yelled cocking her rifle and raising it to show she meant to fire. The men froze and turned towards her. One of the McCarron men gave her a confused look.

"Who's the bitch?" He asked, blood trickling from his mouth.

"Hands up," she ordered, ignoring his slight. When no one raised their hands, Seylah sighed and raised her gun firing into the space just above the men's heads. "I said," she cocked her gun once more, "hands up."

Five pairs of hands shot into the air and she sighed giving August and her Daddy a roll of her eyes. "I meant the McCarrons."

Will spit out a mouthful of blood and grinned at her. "Not takin' any chances with you, sweetheart." He looked at her with admiration, she saw it, he now knew she could do as she had pleaded. That she was meant for more than a desk position.

Seylah smiled in spite of the circumstances. As far as shootouts went she supposed her first had gone as well as could be expected.

"Tie 'em up," Forrest ordered, throwing a length of rope towards August. "We'll take 'em in with the wagon they brought us here in."

Will glared at the remaining three men. "Make sure the ropes are tight."

"You'll pay for this," a man close to Will said and then he looked at Seylah, "gonna enjoy making your girl pay the most for it though. Ain't she pretty boys?" Seylah's blood ran cold, her thoughts flying to Ruth and she did her best to remain stoic despite the threat.

A dark chuckle went up from the other two men, but the laughter was cut short by Forrest striding forward and firing off a shot as casually as if he were asking the time. The bullet hit the man in his knee and he went down with a howl.

Forrest crouched down and jerked the man's hands

behind his back to tie them with the rope he had. "Talk like that will get you hurt, son."

The men fell silent and thankfully all were tied and deposited in the wagon Will brought around in short order. Seylah was shaking, the earlier high of the shootout leaving her both exhausted and restless. How she was able to be both things at once she didn't know. She closed her eyes and sucked in a deep breath walking away from the men. She needed a moment to get herself together. She leaned against the building, the wood at her back making it easier to focus on slowing her breathing, on grounding herself into the moment. When she opened her eyes she felt steadier, she would be able to face her fathers now as a rational adult and--

"Seylah. Are you all right?" Forrest and Will were there in front of her. To everyone else these men were law men, ex-soldiers, keepers of the peace, but to her they were her parents. Two men that she saw were tired and hurt, but still looking to her comfort.

She nodded and flushed at the tears that escaped her eyes. "Yes," she croaked and gave them a jerky nod. "Yes, I'm all right."

Forrest enveloped her in a tight hug. "Sweetheart, you were amazing."

"Oh, Seylah. I'm so proud of you." Will joined the hug and the joint pressure of her father's arms around her set her to sobbing, albeit quiet sobbing. She couldn't have the McCarron gang knowing she was soft.

"I was so scared. We went after you when there was no word and then I saw your horse," she told Will, drawing back to give him a tearful look. "I thought I'd lost you. We had to come after you."

"Came up on an ambush, lost the horse that way," Will told her with a frown.

"Would have let it go but you know how your daddy is," Forrest added, earning a glare from Will.

"That was my favorite horse. If you think I was about to let them get away with it, you've got another thing coming."

Forrest shook his head and gave Will a hard eyed look of his own. "And that's how he ended up here worrying our daughter to death."

Will winced. "Didn't mean for that to happen. Things went astray this morning with them."

"As in very wrong. We're getting too old or this, Will."

"I know."

"Can't keep chasing after every outlaw that kills a horse."

"You repeatin' what you said a hundred times this morning won't change that we did."

"Does that mean you're going to stop?" Seylah asked, looking between her fathers who were locked in a battle of stares. She'd grown up with this sort of bickering between the men, knew it didn't mean much other than a normal parents' spat but that didn't change the fact that Forrest was right, they couldn't keep on as they had been.

Will looked towards her then, his gray eyes softening. "Suppose it does."

Forrest reeled as if he had been slapped. "Truly?"

Will gave a nod of his head and then looked back to Seylah. "Truly. And I think from what we saw here today that Gold Sky is going to be in capable hands. Don't you think so, Seylah?"

This time it was her turn to gape at Will. "What?" she whispered not trusting herself to speak any louder.

"You did amazing here. As good as any man, as good as any deputy would have hoped to perform." Will put a hand on her shoulder and squeezed it. "How do you feel about becoming Gold Sky's newest deputy?"

Forrest chuckled at the strangled sound that escaped his daughter's lips. "I think she likes that fine," he said and Seylah nodded vigorously.

"Yes," she said, bobbing her head and throwing her arms around her parents. "Yes, I--oh, Daddy you don't know how happy that makes me!"

The men hugged their daughter and looked at the other over their daughter's head. "I think," Will said after a moment, "I think it's time we talked about retirement."

Forrest's eyes softened, and he leaned close to drop a kiss to his husband's mouth. "It's about time, old man," he said. Will sighed, but said nothing, preferring to hug their daughter and enjoy the moment before they resumed their roles as sheriffs.

This was a family moment. A time of bliss each other them would remember and cherish. This was their heart.

Outlaws deserved to witness no such thing.

CHAPTER 16

"Tell us again!" Rose was bouncing on her feet, and asking for what Seylah suspected was the fiftieth retelling of how she had rescued their fathers earlier that week.

"Oh, Rose, not again." Seylah closed her eyes and rubbed her temples. "My throat is sore from all the story-telling."

Rose flung her arms out and sighed dramatically. "But I love it so."

"It really is a wonderfully dramatic story," Florence chimed in while Delilah laughed and gave Seylah a shrug.

"They aren't wrong, dear sister. It's a dashing story of you saving the day, like we knew you would and could." Delilah reached out tapping a finger against the silver badge pinned to Seylah's vest.

"And this does look absolutely perfect on you."

Seylah beamed at her sister's words. "Thank you, Del."

Delilah inclined her head with a smile. "You do know how proud we all are of you, don't you?"

"Of course, I do. You've made me so happy. I never thought my heart could be this full. Everything is just perfect," she said meaning every word of it. Since their return to town, things had been different and the same, an interesting combination to say the least. But it was a life more suited to her as a woman.

People no longer stared and whispered when she and August carried on, just smiled and waved to them in passing. It was common knowledge the two planned to marry, she had left her place as a secretary and been deputized in a quiet little ceremony with her family. Her mother had sobbed through the entire thing and could still be found sniffling over her "baby girl" when she thought no one was looking.

They hadn't the heart to tell their mother that they all knew each time she went into a sniffling fit, and the sister had worked out a system of steadfastly avoiding their mother or looking the other way conveniently when Julie began to dab at her eyes.

But for all the tears, her parents were proud of her. All three of them. And Seylah finally felt as if she were becoming who she had always been meant to become.

The town was not the same, and neither was she. A knock at the door pulled their attention away from Rose who had just mustered up the strength to try her hand at demanding another re-telling from Seylah.

"I'll get it!" Florence shouted rushing from the room as if she were being chased and the sister's exchanged a look.

"What has her so eager to answer the door?" Seylah asked.

Her other two sisters gave her confused looks. "No

idea but it is out of character," Delilah remarked rubbing her chin.

"We shall have to get to the bottom of it," Rose added creeping towards the doorway but no sooner had she taken a step did Florence re-enter the room with her shoulders slumped.

"It's for you, Seylah. You have a caller." Florence threw herself down onto the settee and stared morosely at the ceiling. "You have a wonderfully suited caller and I have none. Not even one."

"As opposed to what? Two?" Rose asked with a laugh, but when Florence did not laugh, her sister sat and pointed a finger at her. "You do mean two, you little chit!"

"Oh, please, I am woefully nothing of the sort."

"Liar! Who are you trying to lure over here? Two men? Rose!"

"Go on," Delilah said waving a hand at Seylah. "They will still be carrying on when you return and we can see what she means."

Seylah laughed and made for the door. "Good luck. I'll be back as soon as I can."

Delilah nodded but her sister was already bustling over to stand between the two sisters who were now bickering in earnest. Seylah made her way to the door and wasn't surprised when she saw August waiting on the porch for her.

"Hi," she greeted him, shutting the door to block out the sound of her sister's raised voices.

"Just another quiet night at home, I see," he said with a grin and she rolled her eyes.

"Let's walk?" she asked holding out a hand to him. "I

fear we won't get much talking done if we are within earshot of them." August took her hand and hummed in agreement when a loud thump was heard from inside the house. What her sisters were doing now was a mystery but Seylah offered up a quick prayer of aid in Delilah's name.

"It's good to be home," August said when they were on their way.

Seylah leaned into him. It was winter now, the chill of the evening settled upon her and she wished she had brought a coat. She glanced back at the house with a frown. "It is but I wish I had brought a coat."

"Take mine." He took off his coat and draped it over her shoulders.

"Thank you." Seylah raised a hand up to touch the leather jacket. It was still warm from his body, still smelled like him and she blushed as thoughts of their night together came rushing back to her.

"I appreciate this," she said ducking her head and willing her mind to go to more pure thoughts than what it felt like to be in August's bed.

"I wanted to ask you something, or rather give you something," August said blissfully unaware at where Seylah's mind had strayed. She smiled brightly at him and sucked in a lungful of chilly winter air and straightened her spine standing taller. She would not think of sex with August. She would be perfectly chaste and listen to August. Her mind would remain in the present.

She must compose herself, she must compose herself, she must--

"Will you marry me?"

Seylah jerked to a stop her silent chant interrupted by the four small words. It was then that she realized she had been walking on alone down the lane, her hand woefully empty of his. In her lust addled haze, she hadn't noticed when August had dropped back, when he had gotten down on one knee.

She turned back to see him in just such a pose, one knee bent to the ground, a small box in his hand that he held out to her with the most beautiful smile she had ever seen on his face. It was beautiful to her because she could see every moment of their lives in his smile, the happiness and the longing, the steadfast friendship that had grown between them, that had blossomed from childhood adoration to love.

August was vulnerable to her. Every bit of love between them was reflected to her in his eyes, and the winter chill was suddenly unnoticeable, a small favor as his coat fell from her shoulders in her rush to reach him.

"Yes!" Seylah exclaimed throwing her arms around him and all but flinging herself at him. They fell back into a heap and she peppered his face with kisses.

"Yes, yes, I'll marry you, August."

He laughed and caught hold of her hand, holding it up in front of them. "You have to let me get the ring on your finger, honey."

"Oh, right, the ring." She forced herself to hold still long enough for him to slip the beautiful ring, a simple but tasteful gold band with a ruby inset into it.

"It's beautiful," she whispered bringing her hand close to stare at the ring.

"Not as beautiful as you," he replied and she blushed. "I

know we said we wanted to marry but I had to ask you again when I had a ring for you. I was waiting on them to get this in from New York. Took months to get it here."

Her eyes widened at that. "Months?"

August nodded sitting up with her in his arms. "Yes, months. I ordered it in March, and it just arrived. If I'd known it would take this long I should have just planned to go to New York and get it myself."

"You knew then you wanted to marry me?" she asked in disbelief. "That's so long ago."

He snorted and kissed her. "Seylah, I knew I wanted to marry you when we were sixteen. You say it's early but I can't believe I waited this long. I was pig headed to not ask you sooner. You don't know how happy you've made me knowing that I get to spend every one of my days with you as my wife."

She laughed and closed the space between them. "I love you, August."

"I love you, Seylah." He pulled her into his lap and kissed her. There was tenderness and love in their kiss. The kind of joy that only love, born from years of closeness and friendship, could produce, and Seylah's heart was full. Yes, things had changed, but even so, they were so much the same.

August Leclaire had always been the one for her, had always been her best friend, and now, was to be her husband. She was in his arms, his ring was on her finger, and there wasn't a place in the world Seylah wanted to be more than sitting on this lane, kissing August.

It seemed that August was of the same opinion and when he lifted her into his lap, Seylah was not surprised.

She wrapped her arms around his neck, and she moaned when he deepened the kiss in a promise of what was to come, of what might have come if not for the exaggerated cough that broke them apart. They looked up to see all three of Seylah's parents standing in the lane.

Her mother stood between her fathers, arms linked with theirs and gave her daughter a wink.

"Well, isn't this just the sweetest thing."

"Since when is our child being violated in public sweet?" Will asked with a pinched look on his face.

Forrest sighed at August. "Son, when you said you were going to ask her to marry you, this isn't quite what we had in mind."

August blushed and leapt to his feet pulling, Seylah up with him. "My apologies. I didn't, ah, know you were coming home so soon."

Will rubbed at his temples. "Good thing we did or you'd be makin' us grandparents by now."

Seylah flushed, and August glanced away, but said nothing.

Will's eyes widened. "Did you—"

"Oh Daddy, stop." Seylah rolled her eyes and linked her arm through August's in a mirror of her parents' position.

"Come on, lets get home. The girls will be so happy to hear the good news!" Julie started marching forward, dragging her husbands behind her while Will, still spluttered, looked woefully behind him at Seylah.

"Will, move it!" Julie ordered.

"But that's my little girl," he protested, but was dragged along all the same by his wife and husband.

"Let her live her life," Forrest supplied, and Will jabbed a finger at him.

"You are to blame for this."

"For what?" Forrest wanted to know while Julie continued to drag the now bickering men forward.

"Your sisters won't be any better," August told her with a chuckle when he saw the mortified look on Seylah's face.

"I know."

"But that," he said, bringing her hand up to his lips and pressing a kiss to her knuckles, "is what family does."

She laughed and leaned her head against his shoulder, watching her parents continue to drag Will ahead, even as he shot desperate looks behind him. Her sisters would be in a tizzy over her news. They would love the ring, she knew. There would be no rest in the Wickes-Barnes household, not tonight.

"Yes, *our* family does it very well." She glanced over at him, willing him to hear what she meant in that simple word: *our.* August had, in truth, always been hers and she his, and now with a wedding on the horizon, it would be official.

August's eyes softened, and she knew he understood her meaning. He kissed her forehead. "Yes, yes they do, honey."

THANK YOU!

I hope you enjoyed Honor and Desire!

Writing Seylah and August's story felt surreal to me. Sharing it is a dream. I never intended to write a multi-generational series, but here we are. I am in love with the world of Gold Sky and hope that you're ready to follow each of the Wickes-Barnes daughters in finding their HEA!

Florence's story is next and she is a young woman who knows precisely what and *who* she wants. Florence's love story is a MFM menage and pairs sweet and steamy for a perfectly romantic frontier adventure.

Thank you for reading the Gold Sky series. It means the world to share this with y'all.

Sign up for our newsletter e-mail list at https://bit.ly/

2PCKCZl and *don't be shy about reaching out through social media! I pretty much live for that stuff.*

Reviews help eager readers find new authors to love and I welcome all reviews, both positive and constructive. Drop me a shout and I'll love y'all to the moon and back!

   Turn the page and enjoy a sneaky peek at Florence, Anselmo and Brendan!

EXCERPT: FLORENCE, ANSELMO & BRENDAN'S STORY

"*T*hat isn't how that works. That isn't how any of it works."

"And why exactly not?" Florence asked, eyes moving from her reflection to her sister who stood behind her. She'd been painstakingly applying rouge to her cheeks. She paused, the small pot of rouge in one hand, her powder puff in the other, and raised an eyebrow at Delilah. Her older sister was looking none too pleased with her at the moment, which could be truly vexing.

Clearing her throat, Florence thought quickly, trying to redirect her forward question into something...softer? A turn of phrase more palatable to Delilah's delicate sensibilities. Her sisters always had a way of getting in between her and her beautifully laid plans when they didn't agree. This would not do.

"Ah, what I mean to say is, whatever do you mean dear sister?" She asked, keeping her voice in as gentle and agreeable a pitch as she could manage.

Delilah frowned at her and took a step closer. "Flo.

Absolutely not. I know what you're trying to do."
Evidently, she had missed the placating-meddlesome-
and-disapproving-older-sisters pitch by a mile.

Drat.

Florence lowered her hand and set down her makeup
with a heavy sigh. "Delilah, I have no idea what you
mean."

"You do you little brat."

Florence turned away from the mirror and toward
Delilah with her arms crossed. "Now there's no need for
name-calling, Del." Her voice was flat, her face colored
with a slight blush and her lips pushed into a thin line.

Del's eyes moved over her face slowly before narrow-
ing. . "You're up to something. I don't care how mad you
get at me. I know it."

"Oh, you do, do you?"

Del gave a quick nod and pointed at the dress she was
wearing. "You're absolutely fit for a ball in that outfit.
Don't think I didn't notice just because Papa and Daddy
are too preoccupied to truly understand what's going on."

Florence smoothed a hand over the velvet skirt of her
gown. "Oh, this old thing?" She scoffed and patted at the
silk of her neckline, which was a touch beyond daring for
Gold Sky. The crimson silk and velvet dress left her arms
bare and her decolletage on display in an enticing way
that would have been pushing the envelope even in New
York. In the setting of the city, her outfit would have been
seen as fresh,the marker of high fashion But here? On the
frontier? It was positively scandalous.

Florence loved a good scandal.

She should. She'd been raised with a family that raised

no shortage of eyebrows and whispers outside of their bubble of happiness in Gold Sky. Here, in this westward town, she and her family had a place of acceptance and belonging. That was the way of all those who called the town home.

Life and society may not have agreed with the lot of them in the big cities, but in Gold Sky they were able to choose their own way. Free to love whom they pleased. Free to grow into whomever they might wish to be.

Florence knew she was fortunate to be blessed with such a home. That not every place was like Gold Sky. She knew there were rumors in New York but that due to her mother's family, the Baptistes, they were simply written off as *"eccentric."* New York's Four Hundred may not understand the life her mother had chosen, but first and foremost, her mother was a Baptiste, and that meant her choices were to be accepted, even if strange.

It might have bothered her if the joy and love of her family had been anything but sincere. But as it was, the affection and loyalty between her parents, all three of them, had served as an example of the very thing Florence hoped for as a young girl.

One person to love was fine and a rare thing indeed, but two? Two hearts that beat for yours? Now that was a miracle--a gift of untold value, and it was what Florence wished for herself now that she was a woman of marrying age. She was a woman in her prime and a good looking one at that. This would normally be an advantage in the ways of love, but Florence's needs were specific. She wanted those two hearts beating for her. To give herself in the same way and have her love multiplied, not divided.

However, Gold Sky was not the place for such romantic overtures to be explored. Woefully lacking in eligible men for a lady seeking only one, but two? That was positively Herculean, even in such a place as Gold Sky. Florence patted the ribbons she'd intertwined in her updo and straightened her shoulders.

The women in her family were accustomed to taking on the insurmountable and making it their own. This would be no different. There was a dance tonight, and Florence was determined to make her best showing. Hence, her daring attire and efforts with makeup and hair.

"Where are you going tonight?" Delilah asked, tipping her head to the side. She could see from the set of her sister's shoulders, and the gleam in her eyes, that she was hatching a plan. But for what?

"To a social event."

"Which social event would that be?"

Florence turned back to the mirror and smiled at her reflection. She looked lovely and fresh--perfect for drawing the eye of two suitors. It was what she wanted. Two suitors, and one way or another, Florence was going to get what she wanted.

She raised her eyes and smiled into the mirror. "Why a dance of course."

It was common knowledge that a dance was the perfect setting for romance. Tonight more so as it was a very special dance. Tonight's event was a singles dance. An opportunity for the unattached to mingle and enjoy an evening of frivolity. It would be the right atmosphere for casting her nets a little wider than she'd been previously afforded in her romantic efforts. Florence had been industrious, and was known for her enthusiasm in the pursuit of a goal, but for all her energy, there was little forward progress in her quest for two husbands.

"You cannot mean to entice two men into such an arrangement."

"Such an arrangement?" Florence's hands went to her hips and she pursed her lips. "It's a dance, not some sordid crime ring, Delilah."

"A dance? You really think I'm so naive as to believe that's all you have in mind for tonight?"

"Yes, yes, I do."

Delilah crossed her arms in answer, her sharp eyes missing nothing, so flinty was her sister's gaze that Florence nearly buckled.

Nearly, but *not quite.*

Instead, she beamed at Delilah, gray eyes practically sparkling. "Unless the town-sponsored singles soiree intends to be the site for a nefarious syndicate, which it does not, then yes, it is just a dance. And I haven't a clue what two men you are referring to." Her voice was cool, even, it was the picture of collected respectability, but Delilah remained unconvinced. Florence abhorred her sister's attention to detail.

"I know very well that you've been on a spree of getting acquainted with the eligible men in town," Delilah said shaking a finger at her sister and making Florence frown.

"I wasn't aware that I was expected to keep a nun's hours. I am, after all, a woman in her prime."

"You are, Flo, and I know what your preferences are in

the way of matrimony. We all know that you wish for what our parents have, but you are going about it entirely wrong, and this dance will not fix it."

Florence stepped back as if slapped and blinked rapidly against the prickling sensation of her eyes. She would not cry. She knew her sister was only looking out for her. Delilah always did, always would, in her role as the protector, the sternest and most serious of them all. But Flo did not want practicality and rational planning or forethought. Not tonight.

Tonight was about her heart and giving in to all the soft possibilities that came with believing in love. Florence rejected her sister's logic, and instead, chose romance and drama. She chose the chance that she would meet her matches--two men with room in their heart for her.

"That is your opinion, and you are welcome to it." She shook her head and smiled, pulling the drawstring of her evening bag tight over her knuckles as she continued to speak, feet moving her over the creaking floorboards of her room until she was at the door. "I intend to enjoy myself this evening, and I hope to see you there, Delilah. You might even have a bit of fun at such an event."

Florence turned and left the room. Her parting words to her sister were meant to sting. They both knew it, and she bit her lip at having said them. Delilah was well aware of her penchant for severity, and it wasn't kind to poke a sore spot she knew her sister to have.

The same could be said for Florence's romantic nature. Her sister knew that truth, too. She sighed heavily, walking towards the door. Her dress no longer felt so grand, nor her steps as light. She had meant to leave earlier in the evening when her sister and fathers had been present, but she had been distracted at the thought of what wonder a carefully applied coat of rouge might do for her complexion. She wished she had left and avoided the discussion of tonight, and Florence's marital preferences, all together.

She continued walking, mind swirling darkly around her conversation with Delilah, when a pointed *"ahem"* caught her attention. Florence had just been crossing to the foyer when she turned to look through the archway to the parlor on her left and froze seeing her mother sitting beside the fireplace in one of the three ever-present hearthside rocking chairs. Her mother's dark head was bent over a book, reading glasses perched on her nose as she "read," though Florence noticed that her mother did not turn the page.

"Mama, I didn't know you were home." Florence went to the door.

"I've been home for some time," Julie said, her brown eyes fixed on her in reproach. Ah, so her mother had heard her argument with her sister. *Drat it all.* She'd never be able to enjoy tonight's dance after this conversation.

"That's...good," Florence ventured, and her mother hummed, closing the book in her lap and taking her reading glasses off with a sigh.

"She only loves you--wants the best for you," Julie said.

"She doesn't understand, Mama."

"Might not, but do you, Flo?"

Florence's eyebrows knit together in confusion. "What do you mean?" She walked into the room, unsure of what her mother was getting at, but she was sure it would take longer than a quick chat. She sat in her father's rocking chair and leaned toward her mother. "I don't understand the question," she ventured when they had both been silent for a moment.

"I mean, do you know what it is that you wish for in a marriage?"

"I want what you have," Florence blurt out, the thought escaping her lips faster than she could follow it, and she blinked in surprise. "I mean.. I want the love and happiness you and Daddy and Papa have, but it's..."

"It's what?" Her mother put a gentle hand on her shoulder, and Florence gave her a weak smile.

"It's difficult to find a match, or in this case, matches."

"Suitors are hard to come by," Julie conceded and patted her shoulder gently. "But there is no use rushing it. You do look lovely, though. The finest dress this town has ever seen by far."

Florence smiled, this time it was genuine and warm. She caught her mother's hand and kissed the knuckles. "Except for you on your wedding day."

Julie waved her other hand. "Oh, I don't know about that, sweetheart."

'That's not what Papa says.'

"Your papa's soft-hearted, Flo. We all know it."

Florence giggled and leaned back in the rocking chair. It was Forrest's and suited the big man just fine, one who still needed plenty of room even in his advancing years. She ran a finger along the worn wood and smiled. It was familiar and comforting, the place of so many happy memories. The hearthside with all three of her parents had always been the center of joy for their family and oh, what she wouldn't give for such a place in her own home.

"It's true, but he loves you and Daddy. Loves us, too, and I just," Florence swallowed hard and looked up from the chair to her mother. "That's what I aim to have for myself. I know Delilah doesn't understand it, but I hope that you can, Mama."

"I do understand, sweet girl, but it is a difficult thing to find. The men you match yourself to must, first and foremost, love one another. It cannot be lopsided," Julie motioned with her hands in the way of a scale tipping. "For a marriage such as ours, you cannot be what binds them together. They must choose and love each other as well. That's where you've been erring, Flo."

Florence tipped her head to the side and froze. How could she have not seen that one crucial step? "Oh heavens no, what have I been doing?"

"You've been finding two men that you think are compatible and attempting to push them together. Do not think I haven't noticed your matchmaking tendencies as of late."

Florence frowned. She had taken an interest in the male friendships of Gold Sky,but with far less pure intentions than the men involved realized. They thought she meant to increase the amount of fraternal companionship and camaraderie of the community, or so she had proclaimed. Florence's intentions were nothing of the kind and were, at their heart ,purely romantic, even if she had failed miserably.

In the weeks she had been seeking a suitable pair of men, she had only managed to create four lasting friendships and what she thought was the start of a new business venture amongst them. The business would be a success, whereas her love life was quite the opposite.

"At least the men of Gold Sky have been finding common ground more easily these days. There's been a decided downtick in the number of duels and gunfights," she finally said. Her mother burst into a hearty round of laughter, and the sound made Florence feel lighter after her argument with Deliliah. It was hard not to smile when her mother laughed as she did now, and before long, Florence was laughing along with her.

"Your act of civil service aside, of which Seylah and your fathers will be appreciative of, I have this advice for you, Flo." Her mother's voice was serious, her brown eyes contemplative as she looked at her daughter who was now wiping the mirth from her own face. She sat up and looked at her mother with a quick nod.

"I'm ready, Mama. What is it?"

"Do not force the connection. Find the place where love exists and ask for room."

Florence blinked at that. "Ask for room?" She tried, not sure how the words were meant to be taken, but knowing that they sounded as confusing as she felt.

Julie nodded, sensing Florence's confusion. "Yes, ask for room. Be patient in doing so, but find the love first. Take that with you tonight. Do you understand?"

"Yes, I do," Florence lied, hoping the words would make more sense on her walk to town. She stood from her seat and smiled at her mother who was beaming at her from where she sat. "I'll ask for room."

"And look for love," Julie helpfully added.

Florence nodded. "Yes. Look for love and find it before anything else."

"That's my sweet girl. Now don't take your argument with Delilah to heart. I suspect she'll be along tonight. Enjoy yourself and apologize when you can to the other. I expect you at an appropriate hour."

Florence pursed her lips. She hated appropriate hours and curfews, but she said nothing, instead opting for a quick bob of her head and a barely there: "Of course, mama." She turned to go but, stopped. "I love you," she said over her shoulder, looking back at Julie where the older woman sat with her book in hand.

"I love you too, Flo. Now go and find your loves. Tell Rosemary I said hello."

FLORENCE ROCKED BACK on her heels, hands tucked behind her back, as she surveyed the dance floor. It was being held in the grand hall of the town theater. The space was normally reserved for high profile events, such as speeches from the mayor or other elected officials, when they saw fit to have a gala, wedding receptions, and to celebrate any productions that came to Gold Sky. Florence remembered the construction of the building, she had been a girl of six, and there had been plenty in the town that had laughed at the efforts to bring such an ornate and delicate building to the town.

"This is a working town. Not a frilly city."

"A waste of timber is what it is."

Mrs. Rosemary had been undeterred in its construction. The snide comments of some townsfolk sliding away like water off a duck's back. The woman was never one to be concerned with the opinions of others. She did as she pleased--always had and always would.

Florence was enthralled by her. She raised a hand and waved at Mrs. Rosemary when she spied her across the hall. Mrs. Rosemary's blue eyes lit up, and she bustled across the room with arms outstretched.

"Flo, oh you look ravishing! I am so pleased we chose to go with this color. It suits you perfectly." Mrs. Rosemary enveloped her in a tight hug. The smell of jasmine and cinnamon that was uniquely Mrs. Rosemary surrounded them, and Florence sank into the other woman's embrace.

"You are a wonderful designer. It's not difficult to look ravishing when you are the one dressing me." She gave a little twirl which delighted Mrs. Rosemary to no end. She laughed and gave a little clap.

"It's even easier to look skilled as a designer when the model is so lovely. You and all your sisters take after your mother. I could dress you all in plain linen and every man in this town would lose their hearts."

Florence blew out a raspberry. "I am unconcerned with every man. I search only for two."

"Oh, is that so?"

"Yes, but I can't seem to find a pair that are," Florence looked out at the dance floor and paused. All around the walls of the hall were hung with ribbons and glittering streamers which were pulled into the front of the room to delicately frame the crystal chandelier that hung from the middle of the room. Paper and silk lanterns added drama and warmth to the room. Tables laden with finger foods and crystal bowls of red punch were on theme, as were the paper heart cut-outs that covered every surface. Florence was surprised the servers were not attired as mini-cupids, and she smiled as one appeared in front of her offering her a refreshment. She nodded her thanks, accepting the small glass and took a sip before letting out an appreciative hum at the sweet taste.

"That's love's arrow," Mrs. Rosemary told her, nodding at the glass. "A little like a gin blossom, but with a touch of amaro."

Florence raised an eyebrow, taking in the ruby-colored drink. "How much of a splash?" She asked, taking another sip.

Mrs. Rosemary waved a hand and plucked a cup from the server's tray for herself. "Oh, measurements are such a dreadfully droll thing. You can never have too much amaro. Royalty drinks it, you know. It must be good for one's constitution."

Florence giggled and nodded. "Sound logic as any that I have ever had the pleasure of hearing." She sipped her drink and Mrs. Rosemary stepped closer to her, a hand going to Florence's arm.

"Now, Flo, you were commenting on romance and men and," she raised her eyebrows and inclined her head. "I am not one to let that conversation slip away. What were you saying?"

"I was commenting on the lack of pairs that I can..." She bit her lip, remembering her mother's words, "ask for a place in."

"A place, you say? I could think of a pair of suitors who might be...amenable to such an arrangement."

Florence nearly spit her drink out. She whirled towards Mrs. Rosemary, nearly spilling her cocktail. "Do you mean that? Truly?"

Mrs. Rosemary smiled and gave a tiny dip of her chin in a nod. "I do."

"Where? Who? Are they in attendance tonight?"

"They are, but you might find it a bit difficult to get them to admit what they are searching for."

"But why?" The incredulity in Florence's question was palatable, and a few bystanders looked towards them in confusion.

Mrs. Rosemary gave a little laugh and looked at Florence then. "Not everyone was raised to be as outspoken in their preferences, nor did they have the kind of home life you did or have the gift of growing up in a town such as Gold Sky."

"Ah, you do have a point there." Florence forced herself to be calmer. It was true that she was blessed to have been given this place as a home. She turned, scanning the dance floor, hoping to be able to spot the men Mrs. Rosemary meant. Surely she should be able to find them on her own.

"I see you straining your eyes, Flo. Look to the left corner by the silk lamps. The pair of young men there are very much in love, but have it in their mind to find wives when I'm quite sure they would do well with just one."

Florence's mouth went dry. She saw them. "They're beautiful." A pair of men in fine suits, cut just right and no doubt the work of Mrs. Rosemary's hand. Florence could spot the other woman's touches anywhere and saw it now in the matching charcoal suits they wore. One was red-haired, his hair pulled back in a fashionable knot, and fair-skinned. She wondered if he wore his hair loose and what it might feel like under her fingers. The other, a brunette with hair as dark as night. She suspected him to be of Mexican descent from the warm brown tone of his skin. He turned toward her, and Florence nearly dropped her drink. High cheekbones, full lips, and dark brown eyes met hers from across the room.

"Oh," Florence breathed when he smiled at her. The man beside him turned at a slight nudge and he too smiled in her direction, green eyes lighting up when they met her shocked gaze. She had thought she would be able to withstand the attention of two men, but here she was nearly melting like a candle from warmth in these two men's smile.

"Come with me." Mrs. Rosemary took her elbow and began forward startling Florence out of her smile induced stupor.

"What are you doing?"

"Introducing you. Every proper lady needs an intro-duction when there are eligible men to be considered."

"But--" Florence made to dig her feet in and found out that Mrs. Rosemary was surprisingly strong.

"But nothing. You wished for two suitors. I have found them."

The march toward the men was quick, passing in the blink of an eye. Florence was tongue-tied as she found herself suddenly standing in front of them. Mrs. Rose-mary inclined her head to the men.

"Hello, gentlemen. I'm so happy to see you here."

They both dropped at the waist in exaggerated bows that Florence might have found silly on anyone but them. She watched as they took turns kissing the offered hand Mrs. Rosemary held out.

"We thank you for creating such an opportunity for us, Mrs. Rosemary. We are forever indebted to you for all your hard work." The red-haired man spoke, and Florence nearly swooned at the Scottish brogue she heard in his voice.

"Brendan, you are too kind. Now, it is time for me to return the favor you bestowed upon me by introducing you to one of my dearest friends. Florence Wickes-Barnes. She's the sheriff's daughter and a fine young lady. She works for me in the dress shop as a seamstress and is one of the most talented I have ever had the pleasure of teaching. Sharp as a whip. And," Mrs. Rosemary paused in her praise, "very welcoming to different expressions of love."

The trio stared at one another with slightly rounded eyes. Neither man moved, standing stiff as boards, and Florence swallowed down the feeling of an impending shriek in Mrs. Rosemary's direction. The other woman did what she wanted. That included having a blunt manner of speaking. One did not get the luxury of accepting Rosemary Stark piecemeal. It was either the whole woman or nothing. As such, Florence forced a smile to her lips and cleared her throat, stepping forward.

She would smooth this over as well as she was able. "Pleased to meet you both." Florence held out her hand to them, anticipating a handshake, but neither man moved, still staring at Mrs. Rosemary as if expecting the other woman to suddenly perform an acrobatic routine. Her hand shook slightly from holding it out, and Florence fought against the wince she wanted to give. Her plan for recovering the introduction falling flat as neither man came forward to take her hand. She would have to think of another way to form some kind of relationship with them.

Florence cleared her throat delicately and moved to step back but was stopped when a hand reached out to clasp hers. It was a gentle grip but firm. The feel of calloused fingers on her knuckles had her heart beating wildly. She wanted to thread her fingers with his but instead, she stood still and smiled at him, waiting for him to speak like the lady they all supposed her to be.

"Pleased to meet ye Florence Wickes-Barnes. My name is Brendan Black." His voice was lovely. Dark and warm, rich like honeyed whiskey and Florence blushed at the warmth of his hand on hers. There was something about the man that was closed off slightly even as he touched her. Florence could have sworn he was in a different room, not a foot in front of her with an air of indifference that clung to him like the wool of his suit.

"Good evening, Brendan."

"This is my partner, ah," Brendan stopped and cleared his throat. "My *business partner*. Anselmo Ortega."

She looked to where Brendan gestured and Anselmo smiled at her, taking her other hand in his. Her fingers twitched in his grip and breathing was suddenly a feat. How was she to maintain the facade of a lady with both Brendan and Anselmo holding onto her hands.

Smiles were one thing, but touch, that was an entirely different matter.

"Pleased to meet you, but there is no need for you to call me Anselmo."

"Oh?" Florence asked, voice dropping an octave when he came forward and placed a kiss on the back of her hand. "Then what am I to call you?"

"Beautiful women get special privileges with me. Call me, Ansel," he told her, smiling up at her where he was bent over her hand.

Florence managed a nod of her head. "Ansel."

Mrs. Rosemary tittered beside them and leaned close, kissing Florence's cheek and pinching it as she drew away. "I'll leave the three of you to it then. Please enjoy the singles dance." She turned and swept away with a flick of her skirts before any of them could speak. When they were alone, Ansel squeezed her hand.

"Florence is a lovely name." He was still holding onto her, and Florence cleared her throat, drawing her hand away before anyone noticed. Though she wanted two suitors, two husbands, she did not wish to draw anyone's attention before she was good and ready.

"Thank you," she demurred and aimed a smile at both men. "When did you arrive in our fair town?"

"Month before last, but we have mainly been at work. Brendan here is absolutely horrendous at keeping us working. This is our first true reprieve from the business."

"And what business might that be?"

"Mining," Brendan said then, his voice had gone a touch gruff. "We're here to mine. There are some promising sites outside of town and with the railroad, it's a lucrative move for us." He touched Ansel's arm then stepped back from her. "If you'll excuse us, Miss Florence."

"But only for a moment," Ansel interjected, quickly shooting her a wink. "We would never leave a fair lady such as you for too long, Florence."

She nodded, watching the men step away. Their heads were bent together as they spoke. Whatever the subject was, it was serious. She edged closer on the pretense of looking at the cluster of silk lamps beside her, but was unable to catch their conversation other than the hushed tones of their voices. Somewhere behind them on the stage, the band began to play a waltz and she nearly cursed. Now was not the time for music. She was trying to eavesdrop and how was she meant to do so with that infernal music playing?

Florence turned to the side casting a furtive look in the men's direction. Brendan was touching Ansel, his hand splayed across the small of the other man's back. The touch was slight but it was intimate as was the way Ansel turned leaning into the other man as they spoke. These were the touches of lovers. Mrs. Rosemary was right.

"How am I to ask for a place with them over there?" Florence whispered, sipping from her drink. The burn of the liquor was masked by the sweet flavor but it warmed her all the same as she contemplated her options. Ansel was amenable to her, she could see that. Brendan would take a bit of effort but she could manage it if only they were to--She stopped her spiral of thoughts when they turned and started back towards her. The men were

281

coming and she needed to collect herself if this was going to go right.

She smiled at them when they came to a stop in front of her. "Is everything all right?" she asked.

"Yes, of course, nothing but a bit of business," Ansel replied taking a glass from a passing server. He held out a drink to Brendan and smiled at the man. "Isn't that right?"

The other man nodded sipping from the drink but saying nothing.

"Ah, well, I hope you've been having a lovely time in Gold Sky. I grew up here and there's no other place like it."

Ansel nodded sipping his drink. "We've come to see that. Mrs. Rosemary has made it abundantly clear that all styles of living are welcome here."

"She does take it upon herself to be the unofficial welcoming committee," Florence conceded.

"You have two fathers," Brendan said suddenly, startling Florence. It wasn't a question. It was an observation and she paused, giving the man a shrewd look.

"Yes, that's right. I have two fathers. The sheriffs in town."

"Is that what Mrs. Rosemary meant by you being accepting of all types of love?" Brendan asked, earning an elbow to the gut from Ansel.

"Brendan, this is not what we talked about," he hissed but Brendan shrugged and rubbed his side.

"We are not fighting over one woman," he shot back and Florence raised an eyebrow.

"And why would you be fighting over anything?" she asked in confusion.

"Because we aim to marry."

"As do I," she informed them.

Brendan crossed his arms and took a step closer. His emerald eyes were intent on her and she found she enjoyed the attention. "And there is only one of you, but the two of us. How could we not fight over you?

Florence laughed, raising her glass to her lips and taking a sip. "That's quite easy, gentleman. I aim to marry the pair of you."

ABOUT REBEL CARTER

Rebel Carter *loves* love. So much in fact that she decided to write the love stories she desperately wanted to read. A book by Rebel means diverse characters, sexy banter, a real big helping of steamy scenes, and, of course, a whole lotta heart.

Rebel lives in Colorado, makes a mean espresso, and is hell-bent on filling your bookcase with as many romance stories as humanly possible!

ALSO BY REBEL CARTER

Heart and Hand: Interracial Mail Order Bride Romance (Gold Sky Series Book 1)

Hearth and Home: Interracial Mail Order Groom Romance (Gold Sky Series Book 2)

Love and Gravity: Multicultural STEM Romance

New Girl in Town: Older Woman Younger Man Romance

Auld Lang Syne: Highlands Holiday Novella